"WHAT?" SHE STEPPED BACK.

"I just like saying your name. And I like your hair, the way it feels so cool. It looks as if it should feel like fire in my hands but it doesn't. Just like your skin, so smooth, like porcelain. Even when it shows the fire inside, it's cool to the touch."

"I don't feel cool," she said.

"No? What do you feel?"

"A little bit scared," she whispered. "And a lot on fire. Wondering what will happen when . . ."

He watched the fire rise, saw it spark in her eyes, saw her part her lips, lips he couldn't resist. He bent and brushed them with his. "When I do this?"

WHAT ARE *LOVESWEPT* ROMANCES?

They are stories of true romance and touching emotion. We believe those two very important ingredients are constants in our highly sensual and very believable stories in the LOVE-SWEPT line. Our goal is to give you, the reader, stories of consistently high quality that may sometimes make you laugh, sometimes make you cry, but are always fresh and creative and contain many delightful surprises within their pages.

Most romance fans read an enormous number of books. Those they truly love, they keep. Others may be traded with friends and soon forgotten. We hope that each LOVESWEPT romance will be a treasure—a "keeper." We will always try to publish

LOVE STORIES YOU'LL NEVER FORGET
BY AUTHORS YOU'LL ALWAYS REMEMBER

The Editors

TWICE
THE
TROUBLE

JUDY
GILL

BANTAM BOOKS
NEW YORK · TORONTO · LONDON · SYDNEY · AUCKLAND

TWICE THE TROUBLE
A Bantam Book / July 1995

*If you would be interested in receiving protective vinyl covers for your
Loveswept books, please write to this address for information:*

Loveswept
Bantam Books
P.O. Box 985
Hicksville, NY 11802

ISBN 0-553-44457-3

Published simultaneously in the United States and Canada

PRINTED IN THE UNITED STATES OF AMERICA

OPM   0 9 8 7 6 5 4 3 2 1

ONE

"Dr. Martin, I'm sorry to interrupt . . ."

John glanced up from the government forms he was filling out during a break between patients; or, as he secretly believed, between curiosity seekers wanting not so much medical advice as a glimpse of old Dr. Blaine's replacement. Though he'd asked not to be disturbed, he was relieved to see his office nurse poke her head around the door. He hated paperwork.

He leaned back and stretched. "What's up, Nora?"

"A call from your daughter's school. The principal says Andi's had her eye blackened and her nose bloodied in a fight. They'd like you to come."

John groaned. While it didn't surprise him that Andi had been fighting, he'd have thought she might get through her first day in her new school without taking on the world. He rolled his chair back, stood, and shrugged out of his white lab coat.

"Okay," he said. "I suppose I better go bail her out and offer my services to the other child."

"Doctor, she's the injured party," Nora said, her pleasant face wrinkling as she scowled.

John laughed. Nora hadn't met his daughter yet. "Don't you believe it. If she's got a bloody nose, the other kid is likely to be in need of reconstructive surgery. Andi is not what you might call a shrinking violet."

He pulled on a jacket, snatched up his bag—just in case—and strode the three tree-lined blocks to the elementary school. His daughter had entered it for the first time scarcely two hours earlier on this first Tuesday after Labor Day. A black eye and a bloody nose seemed excessive this early in the school year, but maybe, in this new environment, Andi had finally met her match. It might be that she'd learned a valuable lesson that morning. He certainly hoped so. It was one he'd not yet managed to teach her.

Maggie laughed into the telephone. "Jolene? Fighting? Lou, you're kidding!"

"Would I kid about something like that?" asked Lou, the school secretary and a longtime friend of Maggie's. "She blackened another kid's eye and bloodied her nose."

"What?" It was ludicrous to imagine this as anything but a mistake. The first day of second grade and she was getting a phone call like this? She must be dreaming. "Are you sure?" Maybe Lou had snapped completely under the pressure of working for that dork, Elmer Abernathy.

"All I can say is, you better get over here, because Mr. A is on the warpath. He's highly incensed because . . ." Lou lowered her voice, and Maggie got a picture of her turning her face away, cupping the phone, "because Jolene stepped out of her mold."

"About time, too, I'd say." Maggie couldn't supress a

proud grin. "Who'd she paste? Someone who deserved it, I hope."

Lou laughed. "Little girl by the name of Andrea Martin. New kid in town. She's in the first-aid room being treated for her injuries.

"According to the teacher on playground duty," Lou continued, "Jolene accused Andrea of stealing something from her, and laid right in. By the time the teacher and another had separated the pair of them, the damage was done. As of this moment, Jolene's cooling off in the isolation room. I put her there myself until she gets over her tantrum."

"Tantrum?" Maggie echoed. Not her polite, submissive little seven-year-old daughter! That was as hard to believe as Jolene's fighting—Jolene, who cried if she saw a cartoon character squashed by a falling rock.

"Yes, a real, honest-to-goodness tantrum," Lou said with another laugh. "Kicking Mr. A, screaming at everyone, and swearing at me."

"*Swearing?*"

"Definitely swearing." Lou did a great impersonation of the principal. " 'We will require a full conference to discuss this matter. Please so inform Miss Adair.' "

"Miss Adair considers herself so informed." Maggie frowned, her head reeling from the notion of her daughter doing any of the things she was accused of. "When do I put in my appearance?"

"ASAP, kiddo."

Maggie sighed and cast a glance at her computer, where she'd spent the last couple of hours working on the accounts of one of her clients.

"On my way."

Minutes later she'd changed from her shorts and T-shirt to a pair of leggings and a long top and was heading for her Cherokee. After a brief stop at the end of her rutted driveway, she swung the truck onto the highway, apparently giving an oncoming bus driver the impulse to jump on brakes and horn simultaneously. She glared at him in her mirror. There'd certainly been no need for his overreaction. She sped along the two miles between her house and the school, with the warm latesummer breeze whipping her hair back. She took pleasure in the bright sun, in the novelty of being out in it in the middle of the morning, although normally she hated having her routiine interrupted. Luckily, Jolene had never been the kind of child whose behavior required calls like this from the school. Until today.

Maggie screeched to a stop as a long-legged man emerged from the shadow of a tree and strode directly in front of her, walking across the school's circular drive. The breeze ruffled his dark brown hair, whipped open a tweed sports jacket, and flattened his slacks against strong thighs. Since she was taking so much pleasure in other aspects of nature that morning, she gladly took pleasure in watching his brisk, masculine strides. When she realized that the black bag he carried was a dead giveaway of his purpose there, her heart sank. She slotted the truck into a parking space.

If the kid Jolene had slugged required medical attention, this matter was a whole lot more serious than she'd thought.

She saw him again as she rushed along the corridor toward the school office. He was crouched in front of a child whose face she couldnt see, examining her eye. Maggie winced and felt sick. What could have come over Jolene? This was so unlike her!

"The boss is in his lair, Maggie," Lou said, gesturing toward an inner door. "He wants to see you right away."

"I want to see Jolene first," Maggie said. "Where is she?"

Lou shrugged and pointed at the half-closed door of an anteroom. "In there." She grinned. "Supposedly contemplating her sins at the isolation desk. But she's not the least bit repentant and is still hopping mad. When I poked my head in a few minutes ago to say that you were on your way, she consigned me to a place I didn't suspect Jolie knew about, and informed me that she didn't even *have* a mother."

Maggie gaped in disbelief. "You're kidding!"

"Sorry, I'm not. I've never seen Jolene in this frame of mind before. She sure has changed over the summer. Good luck."

Maggie composed her face and pushed the door open.

"Hi, honey," she said. "I understand you're in a bit of trouble."

"Not me," said the little girl who stood beside a child's desk, fists clenched, her blue-gray eyes glaring up at Maggie from under a mop of chocolate-brown curls. "But that other kid better watch her step." She scowled darkly. "Who are you?"

Maggie took half a step back, staring at her daughter's face while her mind tried to sort out a hundred different impressions, a dozen crazy questions, and a bunch of impossible answers. The one that her reeling brain focused on was a swift and unlikely diagnosis of Multiple Personality Disorder. Otherwise, who was this defiant stranger staring at her out of Jolene's eyes?

She said the first thing that popped into her mind. "Honey, who cut your hair?"

The first-aid room lay opposite the administrative offices. John knocked briefly on the opaque glass door without announcing himself to the authorities across the hall. Probably better if he had a quiet talk with Andi before hearing anyone else's side of this newest battle. He tried always to support Andi, always to be fair to her and give her the benefit of the doubt, though he had little doubt but that she had earned that poke in the eye.

"Oh, you must be Dr. Martin." A woman stood from the cot where she'd been sitting, helping Andi hold an icepack to one eye.

She smiled, looking him over, the way women always looked over a new man in town, wondering if he was lonely, if he was interested, if he was available.

"That's right." He gave her a polite nod. New man in town or not, lonely or not, he wasn't interested, nor was he available. The only female he wanted in his life sat without looking at him, her head bent in an uncharacteristic pose. Sprinkles of blood splattered her white top.

He strode across the brightly lit room with its primary-color decor and crouched before her, setting down his bag. "Hi, baby doll." He ran a hand over the back of her curly hair, wondering how it gotten so long without his noticing. He wondered, too, why she refused to look at him. He'd expected her to meet him with clenched fists, jutting chin, and a furious spate of words to justify the fight.

She cringed away from him while giving him a sidelong look. Her lower lip quivered. "Are you going to give me a shot?"

"Give you—" He stared down at her. "Of course not. Now, do you want to tell me what happened, or do I have to get the story from the principal? I'd rather hear it from you."

She lifted her head, lowered the towel-wrapped ice, and looked at him from one tear-drenched, smoke-colored eye, the other being swollen shut. He winced and cast a swift, professional glance over her face. He saw no broken skin, no evidence of gross trauma, though the shiner was going to be a doozy.

She flinched away from his touch, whimpering, and he said, "Hey, where's my tough little tiger? Sit still, sweetheart. I'm not going to hurt you, but I do need to check the damage. What does the other kid look like?"

His carefully probing fingertips confirmed the snap diagnosis. Of course, a small child's fist wouldn't pack much of a wallop, though a smear of dried blood caked one of Andi's nostrils, confirming the earlier nosebleed. As he took out his ophthalmoscope and shone the light into her eye, he asked, "What really happened, sweetie?"

"A bad girl hit me in the face." She began to weep in earnest. He frowned. Andi hardly ever cried.

"So I can see. But honey, you must have done something to provoke her," he said gently as he sat beside her and put an arm around her.

"I didn't do anything! Honest!" she wailed, and he picked her up and held her on his lap. She sobbed harder and louder. This was unbelievable. Andi had been a stoic even when she broke her femur trying to fly between two second-floor balconies. "I was turning the rope with Kathy while Monica jumped, and the bad girl just started yelling and hitting me!"

Then she shocked him almost speechless by sobbing, "I want to go home! I . . . want . . . my . . . mommy."

"Oh, my darling." John was moved nearly to tears himself by this unexpected confession. He cuddled her closer, stroking her hair back from her face, feeling her burrow into him as she hadn't done for a long time. She never mentioned Laura. He'd thought she'd forgotten, but of course she hadn't. Hurt, frightened, undoubtedly upset by the move to a new town, a strange house, and an unfamiliar school, she was like any other little girl. She wanted to go home and she wanted her mommy.

He wanted her mommy, too, but Laura was gone irrevocably from them. They had only each other. Somehow he'd have to be enough for her.

He let her cry, enjoying the feel of her warm body, the trusting way she nestled against him, accepted his protective embrace. If for these few, precious minutes, she didn't want to be a tiger, then he was just the guy to let her be a scared and injured baby girl. *His* baby girl.

"Sweetheart, I love you," he whispered, squeezing his eyes tightly shut. "And your mommy loves you too."

From somewhere outside the room, John heard an anguished female voice howl "Jolie!" then the door of the first-aid room slammed open so hard, he thought the glass would shatter.

A tall, slim woman flew in, bright red hair swirling around her head. She came to a halt and stared at him, horror warring with fury, warring with consternation in her face. Fury won hands down as she shouted, "You! Get your hands off my daughter! *Now!*"

John gaped. At the sound of the woman's voice Andi scrambled off his lap and launched herself across the room.

"Mommy! That new girl hit me really, really hard and I bleeded all over my new blouse! Look!" she cried, pointing at the blood. "It's *ruined!*"

"All right, baby, it's all right. Mommy's here." The woman dropped to one knee and cradled the weeping child against her breast. "Don't cry, sweetheart. Don't worry about your blouse. Blood will wash out. Let me look, Jolie. Let me see your face."

While he blinked in astonished, slack-jawed disbelief, John became aware that behind the crouching woman stood the principal, wedged into the doorway with his open-mouthed secretary. Between them crowded another form—Andi.

Unmistakably his daughter, complete with short, curly hair, mutinous eyes, and not a shiner to her name. He groaned and rubbed his eyes. He'd lay odds on her knuckles being battered.

"Andi?" He stood and held out a hand to her. She slipped past the kneeling woman, her head high, her shoulders back, and her eyes snapping with temper.

"You see that, Daddy?" she demanded, pointing at the little girl. "You see? She's got my face on!"

"My God," he said slowly, sinking back onto the cot. He stared from Andi to the weeping replica of his daughter, whom the redhead now held back from her while she examined the damaged eye. "Oh my Lord!"

The redhead leapt to her feet and rounded on him. "You'd better pray, mister." Her eyes—emerald green—blazed into his. "What kind of monster are you raising, anyway, who would do a thing like this? Don't you believe in even the most basic form of discipline, in instilling even the rudiments of self-control? Your child hit Jolene! Injured her! Look!"

Before he could even begin to formulate a reply, she dropped back down to one knee and went nose to nose with Andi. "And as for you, young lady, if you ever, *ever* hurt Jolene again, you will answer to me. Maybe you're allowed to hit people in your home. Maybe you can get away with kicking the principal and swearing at the school secretary, but you are not allowed to hurt Jolene."

She lowered her voice and pushed her face even closer to Andi's. "I am not a nice person when somebody hurts my daughter. Do I make myself perfectly clear?"

To John's amazement, his tough little cookie backed up tight between his knees and said in a small voice, "Yes, ma'am."

"Good. See that you remember it."

She shot to her feet again, scooping up her copy of *Andi*, and whirled, her red hair flying out around her head like a wind-fanned flame—and ran smack into the principal.

"Maggie, er, Miss Adair," he said. "I must insist that you not abuse poor Dr. Martin, a newcomer to our town. I can see I've made a mistake, and Jolene was perhaps not the aggressor, but my goodness, the resemblance is uncanny. The girls could be identical twins!"

"He's right, Maggie," said the secretary. "I got them mixed up too."

Looking from one girl to the other, John knew why the mix-up had occurred, though his head spun with confusion and a thousand question, none of which had answers he could readily accept. The most he could handle at that moment was how perfectly the redhead's name fit her. Maggie. Maggie Adair. Oh, yes, she was definitely a Maggie Adair.

Identical twins . . . Maggie didn't even want to think about the eerie likeness between the children. She flicked a glance at the man who still sat on the cot, his daughter between his knees. He looked as stunned as she felt.

"They're not identical twins!" she shouted, not at the principal, not at Lou, but at the gray-eyed man, as if he were the one she needed to convince.

"They're no relation at all! If they look alike, it's nothing more than coincidence. I—" She broke off, fighting to control the panic that threatened her, but it kept welling up, great waves of fear, of doubt, of irrational dread. She shook off the principal's hand. "Get out of my way. I'm taking Jolene home."

"Now, Maggie, please," the principal said, taking her arm again. "Surely we can discuss this like rational adults. Andrea is also a newcomer. I'm certain she's sorry for what she did and very soon she'll understand that we do not tolerate fighting in this school."

"Oh, but you do, Elmer Abenathy," Maggie said, anger sweeping in to replace the fear. It felt good. Strength returned to her limbs, and she clung to the anger, let it hold her upright like a splint on a shattered leg. Shoving her face right into his, she gave vent to all the frustration this man's philosophies had engendered in her during the two years of his tenure. "Of course you tolerate fighting! Not only that, you actively encourage it, which is why we have this very situation today!"

"No, no." He tried to back away from her, but came up against the desk. "You're quite mis—"

She kept at him. "I'm not the one making mistakes, Elmer! You are. You went off to some fancy college and came back with a lot of crackpot ideas that I don't like, such as your policy that doesn't allow children to hit back if struck first."

"Hitting back only escalates battles, Maggie," the principal said mildly, as if trying to explain a basic tenet to someone who could surely understand if he only got the chance to say it often enough. John actively disliked men who used that wimpy tone of voice. Every time he heard it, it made his hackles rise and he wanted to escalate a battle against them. So, it seemed, did the vibrant Miss Adair.

"By your insistence," she went on relentlessly, "that

kids not be allowed to ask for adult help, which you call 'tattling,' by expecting the children to 'work things out between themselves' you create an atmosphere where it's inevitable that bullies hold sway. That policy, which I mean to see changed, Elmer, even if it means getting you replaced, is directly responsible for the fights that do occur. For the *injuries!*"

"Please, Miss Adair. In school I am addressed as Mr. Abernathy."

"Not by me, you're not, Elmer."

John watched with fascination as the principal turned purple. The man's hands splayed on the desk behind him, and he leaned as far away from his tormentor as he could get. There was no escaping her, though, as she continued her attack.

"My daughter has been pummeled one time too many by the bullies your system produces and protects. I for one am not afraid of bullies, nor am I afraid of you. I remember too well the kind of bully you were until someone named Maggie Adair beat the crap out of you down behind your father's supermarket.

"You were scared of me after that, Elmer, and you'd better get scared of me again, because I just might decide to run for the school board. If I do, and if I win, you and your cockamamie ideas could be in serious trouble. I want firm assurance that my daughter is safe at this school. I demand some concrete evidence that your 'nontolerance' of fighting has some teeth in it. What kind of punishment do you intend to mete out to this . . . *child*"—she glared at Andi, who again shocked John by crowding close to him—"who hurt Jolene, who kicked you, and who swore at Louise?"

"Maggie, Maggie," the principal said soothingly, still tilted back over the desk. "You have to move with the times. Things aren't the way they were when you and I were children. We know more now, know better how to treat aggression, and we don't do it with further aggression. Your problem is you were raised by a pair of very strict grandparents whose ideas rubbed off on you, giving you a two-generation lag in the way things should be done."

"Baloney! The way things should be done is that kids who hurt other kids should be punished."

"It's not our place to mete out punishment," Abernathy said. "As you would have to learn if this town were ever foolish enough to elect you to the school board. We are educators, not police officers or judges. I'm sure Andrea's parents will impress upon her that she's done wrong, as will her teacher and I, at the appropriate time."

"Impress her how?" Maggie demanded. "By having one of your famous little *chats*?"

The principal huffed. "Yes. I expect that will do it."

"And I expect it will not," the redhead snapped. "If little chats had been able to impress that kid"—she jerked her head toward Andi—"I figure she wouldn't have the attitude problem she has now. I am putting you on notice as of this moment: If that child or any other harms Jolene ever again, Elmer Abernathy, I will hold you personally responsible! *Criminally* responsible. Do you understand me?"

"Maggie . . ." Clearly, the principal could find no words with which to continue. He slumped against the corner of the desk, his mouth opening and closing like a fish's. John felt almost sorry for the man, especially considering the crowd of children clustered around the open door, witnessing someone tear a strip off their principal.

With a disdainful glare, Ms. Adair stormed out of the

room, wading through the throng of fascinated kids, oblivious to Elmer's plea that she wait.

She wasn't waiting, not for the principal, not for anything. She was a woman with a mission: the removal of her child from an unsafe environment.

As she thrust open the main door at the end of the corridor, John felt an involuntary and completely inappropriate grin tugging at the corners of his mouth. He wanted to laugh aloud from pure enjoyment, from the pleasure of watching the redhead in action. He wanted to leap up and follow her, look into those blazing green eyes again, and listen to her precise voice enunciate each word with utmost clarity as she vented her anger on everyone she felt responsible for her daughter's injury.

He wanted to lay the backs of his fingers against the warm, pink skin of her cheeks to see if it burned with the kind of heat its color suggested.

Something within him broke loose and soared upward, leaving him feeling euphoric and weak-kneed, as if he'd just witnessed an inspiring event.

Maybe he had. A lioness protecting her cub couldn't have been more magnificent than the fiery Ms. Adair.

TWO

Oh God, oh God, oh God . . . Maggie felt as if her mind had exploded and the pieces had come back together wrong, giving her an oddly linear view of things. Her truck, dead ahead. The pavement between it and her. The door handle, her hand on it, her arms shifting their grip on Jolene, her daughter's bruised face, the seat belt she fastened around Jolene's skinny little body.

Someone tugged at her arm and she wheeled, ready to do battle, but it was only Rodney Watson, face flushed, out of breath. "Here-Miss-Adair," he said in a rush, "I'm-sorry-I'll-never-do-it-again-it-was-just-a-joke-please-don't-be-mad-at me." He shoved something into her hand.

Oh God, oh God, oh God . . . The phrase continued like a stuck record, a prayer with no beginning, no end, only a hope that this was all a nightmare and she'd wake soon to find herself tangled in her sheets, slick with sweat, but safe, with none of it real.

Yet she knew it was real. She could smell the scent of freshly mowed grass, feel the warmth of the breeze, hear the monotonous chirping of a bird in a nearby tree.

She remembered too clearly the straight line of the doctor's brows, the taut shape of his lips, and the exact shade of his blue-gray eyes. Suddenly she could taste the fear again now that her righteous anger was abating. One gray-eyed man. Two gray-eyed children. *No.*

She opened her door and slid onto the seat. She had to think. She needed to reason things out. But first she had to pull herself together. All she heard, though, was her brain ticking over those two repeated words, an expression of horror and heartfelt prayer. *Oh God . . .*

Still reeling from shock, she opened her hand and stared at the objects Rodney had thrust upon her. A small rubber man and a Cracker Jack ring with flashy stones meant to emulate an oval sapphire surrounded by diamonds. She tossed the junk into the small plastic trash can on the hump and fastened her seat belt, then sat, clenching her trembling hands around the wheel. She knew she was in no condition to drive. She didn't think she'd be in any shape to drive for the next thirty years. She took a quick glance at Jolene's sweet, familiar face and wondered how, even for an instant, she could have made the mistake she had.

She'd known on one level almost the second she saw the other child that she couldn't be Jolene, but her mind had refused to accept the unacceptable. How could anyone who looked exactly like Jolene be somebody else? Then, what had seemed impossible at first glance had suddenly, in the moment the little girl said "Who are *you?*" become a shocking reality.

Motion reflected in her side mirror jerked her head up, and she saw the father of the other child approaching. His long legs carried him across the parking area in a determined stride. His mouth formed a thin hard line above a square chin. He towed his daughter by one hand; she hopped and skipped and half ran to keep up.

Maggie shoved the key into the ignition, started the engine, and wheeled out of there with scarcely a glance over her shoulder. Behind her the man slapped a hand on the back of her Cherokee and hollered, "Wait! We need to talk!"

"Like hell," she muttered. Maybe he needed to talk. *She* needed to escape.

A glance in the rearview mirror showed him standing there staring after her, as if memorizing her license plate so that he'd recognize her truck if he saw it again. She had no doubt she'd recognize him if she saw him in Timbuktu sixty years from now, and since she never wanted to see him again, she fixed her eyes to the front and drove like mad. She was running away, away from the child with her terrible likeness to Jolene, away from the man that other child called Daddy, away from the questions, away from the answers, away from the fear.

It struck here then with the force of a blow that he'd probably made the same mistake she had. He'd thought the injured child was his own. What had he called her? Andi. He must be as confused as she was, asking himself how there could be two Andis, as she asked how could there be two Jolenes. Maybe they did need to talk. But was she going back? Not a chance!

How could there be two identical little girls in the same school where last year there had been only one edition of her daughter?

The answer was obvious. Though it might be true that everyone had an exact double somewhere, it also seemed entirely too possible that since Jolene was Maggie's adopted child, she could, indeed, have an identical twin. And that that twin had just punched her lights out.

But if there had been two babies born on the same day, in the same hospital, of the same mother, why hadn't they been adopted by the same family? Someone who could love one child, make her their own, could surely have been trusted to love two! She could have. Would have, if offered the chance, but . . .

A chilling thought occurred, and on its heels, an explosive denial. *"No!"*

"Mommy? What's wrong?"

"Nothing, sweetheart." *And everything.* Because the thought persisted. It gave justification to the fear she'd been calling irrational. Her subconscious must have come up with the explanation and acted upon it before her conscious mind recognized the full implications of the situation. Fact: Jolene's birth mother had not been a scared teenager whose boyfriend refused to acknowledge or help support his child. Fact: The birth *parents* had been a young married couple attending college on a shoestring, who'd decided they couldn't afford a child. Fact: They had been emotionally overwhelmed by even the contemplation of the awesome responsibility of raising a baby.

But . . . what if the facts Maggie had been given were incomplete? What if there had been two babies? What if the "awesome responsibility" the caseworker had spoken of had been not of raising *one* child, but of raising two? What if that man back there was the natural father of both girls and now that he'd seen her again, had decided he wanted Jolene back?

She glanced at Jolene, at her blue-gray eyes, and remembered the dark, slatey shade of the man's eyes.

Her foot squeezed down on the gas pedal, sending the Cherokee shooting out and around a slow-moving gravel truck.

"Mom?" Jolene's voice was small. "Are you mad at me?"

"Jolie!" She slowed considerably as she smiled at her daughter. She never exceeded the speed limit with Jolene in the car. "No, baby, of course not. Why would I be mad at you?"

"I talked to a strange man. I sat on his lap."

"Yes, well . . ." Maggie didn't know what to say. Obviously, Jolene knew it was wrong to do that, but she'd been hurt. He'd offered solace. And a teacher's aide had been present, so . . .

"I'm not mad at you," she said. "It was okay for you to let him look after you because he's a doctor and Mrs. White was there."

"He's real nice, Mom. I was afraid he'd give me a shot, but he didn't. He just touched my face and called me sweetie and asked me a bunch of stuff."

Maggie went instantly on the alert. "What kind of stuff?"

"What the other kid looked like. What the fight had been about."

Oh. Relief made her light-headed. "What did you tell him?"

"That me and Kathy and Monica were playing jump rope and the bad girl came up and hit me for no reason at all." She frowned, her faint, wispy brows drawing together, and Maggie braced herself for the inevitable questions about why the "bad girl" looked so much like Jolene. To her surprise, they didn't come.

"Then I said I wanted you," Jolene continued, "and he picked me up and rocked me and talked real soft. He said he loved me and . . ."

Alarm bells rang in Maggie's ears, but through their

clamor, she heard Jolene go on, ". . . and that you loved me too."

"Oh," she said weakly. "Well, he was sure right about that."

Jolene sighed and Maggie glanced at her again, seeing a wistful smile curving her mouth. "I wish he could be my doctor. Dr. Klein doesn't cuddle me."

Everything protective in Maggie rose upright like the quills on a porcupine. "Dr. Klein has been your doctor since you were one year old and we came to live in Maples. He takes good care of you. It wouldn't be right for him to cuddle you. That's not what doctors do. They make you well when you're sick. Moms are for cuddling, and Mr. Bear, of course."

Jolene nodded, and Maggie hoped that would be the end of it. Naturally, it wasn't.

During lunch, Maggie again expected questions about Andi, but they weren't forthcoming. She tried to introduce the subject, but Jolene evaded the issue. While Maggie rolled out pastry for an apple pie, finding the action soothing and relaxing, Jolene knelt on a stool and nibbled apple peels. She chattered happily about being in Mrs. Amberg's second-grade class and complained about the first day of school only being half a day. As compensation, Maggie suggested that after the pie was out of the oven, they take their horses out to the lake, just for fun, not a riding lesson or anything. Jolene surprised her by asking if she could have a nap instead, though she'd stopped taking naps the year she went to kindergarten.

Instantly mindful of the dangers of a blow to the head, Maggie looked at her daughter sharply. "Do you feel sick? Does your head hurt?"

"No. I'm just tired. I want to snuggle with Mr. Bear."

Maggie managed to distract her for half an hour

while they fed the apple peels to the chickens, then picked more apples and some of the last of the green beans. The subject she most wanted to discuss with her daughter was the one Jolene continued to evade. By the time the pie was out of the oven, Jolene was insisting on that nap she wanted.

Maggie agreed, on the condition that Jolene not beg for extra time out of bed that night as a result.

As she curled up under a light blanket Jolene looked up at her mother. "You know, *he* was all warm and snuggly, and I could hear his heart beating." Maggie did not need to ask whom she meant, but she did so anyway, to keep the conversation going.

Jolene smiled. "That nice doctor. He rocked me and rubbed my back and talked in a growly voice just like Mr. Bear." She hugged Mr. Bear, who growled in response. "He smelled nice too."

"As nice as Mr. Bear?" Maggie teased. Mr. Bear had reeked of cheap perfume since Brownie camp last month.

Jolene's thumb hovered just an inch from her mouth. She never sucked it anymore when Maggie was present. She closed her eyes and said sleepily, "Maybe that's what it would be like to have a daddy's lap to sit on."

There was nothing, when it came right down to it, that Maggie could say, so she merely cradled Jolene close for a few minutes, then left her to sleep.

She was heading for her computer and the accounts waiting for her when her rusty-sounding doorbell rang. She didn't have to wonder who it was, didn't even question how he'd learned where she lived. In Maples, Nova Scotia, it wasn't hard to learn anyone's address.

She simply opened the door, feeling resigned, and there he stood, all six feet plus of him, crisp dark brown hair curling over his forehead, blue-gray eyes smiling at her. The color of them, only a shade or two darker than Jolie's—or Andi's—sliced into her like knives through her heart.

John stared at Maggie. Her house didn't suit her. Though he'd known this was her address, had expected her to open the door, he realized as he looked at her that he hadn't expected such a sense of incongruity. She stood in the doorway looking young and clean and vibrant, a direct contrast to the peeling gray paint on the clapboards, the sagging roofline he'd seen as he navigated between potholes in the rutted, weedy drive. The porch felt as if it might collapse under his feet, and he could see a distinct gap where it should have met the front of the house.

He frowned, offended in some way that she had to live there, almost overcome by a surge of protectiveness that made him want to take her away from it. Protectiveness? He nearly laughed at the idea. He didn't think he'd ever met a woman less in need of a protector than Maggie Adair.

Her wooden expression told him she, too, was offended, but by his presence. Swiftly he took in the rigid posture, the white knuckles of her hand clenched on the door, and the taut line of her jaw. Uh-oh. This was not a lady who had, as the school secretary had promised him, "cooled down by the time you get there."

"Hi." He tried a smile, hoping it might soften her visage.

It did not. "What can I do for you, Doctor?" Her tone was icy, her expression giving nothing away. Her arm barred his entry.

"I think we need to talk," he said. "May I, uh, come in?"

She eyed him with dislike. "No."

Her blunt refusal made him feel big, stupid, and awkward; foolish for having asked. He blinked. "I, er, well . . ." He cleared his throat. "Okay, then, we can do it here. How is your daughter?"

Her perfectly chiseled nose rose a fraction. "Are you asking in your professional capacity, or as a concerned parent of the child who did the damage?" Animosity emanated from her like a visible aura. Clearly, she was going to hold a grudge.

"Whichever you prefer."

She flicked her hand at a fly seeking entry, brushing it away as she would obviously like to do with him. With as little success. It buzzed right by her and into the house. "What I'd prefer," she said, "is for you not to be here at all."

Maggie watched his eyes narrow, watched a dark stain of color rise up his cheeks as her bad manners got to him. Good. Maybe he'd leave. "I'd prefer to be elsewhere, too," he said, "but circumstances dictate otherwise. We need to talk, whether you like it or not. Now, do we conduct our conversation on the doorstep while flies fill your house, or do I come inside where we can discuss this very serious matter in a civilized manner . . . to say nothing of privacy," he added, raising his voice as a slow-moving truck ground its noisy way up the hill.

"We have absolutely nothing to discuss!" Maggie kept her own tone low so as not to disturb her daughter. The less Jolene knew about this entire mess, the better, and since she hadn't started asking any questions yet, maybe she'd go on pretending there was nothing amiss. If she did, then Maggie could too.

"If you're concerned professionally about Jolene's condition," she continued, "I assure you she's fine. If I weren't certain of that, I'd have taken her to her own pediatrician. If you're here for any other reason, I'll have to refer you to my lawyer."

"Lawyer?" His eyes widened. "Are you planning to sue me over a playground fight between two seven-year-old girls?"

"What?" She stared back at him. "No, of course I'm not planning to sue. Why do you say that?"

"Why did you bring up the subject of lawyers?"

"Because—" She broke off, brushed another fly away from her face, and chewed on her lower lip.

Into her silence he said, "Ms. Adair—Maggie— please don't be afraid of me. I'm not here to hurt you. *Or* Jolene. In any way."

She tossed her hair back with a quick gesture. "Afraid? What gives you the idea I'm afraid of you or anything else?"

"For one thing," he said, "you look scared. And you act scared. Anger is often a cover for fear."

She dropped her hand from the door, stuffing it behind her lest he see it trembling. "I hope the snap analysis is free, doctor, because you are completely mistaken, and I'd hate to get a bill for an incorrect diagnosis. It takes a lot of nerve to peg someone as 'looking scared' when you don't know her, can't possibly tell how she might look when she's scared."

He swept another searching glance over her. "There are signs that are considered universal. Extreme pallor, fine tremors, damp upper lip."

Maggie caught herself as she was about to wipe her upper lip.

"Why are you really here, Doctor?" she asked with exaggerated patience. "What do you want from me?"

"I told you. We need to talk. About Jolene and Andi. And the name is John."

"I have nothing to say to you about my daughter."

"Maybe she has things she'd like to ask me about her sister," he said. "My daughter certainly wanted to come with me to see you and Jolene. I'd have brought her, but her behavior today has her grounded after school for the rest of the week."

"Jolie is sleeping and has no desire to know anything about you or your daughter. Understand this, Doctor, once and for all. I adopted Jolene legally and irrevocably, and that being the case, we have nothing more to say to each other. I suggest you leave."

He shook his head. "This is too important an issue to our two children for us to ignore it."

"I'll ignore it as long as my daughter chooses to do so." Maggie's voice rasped. "And when—if—she decides to ask questions, I'll find some way to explain it to her satisfaction. Now, I have work to do, so if you'll excuse me . . ."

"How?" he demanded, leaning a shoulder against the door she would have shut. "How do you explain to your child that she has an identical twin sister she's never heard of—that you've never heard of—until today?"

His stubborn refusal to leave elicited a strong desire in Maggie to yell at him, to pound him with something, to make him hear what she was saying. She was saying no, no to a discussion, no to his presence on her doorstep, no to the very thing that had brought him there. She was saying no, but he was acting as if she'd said yes. There was a dogged quality about him that frustrated her, because she recognized it as one of her own less charming characteristics. If she was an immovable object, then he was an irresistible force.

"Believe me," he went on, "my daughter's not ignoring the situation, and I can't either. She wants an explanation. They are *twins*, for heaven's sake. Sisters. They need each other. We have to deal with that."

Maggie lost the tenuous control she'd had on her temper. Planting her fists on her hips, she said, "No, dammit! What you and your wife have to deal with is that you gave her up! *I'm* her mother now and nothing is going to change that. How dare you come to me whining about your child 'needing' her sister in her life? You should have thought of that seven years ago and—"

"Wait a minute!" His eyes darkened as his brows drew down. He took one step through her doorway, coming within a few inches of her as if he expected her to move. "Do you think *I'm* their biological father?"

Maggie stood her ground, arms crossed over her breasts. "Aren't you?"

"Good God, no! Is that what all this animosity is about? My late wife and I adopted Andi when she was an infant. We—" He broke off and wiped a hand down his face. His wedding band glinted.

"It never occurred to either of us that there might have been two. If we'd known, we'd have wanted them both, but—" He spread his hands in a helpless gesture. "I'd never try to take your daughter from you."

Relief made her knees sag.

She backed up a step, aware of her breath jerking in and out as if she'd been running. He wasn't Jolene's father! He had no claim.

He came fully over the threshold and caught her as she swayed, his eyes expressing concern as she stared into their depths. His hands were large, warm, secure on her shoulders, and Maggie was jolted by a sudden and insane desire to step forward and rest her head against his chest.

In the silence, she could hear—she was sure she could hear—his heart beating, slowly, steadily, rhythmically, in time to the pulse she could see in his throat.

Suddenly she understood how her daughter had been comforted by this man's embrace. He said nothing. A breeze wafted in through the open door, lifting a strand of her hair and blowing it across her face. He slid a finger under it and lifted it away.

As her gaze clung to his, his palms flattened on the backs of her shoulders, and for a wild, heart-stopping moment she thought he would pull her into an embrace. It shocked her, the strength of that part of her that wanted him to, that wanted to take comfort in his closeness.

She told herself to move away, but felt like a marionette in inexpert hands. Excitement rose in her like licking flames. If he put his arms fully around her right this minute, would she melt, or would she ignite?

She lifted a trembling hand to his face, but then, without her knowing how it had happened, he was three feet away from her, his expression distant, even cold. It left her feeling somehow ashamed.

She swallowed quickly and shook her hair down over her face before pushing it back behind both ears.

"Circumstantial evidence," she said, finding her voice at last, pressing her back to the wall. "I can't believe I got caught in that trap." She managed a creditable laugh. "It's your eyes, you see. They're so much like Jolene's, I couldn't help jumping to conclusions and—" She stopped, swallowed, glanced down at his hands. They were curled into fists at his sides.

Her gaze moved up, over his wide chest, past the open neck of his shirt to that pulse again. It still hammered there, though his breathing was slower. She conjured up a smile that he didn't return.

"And I think you've fallen for the same thing here," she went on quickly. "Circumstantial evidence." She was clutching at the idea she most wanted to believe as she wrapped her arms around her middle. "That's all you're basing your assumptions on. Maybe the girls *aren't* twins who were separated at birth, but simply two little girls who look alike."

"Maggie," John said, and his voice cracked on her name. He cleared his throat and tried again, wondering if she had recovered so much more quickly from that momentary insanity they'd shared because it hadn't gone as deep with her. In the blink of an eye, she'd shaken her head, fixed her hair, and gotten right back to the subject at hand as if the roof hadn't just blown off the world.

He drew in the subtle scent of her perfume, and his throat went thick, his body heavy with a renewed surge of the kind of longing he'd thought he'd buried with Laura. It shocked him, brought him up short, forced him to take another deliberate step back from Maggie Adair. She was a stranger and not his type, nothing like his serene Laura had been. He had no business feeling these spikes of physical need where she was concerned.

"Maggie, they are twins."

"You can't know that for sure."

"Oh, come on," he said, recovering his equilibrium. "There's not a shred of doubt in my mind, but if any remains in yours, a simple blood test would prove it beyond question."

"No!" Her teeth clacked together as she bit out the word. "Jolene hates needles. I won't subject her to that."

"All right. I don't think it's necessary anyway." He wondered if it was so much her daughter's fear of needles, or her own fear of the outcome, that made her refusal so adamant. "But if you want to be sure, one way or the other . . ." He let his voice trail off, let the decision be hers alone.

"We have two children," he went on after a minute, "who are going to be put through all kinds of hell as the kids at school treat them like freaks—at least for a while. They're going to need us to stand with them, to help them come up with answers to the inevitable questions. We're going to need to work together on this, Maggie."

"What we have are two children who happen to look alike," she said. "They'll get used to it, their classmates will get used to it, and so will we. It will cease to be remarkable if we don't treat it as remarkable."

"Dammit, Maggie . . ." Before he could prevent its doing so, his hand rose and stroked her pink cheek. *Satin.* And despite the rosy color, her skin felt as cool as porcelain. The warmth, he sensed, would be elsewhere. Deeper. He snatched back his hand. "What's it take to convince you? Facts, figures, dates?"

She said nothing, only looked at him challengingly as if certain his facts, figures, and dates couldn't possibly stack up. He quickly told her Andi's birth date.

She bit her lip. He watched her white teeth make clear depressions in the pink flesh. Aware he was staring, he forced his gaze away.

He told her the name of the hospital.

She winced, and he felt as bad as if he had deliberately caused her pain.

He cited the name of the attending physician and saw a wave of shock cross her expressive face. He wanted with every fiber of his being to tell her it was all a mistake, that she didn't have to stand there looking as if he were sentencing her to death. Honesty made him continue. "Andi was born at 12:15 P.M."

Her voice was a fine thread of sound. "Jolene, at 12:27. Also attended by Dr. Rebecca Long."

He nodded.

She sighed and slumped against the wall.

"Are you okay?" he asked, lifting a hand to touch her again, but dropping it just short of its objective.

As if his fingers had made contact, she tossed her head, swirling a stream of hair around her shoulders.

"Of course I'm okay," she said, pushing away from the wall.

"It's a shock, I know," John said, keeping an eye on her too-white face, afraid to touch her again, but ready in case he must. "I wanted to hold on to my doubts, too, but I've seen enough identical twins in my career to recognize the phenomenon."

"But it's no big deal," she insisted. "Even if they are twins, it's no big deal."

He rammed a hand through his hair. "Dammit," he said, half laughing, "how can I make you understand that we have two innocent girls here whose future well-being is at stake, and we're the adults? We have to take responsibility. We have to find the answers they are going to expect us to provide."

"Answers," she whispered, leaning against the wall again, shaking her head. "Hoo-boy. Answers."

They stared at each other, motionless, speechless, contemplating the answers. And the questions.

To her surprise, Maggie found the desire to fight with John Martin was gone. The need to deny that they had a mutual problem that would take both of them to solve no longer existed. Their children were sisters and he was right. It was a reality they were going to have to deal with.

"Could I offer you a cup of coffee and a slice of apple pie while we compile our list of answers, John?"

For an instant she thought he looked almost trapped, certainly wary, as if he suspected an ulterior motive behind her invitation. However, after a brief hesitation, he nodded. "Yes, I'd like that. Thanks."

THREE

As she led the way to the kitchen Maggie was uncomfortably aware of John following her. She wondered if his gaze was on the motion of her rear end under her tunic-length top, or if it had trailed down her black leggings, taking in the shape of her thighs and calves. Did he think her hips were too wide? Did he see the way she walked as provocative? She knew that trying to keep her hips from swaying likely exaggerated their movement, but she couldn't prevent herself trying not to sway.

It was strange, embarrassing, being this physically aware of her own body. It had been a long time since she'd felt this way, and she wasn't at all sure she liked it.

Luckily, the walk was short.

John stared with curiosity into the living room as they passed it. He liked the ambiance, cluttered though the room was with toys and books. The big, squashy furniture, the faded patterned rug over brown-painted floorboards, and lamps positioned for comfortable reading created a homey atmosphere. It was a room he hoped to be invited into someday, but clearly this wasn't the time. She continued on toward the back of the house, whisking a door shut as she passed it, but not before he caught a glimpse of a sheer pink nightie over the back of a chair, a bra on the dresser, and a pair of jeans, panties included, in a just-stepped-out-of position on the floor.

So. Picking up after herself wasn't one of her strong suits. Oddly, it made him smile.

The kitchen, with 1950s-vintage chrome table and chairs, looked as if it were trying to slide away under the back porch, but John scarcely noticed as the aroma of freshly baked apple pie smacked him in the nose. He breathed it in appreciatively and would have pulled out one of the red vinyl chairs from under the table, but Maggie shooed him toward the back door as if he were one of the flies that had come in at the front.

He wanted to stay in her kitchen. It might be old, it might be dingy, but the aromas of apples and cinnamon made his mouth water, and his eyes were drawn to a huge bowl of mostly blue wildflowers in the middle of the table. There were blue curtains at the windows, which reminded him of a set his mother had made for his bedroom one happy afternoon shortly before he started school.

They'd hung there for close to a week, he recalled, before his stepfather Jack had ripped them down in a rage over something John had long forgotten. There had been too many rages, too much destruction. And too few happy memories of his mother.

Again Maggie waved him toward the back door and the picnic table he saw set on a cement slab just beyond. "Please, go on out and get comfortable. I'll bring the coffee when it's ready."

John obeyed reluctantly. He wondered if Maggie had made her curtains. He wondered if she always picked flowers and arranged them. He couldn't recall if his mother ever had, though there must have been a time . . .

With a quick, impatient sigh, he distracted himself by sweeping his gaze over the unexpectedly spacious backyard. From the front, he'd thought the house sat on a small plot, an anomaly surrounded by farms. Yet, while certainly no farm, it surely had an acre of backyard within the confines of a rail fence. Part of the area was given over to a vegetable garden, some to a chicken run in the far corner where a rooster stood on a perch in a dead snag, surveying his clucking harem. The remainder contained fruit trees and low bushes that he thought bore berries.

Three white rabbits with floppy ears nibbled at the grass along a wire fence surrounding the vegetable garden, clearly wanting in. Their noses twitched as they pressed them to the wire.

He could almost hear Andi's squeal of delight, should she see them. She'd rush at them, full of excitement and impetuous motion, and send them scattering in all directions.

The light breeze ruffled the leaves of pole beans and the fronds of carrots and carried the scent of tomatoes to him. Flowers whose name he didn't know, but that he recognized because they grew up a fence in his own backyard, climbed a trellis ten feet away, trumpet-shaped blossoms bobbing like little dancers in multicolored skirts.

As he continued down the steps and toward the picnic table, the rustle of leaves and branches drew his gaze upward. Large golden apples with rosy cheeks hung in clusters. The scent of them filled the air, mingling with the aroma of coffee brewing in the kitchen.

He turned in response to a whinnying sound. A bay

horse leaned its neck over the fence, dark mane draping forward, nearly black tail sweeping idly at flies; it seemed to think Maggie's grass was sweeter than its own. In the sun its coat gleamed almost as red as Maggie's hair. Beyond, a dainty gray mare cropped grass near a white barn with a red roof.

Pastoral . . . peaceful . . . homey. From the ramshackle dwelling behind him, to the chickens and rabbits and vegetable garden, to say nothing of the overgrown but colorful flowerbeds and the horses next door, Maggie's environment pleased him.

A hugh sigh he hadn't been aware of holding back escaped him in a rush but did nothing to relieve the tightness in his chest. He felt lonely, homesick, envious of what Maggie had managed to create on what was obviously a small income.

Odd how the sight of a real, old-fashioned home affected him. Despite his living in an authentic Victorian house, he didn't feel at home. Neither did his daughter. Maybe that helped account for some of Andi's anger and aggression. Of course, their house in Hamilton hadn't felt like a home to him, either, not since Laura died.

Mrs. Wisdom, their live-in housekeeper, had tried hard there, as hard as she was trying here, having cheerfully made the move with them. It wasn't the same, though. Of course it wasn't. Nothing would ever be the same without Laura. He thought he'd come to terms with that. He thought he'd accepted it, but suddenly the yearning to have a real home again was so strong, it nearly buckled his knees. It made his throat tighten and his stomach twist with an emotion he couldn't name. The stifled sensation clutched harder at his throat as he listened to the voices of the countryside, drew in its scents, and gazed at its quiet face.

A home with Maggie Adair.

What? He spun around and stared at her windows, as if she had somehow implanted the thought. Of course she hadn't, but where in the hell had it come from? He mentally erased the words, squelched the feelings the notion evoked, irritated, disconcerted, angry with himself and, unfairly, with her.

He didn't even know the woman. All right, so maybe he was sexually attracted to her, but he'd been drawn to women that way before and would be again. As for anything else, he wasn't ready for that kind of relationship.

Not yet. Maybe never. Maybe a man could have that only once in a lifetime. But he wanted—

Stop it! he commanded himself. *What you want is a good piece of—*

He shook his head and clenched his jaw. What he wanted was not something he was going to get anywhere in Maples, Nova Scotia. The town was too small for even the most discreet liaison to go unremarked, and he had a daughter to think of, to say nothing of his professional standing. Which meant he had to take his physical needs elsewhere, despite the powerful way Maggie Adair affected him.

He blinked as she came out the door, the sun catching her hair and turning it to living flame. The beauty of it got right down deep inside him and twanged something that had pulled taut again over the past few minutes.

He tried to compose his face into expressionless lines, but knew he smiled, watching her glide over the uneven ground with a sure grace that spoke of familiarity with her surroundings. She carried a tray before her, balancing it easily despite its burden of two brown ceramic mugs, sugar bowl and creamer, and matching plates with slices of apple pie stacked with scoops of melting ice cream.

"Have a seat," she said, setting the tray down and straddling a bench. He took a place opposite her and accepted the mug she slid toward him. He lifted it quickly, taking a swig before he blurted out something stupid. It was too hot and burned his mouth, but he swallowed it anyway, savoring its flavor.

She set a plate before him, then picked up her own fork and dug in. He followed suit.

The pie was ambrosial, hot, spicy with cinnamon, sweet with sugar, and stuffed with thick, tangy apple slices. The pastry flaked and melted in his mouth. The richness of the ice cream soothing the coffee-scald completed the sensual experience. "Mmmm," he murmured, glancing up at Maggie.

She sat watching him intently, fork halfway between mouth and plate, and for a second he had the impression she had been waitng for his approval. "Incredible," he said around another bite. "Delicious."

"Glad you like it," she said, her one-shouldered shrug implying that approval had been the last thing on her mind. Her smile, though, made a lie of the gesture.

Suddenly his heart lifted in that strange, almost dizzying way it had that morning when he'd wanted to laugh in sheer pleasure at the sight of Maggie Adair in action. His delight produced an unexpected sensation of disloyalty to Laura, until he told himself it was nothing more than a knee-jerk response, a normal male reaction to a pretty smile. Still, he had to take a long breath to steady himself before he continued eating his pie.

"This is, uh, nice," he said, then wished he'd come up with a more appropriate word than "nice." He compounded the error. "It's very . . . pretty here."

"I like it," she said, so defensively he got the impression she was ashamed of the way she lived. "And so do my friends over there. They're the prime reason I bought such a beat-up old house that's nearly impossible to keep warm in winter and even worse to keep cool in summer. The darned place is an air sieve, but with two horses, I needed some space. Even that"—she gestured at the paddock on the other side of the fence—"isn't as big as I'd like, but it comes with a nice tight barn."

She laughed. "Sometimes I think Jolene and I should live there and let the horses have the run of the house." Her gaze clung with fond possession to the animals.

John looked, but at her profile. Above, the apple tree limbs moved restlessly in the breeze, casting flares of sun and depths of shade over her hair, her cheeks, her lips. "I didn't realize they were yours."

"They're not mine." She turned a quick grin in his direction. "I'm theirs, but they permit Jolene and me to ride them. I give lessons, as well, to a few local kids."

"So your horses earn their keep."

She laughed. "Not really, but I can't be without them. My father was an Irishman, a horse trainer, and he had me in the saddle before my second birthday. I've always owned at least one horse, though there were times I couldn't keep them with me."

For a moment John saw a shadow cross her face. He wanted to reach out and take her hand. He wondered about those times. Clearly, they had made her unhappy. He disliked the thought of Maggie being sad. Fortunately, before he could blurt out a question he had no right to ask, she went on.

"I'm glad I can now, even if it means making the odd sacrifice." He nodded, thinking of the canted kitchen floor, the likely dangerous front porch he'd crossed so gingerly, and the sagging roofline.

"When I was a child," she continued, "my pony was always boarded over there in that very paddock, along with my grandfather's two racehorses. At one time the property belonged to a man who ran breeding stables. My father worked for him. I like to think that if my dad had lived, his expertise would have made the business fly, but after he died, it went under.

"Bit by bit, the property got sold off. The first owners are long gone now, and the people I bought my house and three acres from own only about one-eighth of the original place. They maintain a fair-sized apple orchard and grow a few vegetables for market, as well as keeping a couple of cows."

John cast around for something positive to say about the home he'd assumed she was only renting. But to have bought it—well, it said something for her judgment. "And you get to keep your horses," he said. "I suppose you're lucky to have found a large enough space for them."

"I think so." She swung her legs over the bench and stood. Her "You like horses?" was an invitation, and he walked beside her to the fence, where the horses greeted her with insistent nudges and soft whickers.

"Medallion," Maggie said, introducing the bay. "And Ghost." Ghost tugged at the bottom of her shirt. She reached up and pulled two apples from a tree, handing one to John.

He fed Medallion, who, clearly not satisfied, nuzzled his armpit and took his shirt in large, yellow teeth. Gently, but with a firm authority that Maggie liked, he broke the horse's grip and pushed it away. "You're familiar with horses," she said, pleased.

"I used to work with them. I was a—"

He broke off with a strangled sound, paling visibly as Gilgamesh, the neighbor's German shepherd, came roaring out from the far side of the barn, his hackles up, his teeth bared, and his voice booming. His tail, however, was wagging. Before Maggie could tell the dog to stop his noise, John had her up in his arms and was swinging her toward the lowest branch of the apple tree, shouting, "Climb!"

"John!" Maggie grabbed the branch because she had little choice, but dropped back down immediately, hushing Gilgamesh with one quiet word. Obediently he sat, tongue lolling, grinning up at John, delighted with the response his greeting had received.

"It's all right," she said, looking into John's white face. "He's okay. Noisy but harmless. Gilgamesh, shame on you. What a goofball you are!"

He hung his head and Maggie relented, rubbing his ears.

John's throat worked. "I'm familiar with horses," he said, "but as you can see, not so with dogs. Sorry. I didn't mean to overreact." Maggie could see the difficulty he had bringing his breathing back under control. "I hope I didn't hurt you, grabbing you like that."

"It's okay," she said. "You didn't hurt me." She smiled, trying to ease what must be an awkward moment for him. "You said you worked with horses?"

It was a few seconds before he answered, a time during which he kept a wary eye on the dog before apparently convincing himself there was no immediate danger.

"Yes. As a stablehand while I was going to college. I got the job by default; no one else applied. What I really wanted was the apartment that went with it." He smiled wryly. "I didn't know a thing about horses when I started. I soon learned and came to enjoy riding, but in recent years there's never seemed to be the time." He paused for a moment, still patting Medallion's neck with rhythmic slaps.

"I'll have to think about getting a couple of horses. I know Andi would love it, and now that I'm back here"—he shrugged—"I guess there's no reason not to."

"*Back* here? You've lived here before?"

The startled interest in Maggie's gaze sent a surge of caution through him. It was so easy to talk to her, he'd forgotten to be wary. It was too late now to backtrack, though. "Yes," he said. "I grew up in the area."

"Really?" She angled her head as she studied him. "So did I. Funny I don't remember you. I don't even recall seeing you around."

He ran a speculative gaze over her, assessing age. "By the time I finished high school, I suppose you might have just been entering junior high. Six or seven years is a big difference between kids. Different crowds, different interests." Not that he'd ever been part of a crowd, or permitted to pursue any interests.

It hardly surprised him that no one had recognized him so far. He'd been counting on it, though he'd found several faces familiar, and many names. His own name was different now, and in twenty years a man's looks can change a lot. If anyone had recognized him, he wouldn't have denied being who he was, but it was easier simply being the new doctor in town and letting it go at that.

"Yes." Maggie's word of agreement cut into his thoughts. "But my grandfather was Doc Monro, and over the years, I thought everyone ended up at our house one time or another, for stitches or cough syrup or hay-fever medication. Where did you live?"

Shock prevented him from speaking for a moment.

She was Doc Monro's granddaughter? Her "our house" suggested she'd grown up in Maples—in the doctor's house. He may have seen her on the rare occasions that he was allowed into town. He didn't recall any redheaded little girls, but then he probably hadn't been looking. Yet he realized she might have been the child he'd heard laughing outside Doc Monro's office window one day, a delicious, joyful sound that had left him feeling both enchanted and sad. Even as a thirteen-year-old he'd known that a life like his, totally devoid of laughter, was wrong. That was why he had gone to her grandfather, seeking help to make it right, help that had not been forthcoming.

"So you grew up in Doc Monro's house," he said finally. "I was there a couple of times. It impressed me a lot." He managed a smile. "So much so, that I've just moved into it."

Her eyes widened momentarily, and John thought he saw a flicker of regret in them. Her tone, though, was light as she said, "Really? That's nice. I believe the previous owner was a dentist. It's a good place for a doctor who wants to run his practice on-site." She leaned against the top fence rail, hooking a heel up over the bottom one. "That's what my great-grandfather built it for."

"And one of the reasons I bought it," John said, assuming a similar position. *One of the minor reasons.* The major one being that he was, like it or not, still playing a secret game of catch-up, and owning Doc Monro's house gave him a feeling of satisfaction little else had in the past several years. He supposed that was part of what had drawn him back to Maples. Even if no one else knew the huge strides he had taken to get away from there and then to return as a successful professional, a general practitioner, *he* knew, and that was what counted.

He let his gaze rest on Doc Monro's granddaughter, wondering how she'd react if she knew he was the stepson of the man who had once been the area's most notorious bootlegger and drug dealer. If they'd been of a compatible age back when he'd lived there, he knew damned well Doc Monro would have gone to great lengths to keep his granddaughter safe from the likes of Jack Porter's kid. Assuming Jack Porter's kid had been permitted to date.

"One of the reasons?" Maggie asked.

He grinned. "Another being that it has lots of room and I'm a collector, so I need plenty of space."

Her eyes sparkled with interest. "What do you collect?"

He laughed. "Junk, mostly, according to my housekeeper. I hate to throw things away. It started with antique surgical instruments, but went on from there to old laboratory vessels like test tubes and beakers, which somehow began to include jugs and pitchers from the Depression era. That snowballed into different specimens of Depression glass, and who knows where it'll end? Oh, and I have marbles, too, lots of marbles."

She tilted her head to one side. "Holdovers from childhood?"

"Not really. I just like marbles." Before she could press the subject, he asked, "The house was in your family for a few generations, then?"

"Yes," she said. "I was the fourth generation to live there. After my grandfather was murdered, it was . . . sold."

"Murdered?" People had certainly mentioned Doc

Monro to him, but no one had said anything to suggest the man hadn't died of old age.

Maggie didn't look at him. Her focus seemed fixed on something across the field, or maybe across the years. "They said he died of a heart attack, probably brought on by stress. When I got home from a school dance that night and found him lying in the hall, he was still alive. His office had been ransacked and it was clear, at least to me, that he'd been trying to stop whoever forced their way in. Two men, he said. They smashed open the drug cabinet, snatched a bunch of stuff and ran, but not before taking the time to shoot themselves full of morphine. He lay there the whole time, and they never so much as called an ambulance or did anything to try to help him. And they never got caught."

She turned and looked at John. "I don't care if they were addicts, sick with a need they couldn't control. To me, they're murderers who killed the best man, the best doctor, who ever lived. If they'd had just asked, Grandpa would have helped them somehow. I know that. He didn't hate addicts, or judge them. But he certainly hated those who profited by creating them." She drew in a ragged breath and let it out in a gust. "And so do I!"

John touched her arm. "Yes."

She pulled away, but not before he saw her chin pucker for just an instant. Then, with a couple of rapid blinks, she collected herself. "Sorry," she said. "It was a long time ago, but every now and then the utter fury I felt at first sweeps over me again."

John nodded. Now he understood why her family had let the house go, though it was a good, solid, sturdy structure, if a bit on the austere side with its dark paneling and small-paned windows. It stood on one of the most prestigious residential streets in town and was convenient to everything—the school, the small hospital, and stores.

But, full of big, drafty rooms, creaking floors, and unexpected staircases, it was not convenient or comfortable to live in. Nor, he was sure, would it be a happy place for any of Doc Monro's family to live.

"Since you grew up there," he said, "you must know all of its secrets. Is there any way to get the cellar door open when it rains?"

He liked the sound of her laughter, liked the way his question wiped the shadows from her eyes. "Nope," she said. "Not short of dynamite or a swift kick from the other side. Many's the time my grandmother dropped me in through the coal chute so I could deliver that swift kick when she needed a bottle of preserves for dinner." Maggie grinned. "I loved it. It was the best—and the dirtiest—slide in town. My friends were forbidden to use it. I was, too, unless Grandma wanted me to do it."

John laughed. He'd looked down that disused coal chute and quickly shut the hatch on it, mentally thanking whoever put in oil heat. He'd spent a lot of backbreaking hours as a youth, shoveling coal. He didn't want to do it ever again.

"I'll have to makes sure Andi never finds out about that. She'd love it too."

Maggie grinned wider. "Only if she loves getting filthy."

"She revels in it! The grimier the better."

"Really?" He thought there was something wistful in her tone. "That's exactly the way I was as a kid. My favorite treat as a child—apart from horseback riding—was to be taken to the shore to dig clams in the mudflats. Jolie's completely the opposite. I love my daughter dearly, but there are times when I think she's from an alien race.

"Last spring I thought she was just the right age to go out and collect frogs' eggs so she could grow tadpoles in a jar. She was completely disgusted with me for getting all muddy and wet. I took her clam digging. Same reaction. She just doesn't find things like that fun. I guess that proves environment doesn't play as big a role as we'd like to think in the development of a child."

"Maybe you're right," he said. "I have a lot of trouble interpreting Andi's moods and actions. I thought it was just a gender-difference thing, but possibly it's more than that."

Maggie met his gaze, finding it somber and brooding. Somehow, now, it seemed easier to let the conversation focus on the girls. "Maybe," she said. "Do you wonder about where she came from, what kind of people, what they liked, cared about, valued?"

"Often. I—"

Medallion chose that moment to hang her head over the rail again, nudging John aside, closer to Maggie. Their arms and shoulders pressed together and stayed that way as if glued all the way down to the elbow.

She felt a tingle at the contact, a surge of sexual awareness, saw an answering flare in his eyes. She wanted to pull away, but could not, wanted to break the hold of his gaze, but it held her captive.

She tried to edge sideways, but there was no room between her and the apple tree. He half turned to her and put his hand on the tree trunk, effectively trapping her in a corner, and all she could do was look into his eyes and wonder . . .

Wonder what it would be like if he put his arms around her. Wonder if their bodies would fit together as well as her eye told her they would, with her head finding a comfortable resting spot on his shoulder, her arms linking about his neck just so.

She wanted him to hold her. She wanted to hold him. She wanted—

"Mom!" Startled by the calling voice, Maggie felt her eyes widen, her knees sag, her spirits slump.

"*Mom* . . . Where are you?" Jolene shieked again, this time closer, as emotions similar to Maggie's played across John's face. Longing, regret, frustration. He backed up slowly, and as if the act of separating himself from her had allowed other feelings in, she saw again that flash of guilt. He gripped the fence behind him so hard, his knuckles went white.

"I'm here, Jolie," Maggie said quickly, forcing herself to move away from the supporting bulk of the tree trunk, hoping her legs wouldn't cave in.

"Oh, there you are. Why didn't you an—" Jolene broke off, her frown replaced by a huge smile as she spotted John. She clasped her hands up under her chin. Her face glowed as if he were Santa Claus, the Easter Bunny, and Peter Pan all rolled into one. "Oh!" she breathed. "You came to see me!"

She swung an accusing look at her mother. "The nice doctor came to see me! Why didn't you wake me up, Mom?"

"I, uh . . ." Maggie bit her lip, astounded by this uncharacteristic behavior. For just an instant she wondered if someone had pulled another switch on her, but of course that was impossible.

"I didn't think you'd want me to," she said to her normally shy daughter, whose sleeping presence in the house she had all but forgotten during the past half hour. "I thought you wanted to cuddle with Mr. Bear."

"I'd rather cuddle with the nice doctor," Jolene said, stepping up close to him, leaving Maggie to gape at her in disbelief.

"Hi," Jolene said, batting her lashes. Good grief! The child was flirting, all but simpering! "My eye doesn't hurt anymore."

He crouched down and peered closely, prodding around the edges of the bruise with a gentle finger and thumb. "Good," he said solemnly. "I guess that means I won't have to give you a shot."

Jolene grinned and said with absolute confidence, "But you're a *nice* doctor. You don't give people shots." She sighed wistfully. "Mom says we'd hurt Dr. Klein's feelings if we asked you to look after me when I get sick, but otherwise I'd like you to be my doctor."

Maggie watched a sappy smile turn his face to mush. "If circumstances were different," he said, smoothing a hand over Jolie's hair, "I'd like that too. But of course I wouldn't want to hurt Dr. Klein's feelings, either. Besides, I'm sure he looks after you very well and only gives you a shot if you really, really need it."

Jolene nodded sagely. "That's true." Then she frowned. "But if you can't be my doctor, why'd you come to see me?"

Maggie was grateful John didn't disabuse her of the supreme conviction that she was the one he had come to see.

"Because I wanted to talk to you and your mom about—" He glanced at Maggie. She grimaced, but then nodded and came to stand on Jolie's other side. "About my little girl," he finished.

Jolene's mouth compressed. "Why?" she asked, pulling her shoulders up to her ears. "She's a bad girl. She hit me and said I stole her face. That's dumb. Nobody can steal somebody's face. Faces are *attached*."

"I think she was talking about how much you two look like each other," John said. "Maybe she was a bit confused by that, and upset by being in a new school. All in all, Andi had lived through a pretty tough morning before she met you."

When Jolene only looked indifferent, and slightly trapped, Maggie knew she had to help out. "What happened to make her morning so bad?" she asked John.

His swift glance held gratitude, but it was to Jolene that he spoke. "A boy stole her Power Ranger eraser. Her teacher, Miss Larkin, wouldn't listen when she asked for help getting it back. Miss Larkin also believed the other kids when they said Andi was you, and scolded her for insisting that she wasn't. So you see, by the time Andi found you skipping rope with your friends, she was really steaming. She's sorry she hit you and hurt your eye."

Jolene wriggled her head a little farther down between her shoulders, like a small turtle trying to hide. "We *don't* look like each other," she said, ignoring all but what she had chosen to hear. "I have long hair."

"You do look a lot like each other," John insisted gently. "Your hair is longer, but it's curly, and so is Andi's. It's the same color. Your eyes are the same color, too, and you have the same little lump-of-putty noses." He tapped her nose with his forefinger. She rubbed it and looked away, catching her mother's glance.

"Dr. Martin is right, honey," Maggie said. "You and Andi do look very much alike."

"I don't like her."

"I know," John said, "but she's very sorry she hit you. She'd like to be friends."

Jolene let her shoulders drop again and edged closer to her mother, looking wary. "Is she here?"

He shook his head and straightened. "No. She wanted to come and visit you and tell you herself that she's sorry, but she's being punished. I told her maybe she could come with me another time. What do you think, Jolene? Would it be okay for her to come and play sometime?"

She hesitated only a moment before saying quite positively, "No. I don't think I'd like her even if she said 'sorry.' " Then, so he wouldn't think her animosity extended to him as well, she smiled charmingly and said, "But I like you. Would you like to come in and meet Mr. Bear? He's got a growly voice, just like yours."

John gave Maggie a helpless look.

Maggie picked Jolene up and sat her on the top fence rail, keeping one hand on her waist until she was balanced and hanging on properly.

Eye-to-eye with her daughter, she said without any kind of emphasis, "Honey, you know that your father and I adopted you when you were a tiny baby, right?"

Jolene looked suspicious, but nodded.

Maggie went on. "Dr. Martin and his wife adopted a baby girl around the same time, and at the same place. Halifax. Remember I told you you were born in Halifax?" Jolene nodded.

"Now, what if there were two baby girls, exactly the same, and they got adopted into different families? Wouldn't that be interesting? And they might still be exactly the same as each other, even now."

"How could they be exactly the same?" Jolene asked, her tone close to scathing, but the hunted expression in her eyes deepened. Maggie knew that Jolene knew what this discussion was all about. She simply didn't want to acknowledge it. "Everyone's different," she insisted. "You said that, Mom. Nobody's exactly like anybody else. Everyone's a separate, individual person."

"That's true," Maggie admitted, "but if two baby girls were born at the same time from the same birth mother, they might look exactly the same, though of course they'd still be separate, individual people, just as you say."

"Okay." Jolene's gaze slid away. "Mom, can I go now?"

"No," Maggie said, trying to control the surge of impatience that threatened to sharpen her tone. John was right, of course. She had to arm Jolene with the facts she'd need, so she could answer the questions she was sure to get at school over the next days and weeks.

"Jolie, this is important." With a hand cupped around her daughter's chin, she turned Jolene's face back, searching for signs of stress. She saw none, only indifference that might be hiding all sorts of uncertainties. Jolene was good at hiding things. Too good.

"Andi was born in Halifax too," she went on. "And her birthday is the same as yours."

"Cindy Ellmore's birthday is the same day as mine too."

"Yes, but Cindy Ellmore wasn't born in Halifax, and she doesn't look anything like you, so what I'm talking about is completely different." Maggie drew in a deep breath and let it out slowly. "Dr. Martin and I both think that you and Andi are sisters," she said, keeping her gaze locked with Jolene's. She saw instant denial rise up, saw Jolene's lips part to protest, and went on quickly.

"*Twin* sisters. Identical twin sisters. That's why you look exactly like each other. And that's why Andi wanted to come and see you today. She wants to meet her sister. Properly this time."

"That's silly!" Jolene exploded, and would have jumped off the fence if Maggie hadn't held on to her. "How could we be sisters? We don't even have the same mom and dad."

She turned and rubbed a small hand over Ghost's right ear as her favorite mare nuzzled her. "Do you like horses, Dr. Martin?"

Maggie caught the sympathetic glance John flicked over her before he said, "I like horses a lot, Jolene. So does Andi, but she can't ride. She'd like to take lessons. Maybe you could help her. Do you know how to ride?"

Jolene favored him with a big grin. "Sure. Watch." So swiftly Maggie didn't have a chance to stop her, Jolene slipped free of her mother's grasp and swung herself from the rail to Ghost's back. Clinging to the mare's mane, she tapped Ghost with bare heels and leaned forward. The two of them were off, flying across the paddock and then, while John gasped aloud, they soared up and over the rail on the far side, heading across the field toward a distant farmhouse. The dog, Gilgamesh, darted out of the shade where he'd been sleeping and followed at a lope.

FOUR

"I'm sorry," Maggie said, but deep inside she wasn't as sorry as she thought she should be. She was glad her daughter had bolted. "We'll have to leave it for a while. I'm sure when she's ready, she'll talk to me about it. I won't push her on this, John. I know her. Pushing won't help."

"If it were just us," he argued, "we could give her time to accept it, but there's a school full of kids who aren't going to drop the issue, and a town full of adults avid for the entertainment of a new bit of gossip. There'll be endless speculation about the girls. And about us. We're going to have to give them the right answers, or they'll be left floundering and helpless in the face of other people's questions. To me, that wouldn't be responsible parenting."

Though Maggie knew he was right on all counts, she said, "They're seven and a half years old! Why can't they simply be left alone?"

"Human nature," he retorted. "Besides, even if Jolene doesn't want to know how all this happened, Andi does. I know her. She's looking for answers. I'd rather see she gets the right ones, instead of those her school-mates may come up with through misinterpreting their parents' theories. Not only that, she's entitled to know the truth and be able to tell it."

In anger and frustration, because she knew he was right and she didn't like it, Maggie slapped one hand on the trunk of the apple tree. "Fine, then!" she said. "Give Andi her answers. Tell her we've discussed it and that as far as we can make out, she and Jolene were born as twin sisters and adopted into two different families. I agree that Jolene may have to be forced to acknowledge the relationship that far, but tell Andi, too, that it takes more than an accident of birth to turn two girls into sisters. Shared blood has nothing to do with shared interests, or shared values, or shared anything. Even parents."

A frown drew his dark brows together. "You speak from experience, I take it?"

Maggie backed up a step and pasted on a smile. "Of course not. It's merely common sense."

John recognized the lie in her words, heard the bravado in her tone, but saw, too, her chin pucker and quiver again. That delicate, almost hidden hint of vulner-ability reached down deep inside him and tweaked some-thing hard. With a soft groan, he obeyed an impulse he couldn't ignore. He bent his head and kissed her.

It was a light kiss, meant to offer solace against a pain whose origins he might not understand, but could easily recognize. It was a warm kiss, intended as reassurance, a promise of friendship, support.

The sensation of her lips parting in surprise, the warmth of them under his, their softness, combined to hammer him in the solar plexus with a breathtaking blow. He heard a sound rumble up from inside him, and slipped a hand around the back of her head, stroking it down over the sun-warmed satin of her hair. He was consumed by a need to deepen the kiss, to taste the heat inside her mouth, to feel her respond.

She did, her hands sliding up his chest, linking behind his neck, body swaying close. It was right, good, to feel her fitting herself to him. He helped himself to a fistful of her thick hair, tilting her head back, needing more of her, from her.

She softened in his arms, and he ran one hand down her back, drawing her more tightly against him, feeling her heat, showing her his need. He wondered if she heard the galloping thunder of his heartbeats. Suddenly she went rigid, pushing against his chest.

"No!" she said, tearing her mouth free of his. "Stop. Jo . . . Jolene's coming back."

"What?" He stared into her eyes. Green and soft as new grass, they were bemused and filled with shock, regret, questions—as he knew his must be. It took him a moment to realize that the pounding sound he heard was not only his heartbeat but hoofbeats as well. Still he couldn't tear his gaze from Maggie's face. Her parted lips, moist and pink, so tempted him, he nearly gathered her close again. A delicate wash of color tinted her cheeks, and once more he was compelled to lay the back of his hand to her skin, seeking warmth. Still porcelain cool, though her breath, wafting across his wrist, was hot.

"One day," he promised himself aloud, struggling to control his breathing. "Soon."

Excitement leapt in her eyes as a pulse leapt in her throat, and John's breath caught. "One day soon . . . what?" she asked, her tone innocent, her expression almost bland, but he knew she knew what he was talking about. The breeze toyed with her hair. A coppery strand curled around his wrist. It felt like a manacle, a silken thread that, if allowed to bind him, could cut him so deeply he might not survive.

"Nothing," he said, dropping his hand, almost snatching it back.

One day soon, nothing.

He knew what would happen if he didn't get a grip on himself. He'd kiss her again and send the two of them up in flames. And while he wanted desperately to explore her body, to enter into a torrid affair with her, Maggie was not the kind of woman for that. He knew it without being told. She was a woman who deserved better, deserved more. And he didn't think he had more to give. Not now. Maybe never. He didn't dare.

He swallowed roughly. "I'd better go," he said as two little girls on horseback came trotting toward them. Students, presumably, ready for their lesson.

She met his gaze for another moment, then nodded, tossed her hair back, and turned from him to speak to the newly arrived pair.

With a murmured good-bye, John left as Jolene came to a halt on Ghost on the other side of the fence.

He looked back before he took the path that led around the side of the house. Maggie was so engrossed with the children and horses, he was sure she'd forgotten him already.

As before, she'd come out of one of their close encounters more quickly, more easily, and certainly more unscathed than he. With one shake of her head, she'd settled her hair down, and seemingly her erratic heartbeat as well. He didn't think she'd so much as noticed his leaving.

It bothered him more than he liked.

❖━━━━━❖

"Mom? Can we have dinner now?"

Maggie looked up from her computer screen, startled to see it was nearly five-thirty. She'd meant only to work for a few minutes after her students had gone, but already more than a hour had passed.

"Hi, chickie. Come on in. I'll print this, then we can eat. You starving?"

Jolene nodded and leaned on the corner of Maggie's desk as the printer went to work on the month-end financial statement of Beverlee's Boutique. She fiddled with a pen, then put it down. She twisted a finger into a curl in front of her ear. She leaned over and took the papers out of the printer as it stopped, and tore them neatly along the dotted line before handing them to Maggie.

"Thanks, hon."

"Mom?"

Something in Jolene's demeanor told Maggie what was coming. "Mmm-hmm?" She was careful to keep her tone neutral. She didn't even look at her daughter.

"Do you think maybe it's true? What the nice—what Dr. Martin thinks?"

"It's not just what Dr. Martin thinks. It's what I think too, baby. Dr. Martin says a blood test would prove it one way or the other. But you only have to have that done if you want to."

Jolene said nothing, only frowned and ran her fingers around the rim of Maggie's coffee cup.

Maggie decided to force the issue, if only slightly. "Jolie? What do you think?"

Jolene pushed Maggie's swivel chair back and forth, back and forth, back and forth. "You don't like your sister. Or your brother."

Maggie blinked rapidly. She'd thought Jolene was

mulling over the idea of a blood test. "I wouldn't say I don't like them, Jolie. I just don't know them very well. Our lives don't really . . . match."

"Because they're rich and we're not and Aunt Katrina looks down on us?"

"No, honey. It's more to do with the different values we learned, growing up in two different families."

Jolene pounced on that. "So, if that girl, Andi, really is my sister, and we're not in the same family, I don't have to like her. Right?"

Maggie sighed silently and nodded. "Of course you don't *have* to like her, but I think you should give it a chance."

Jolene scrunched up her shoulder and her eyebrows. "Sometimes," Maggie said, twirling a finger in one of Jolene's curls, "sisters can be best friends."

Jolene's lower lip trembled for a second before she flung her arms around her mother. "But I'm your best friend and you're mine. We're fine, just you and me, aren't we, Mom? I don't need a sister. I don't want one. If she's my sister, does that mean you have to love her too?"

Her taut little voice held a dozen other, unspoken questions, a distinct need for reassurance, and a plea for her mother to make this whole mess go away.

Maggie pulled her onto her lap and hugged her tightly, thinking of her daughter saying ". . . like having a daddy's lap to sit on." In that moment Jolie's wistfulness had sent a rage of jealousy through Maggie, though she'd struggled not to succumb to it. Jolene seemed to have forgotten having said it, forgotten the feelings that had led to her saying it, but she'd remember if John and Andi Martin managed to insinuate themselves into Maggie and Jolene's life.

"Sure we are, Jolie," she said. "We're great, just you and I together, and I'll never love anybody more than I love you."

"And we don't need anybody else?"

Again the image of Jolene's adoring gaze fixed on John's face intruded. Maggie laid her cheek on her daughter's hair. "We don't *need* anybody else, honey, but there might come a time when one or both of us would want to have somebody else as part of our lives. That would be okay, too, because it would never mean that we meant less to each other."

She wanted it to be true, wanted not to feel this fear that Jolene was about to slip away from her, that the perfect circle the two of them had made for the past six years was about to be broken. She was going to have to share her daughter with this unexpected twin sister, and possibly with the sister's father as well.

She cuddled Jolene closer.

"Love doesn't get cut up like a pie when it's shared," she said, trying hard to convince herself too. "It just grows bigger and bigger, so it can fit around everyone in your heart."

Jolene shoved herself away. "Are you saying you want me to be friends with Andi?"

Maggie hesitated. "No, honey. But I won't be surprised if you change your mind, and if you do, I won't feel left out or sad, or as if you don't love me just as much as you always have." *At least I'll try hard not to feel that way.*

Jolene hugged her again and said in a muffled voice, "I won't change my mind. I don't like her at all."

She was silent for a few moments, then added softly, "But I really do like her dad."

Maggie thought of telling Jolene that she couldn't

have one without the other, but held back the words. It would probably be best for both of them if they had neither, but she suspected that kind of choice had been taken from them by the hand of fate. It remained to be seen whether that hand was kind or unkind.

Unkind. That was how Jolene saw it by the time she got home from school on Wednesday, woebegone, indignant, tearful—almost inconsolable. Hugs and cookies helped. Thursday was a repeat of Wednesday, with a few details added.

"I hate that Andi girl!" Jolene wailed. "Yesterday she said she was sorry, but today she called me a wuss and said if somebody hit her in the eye she'd hit right back and why didn't I go ahead and give it my best shot.

"And I hate having a sister too. All the kids are talking about us. They point and whisper. They make fun of my eye. Paulette said Andi punched me so people could tell us apart. Alison said that her mom says you and Dr. Martin must have been married once and gotten divorced and each took one kid just like in a movie she saw. She's gonna rent that movie tonight so Alison can see it."

Maggie held Jolene on her lap and explained the concept of the "nine days' wonder," which didn't help much, but in time Jolene's tears tapered off.

"Hey, wanna know something funny?" Maggie smiled as she shoved Jolene's damp hair back from her brow.

Jolene looked as if she'd never find anything funny again for the rest of her life, but she sniffled and said, "What?"

"There's only one copy of that movie in town, and Alison's mom isn't going to rent it. At least, not tonight."

She grinned conspiratorially. "Because I did, so you and I could watch it together."

"On a school night?" Jolene's good eye widened. The almost unheard-of treat cheered her immeasurably.

They had just settled down on the couch to watch the movie after dinner when the doorbell rang. Again some inner sense told Maggie exactly who was there before she so much as stood and glanced out the window. John's black Ford sedan was parked right beside her red and cream Cherokee, and she saw his shadow, accompanied by a much smaller one, falling across the front porch.

A chill ran over her as she cast a quick look over her shoulder at Jolene. "It's Dr. Martin," she said quietly. "And Andi."

Slowly Jolene rose and came to stand at her side, her eyes wide and worried. The bell rang again.

"I guess we gotta let them in." Resignation colored Jolene's tone, but something else glinted in her eyes. A tingle of excitement she couldn't help feeling, perhaps? Hidden curiosity, maybe?

As her hand settled around the doorknob Maggie realized that it wasn't purely on Jolene's behalf she had hesitated so long. She wasn't absolutely certain she wanted to see John again, at least not so soon. She'd feel a little more secure if she'd had time to sort through the various emotions he evoked—and a lot more secure if she was wearing something other than a pair of ragged cut-offs and a faded tank top, the latter with nothing underneath. If it hadn't been for Jolene's stricken face and the sure knowledge that for her daughter's sake she had to get this first real meeting between the two girls over with, she'd have pretended not to be home.

She opened the door and looked down at Andi first, sure it would be easier than looking at Andi's dad.

Easier? What a joke!

She met the half-defiant, half-wary smoky-colored gaze of her daughter's identical twin and felt as if she'd been poleaxed. A tight band squeezed around her heart as she tried to smile at Andi. Pain, regret, and unarticulated wishes coursed through her. That little girl, so like her own beloved daughter, should never have been a stranger to her. That she was tore Maggie apart inside. Instinct told her to gather the child close and hold her forever, but common sense told her she could not. Andi might look exactly like Jolene, but she was, of course, a separate individual.

And not Maggie's child.

The wary bravado in Andi's gaze affected her deeply, reminding her to keep her voice soft and gentle as she said hello. In response Andi blurted out an unpunctuated rush of words.

"Hello Miss Adair I'm sorry I hit Jolene and I promise I'll never do it again please forgive me."

Maggie couldn't contain the delighted smile that rose up on her face, nor prevent the tender hand with which she smoothed back Andi's hair. "Thank you, Andi," she said, dropping down to the child's level. "Jolene tells me you apologized to her, too, so that's the end of it. I trust you not to do it again, and of course I forgive you."

Not to forgive Andi would have been like refusing to forgive Jolene.

Then, seeing no way out, she stood and raised her gaze to John's face. His probing stare felt like a physical touch. "Hello, Maggie," he said, and she stepped back involuntarily.

"I understand you got in first and rented the most popularly requested video in town tonight," he went on.

On a tension-releasing laugh, she let out a quick rush

of breath she hadn't been aware of holding. "Wow! There's no way to keep a secret in this little burg, is there?"

"No." He shook his head, his face solemn, but a glimmer of laughter lurked in his eyes. "There's one very bewildered girl at the video store. She couldn't understand the run on *The Parent Trap* and was completely flummoxed by it. When I got there, she was saying automatically before anyone could speak, 'Sorry, Maggie Adair took it this morning, but it's due back tomorrow, so I can put your name on the waiting list.'"

"Oh, poor Cheryl," Maggie said, then fell silent, still looking at his eyes. She was caught by something half hidden in his expression, something she wanted to understand, wanted to fathom, but couldn't. Maybe if she stepped a little closer, looked a little longer, looked a little deeper, looked—

He cleared his throat and seemed to pry his gaze away from hers, glancing first at his daughter, then at hers before returning his focus to her. The elusive, unreadable expression was gone.

"Since there were at least eight people ahead of me on the list," he said, "I wondered—we wondered—if under the circumstances, since our need is as great as yours and all that and . . . well . . ."

He smiled charmingly, shrugged one shoulder, and spread his hands. Big hands. With long, strong fingers that could massage a woman's back, hands that could tangle in her hair and tilt her face for his desire. Hands that—

Maggie suppressed a gasp and stepped back another pace. "Of course," she said, feeling a cold hand steal into hers and grip her fingers tightly. She looked down. "If Jolie doesn't mind."

It wasn't fair, Maggie knew, putting the decision on Jolene's narrow shoulders. Nor was it fair that three pairs of eyes turned to look expectantly, perhaps even pleadingly, at one little girl with a black eye, but Jolene was made of good stuff and she rose to the occasion superbly.

Her chin tilted and she looked up at John. "You can come in," she said, stressing the pronoun.

He waited several beats, then asked, "And Andi too?"

Maggie felt the tremor and squeezed her hand comfortingly around Jolene's. "Yeah. Her too," Jolene said grudgingly, never once looking directly at her twin.

She scurried back to the living room, where she curled up in a chair, her gaze locked on the flickering screen that Maggie had put on pause when the doorbell rang.

Maggie waved their guests to the sofa and reached a hand out to her daughter as she shut off the television. "Come on, Jolie. Let's make a bowl of popcorn and pour some drinks."

Having just finished dinner, they had no need of popcorn, but they did need a moment's privacy.

In the kitchen she gave Jolene a swift hug. "That was very brave of you, honey. And very kind. I'm proud of your for inviting Andi in. I think she'll enjoy this movie as much as you will, and maybe learn something, too, like you."

Jolene nodded, her eyes shuttered behind thick, dark lashes, but her expression was one of pure misery.

John couldn't sit. While Andi checked out the toys and children's books, he paced slowly, peering at the framed photographs on one wall. Horses. Lots of horses, garlanded and beribboned. Winners. Most were ridden or led by a tall, laughing-eyed man with a thick bush of dark-red hair. There was one of the same man steadying a long-legged bay foal, clearly only minutes old, then another shot of him cradling a newborn baby bundled in a blanket, with a frilly knit bonnet covering her head. The same degree of awed tenderness shone from his smile, was evinced by the curve of his large hands around infant frailty.

There was a picture of him with a redheaded toddler —identifiably Maggie—who stood on the top rail of a fence, one hand held in his as she regarded him with solemn adoration. Yet another showed the two of them together, Maggie maybe four years old, wearing a pair of tiny jodhpurs and perched astride his hip. They laughed at each other as if the whole world were a private joke between the two of them.

Another photo had clearly been taken within the same time frame, because their clothing was the same, only this time Maggie sat proudly upon a wide-backed pony, holding the reins in one fist while her father held a protective hand on her back.

And then, though pictures of Maggie at different ages and on different horses continued to mark the progression of years, there were no more of her father.

John scrutinized a rather formal portrait of Maggie in her mid-teens with her grandparents. Her grandmother was stooped by the effects of osteoporosis, but it was her grandfather who intrigued him the most.

He'd remembered Doc Monro as a tall, imposing man, but seen pictured beside Maggie, the old doctor obviously hadn't been more than average height and of a slight build. Yet to a young boy, the man had seemed a giant, an impression that had been strengthened by the lionization of his memory within the community of Maples. Nearly every patient beyond a certain age who'd visited him had something good to say about old Doc Monro.

John paused before a photo of Maggie cradling Jolene in a pose similar to the one of her father holding her infant self. From that point on, the focus fell on Jolene, and John felt as if he were looking at his own daughter's baby pictures. It was a strange, disturbing sensation, seeing what could have been Andi in unfamiliar clothing, unfamiliar surroundings, and with unfamiliar people.

"Can I see, Daddy?" Kicking off her thongs, Andi jumped up onto an armchair to get a better look. "Oh, luck-*ee!*" she said, pointing at a picture of Jolene astride Ghost. "Jolie's got a *horse?*"

She turned an almost accusing gaze on him, then asked, "Think she'd let me ride it, Dad?"

Before he could reply, she hopped onto the arm of the chair and peered at some of the other photos.

"Oh, look, that must be Miss Adair when she was a baby. Is that her daddy? His hair is red too. And *she* had a horse when she was little." Envy rang in her tones. "I wonder why there's no more pictures of her and her daddy?"

"I think he died," John said carefully.

She glanced at him, her expression going flat. "Oh," she said. Andi didn't talk about people dying, not even in general terms. She ignored death as if it were something that, unacknowledged, would go away and never touch her again. She continued checking out the pictures, lingering longingly over every horse, asking questions he couldn't always answer about the meanings of the different awards.

She tapped the formal portrait. "Is that Miss Adair's

grandma and grandpa, do you suppose? They're real, real old, aren't they, Dad?" He nodded, and Andi continued her perusal of the gallery for several moments before saying, "I wonder where her mom is?"

Now that Andi mentioned it, John did too. Maggie's history in photographs had some very notable gaps. How odd.

"Do you figure her mom died, too, Dad?" Andi asked in a small voice.

"I don't know, sweetheart," he said, lifting her down. Taking her hand, he went to the couch where Maggie had offered them a seat. Still gripping his fingers, Andi wriggled in close beside him.

"It wouldn't be very nice," she said, "if your mom *and* your dad died when you were just a little kid."

"No, it wouldn't," he said, more than a bit surprised and wondering where this was going. He wished she'd chosen a different time and place for the discussion, but since she'd started it, he was reluctant to try to distract her. Obviously she was working on something.

Worry underlay her solemn tone. "If you died, would I have to go live with Grandma and Grandpa?"

"Yes," he replied evenly.

"And then, if grandma and grandpa died, where would I live?"

"Honey, I think that's a lot of *ifs*, but if it did happen that way, you'd never be left alone. There's always a family somewhere who needs a little girl to love and look after, someone who'd want to give you a home and keep you safe until you're all grown up."

"Maybe like Miss Adair," she said, " 'cause now I got a sister and she's my sister's mom. If I lived with them, I bet I could ride their horses any time I want."

John stared at her, torn between laughter and exasperation. How much of this had been brought on by genuine concern over what would happen if everyone she knew were dead, and how much by a desire to have a horse?

"At any rate," he said, "I don't plan on dying. I'm strong and healthy and I figure I have a lot more years in me yet."

Andi looked faintly distrustful, as if she weren't convinced, but she fell silent, still clinging to his hand as they heard Maggie and Jolene returning.

He squeezed her fingers in comfort, his feelings mixed over the conversation's curtailment.

FIVE

When they returned to the living room, their guests sat politely side by side on the sofa, saying nothing. Maggie noticed that they held hands tightly, as if this meeting were as difficult for them as it was for her and Jolene. She set down the tray of tall lemonade glasses while Jolene put a bowl of popcorn before the guests and scuttled away with one for herself and her mother.

John smiled at Maggie as she served them, murmuring a word of thanks, but she saw his eyes darken as they swung from one child to the other, regret and the same kind of unspoken longing she had experienced shadowing his face.

She was glad to scrunch in beside Jolene in a big chair at right angles to the couch. She punched the remote control to start the video and sat back, trying to appear at ease. Jolene kept a death grip on the popcorn bowl on her lap, but as the story captured her attention she began to relax. Handing the bowl to Maggie, she hitched her bottom up onto the arm of the chair, feet on Maggie's lap, and sat leaning forward, elbows on her knees, chin in her hands.

Maggie spent little time watching the movie, and much dividing her attention between the two children. Andi's pose went from stiff and uncomfortable to slumped against her father. Halfway through the video she slid to the floor and lay on her stomach under the coffee table, chin on her hands, one bare foot rhythmically kicking the front of the couch until John captured it and held it still.

As Maggie's gaze flicked from one child to the other, it regularly encountered John's. They'd hold for a moment, then both look away. Once, when the two girls laughed aloud at exactly the same moment, in exactly the same way, Maggie's and John's gazes clashed and they shared a startled, bemused smile. "Stereo," he murmured, and Maggie nodded.

During the haircut scene they spoke simultaneously to their daughters.

"Don't you dare!" Maggie said as John ordered, "Don't even think about that, Andrea Jane!"

As the four-way laughter died Andi gave him an impudent grin. "But what if I grow mine, Dad, so it's just like Jolie's? Then no one will be able to tell us apart."

"Hah!" he said, tapping a finger against her nose. "I'd know *you* at five hundred paces."

"Mom?" Jolene looked at her mother. "Would you know me at five hundred paces?"

Maggie smiled. "Six hundred."

Again she and John shared a sympathetic smile, acknowledging those moments at the school when neither had immediately known their own child. They turned their attention back to Hayley Mills and Hayley Mills and the reluctant romance between a mother and father who clearly cared deeply for each other though they might not want to admit it.

In the end, of course, they did admit it, and in true Hollywood style, everyone lived happily ever after.

Maggie hoped her sigh of satisfaction wasn't audible and that the stinging tears the end of the movie always brought to her eyes weren't visible.

It was pure sentiment, she told herself sternly as she blinked the salty burn away. Maggie never cried.

Quickly she got to her feet. "Would you like some coffee?" she asked John. He nodded.

"Jolie," she went on, smiling at her daughter, "when he was here before, you wanted Dr. Martin to meet Mr. Bear. You could introduce them now, and show him and Andi your room at the same time."

She was glad she'd taken the time to tidy up that day, along with putting fresh linens on the beds. The bedrooms smelled of fresh air and sunshine from sheets and bedspreads dried outdoors.

Jolene frowned, but got to her feet, if reluctantly. "Would you like to see my room?" She spoke directly to John, ignoring her twin.

Andi shrugged and John stood. "You show Andi," he said. "I'll help your mom."

"But I don't—" Maggie began, only to be cut off by his pointed stare. She gathered up the two popcorn bowls and glasses and set them on the tray.

"Let me take that for you," he said, whipping the tray out from under her hands before she'd scarcely had time to add the last glass. A quick jerk of his head urged her toward the kitchen. Maggie started from the room, sending a sidelong glance at the girls. They stood like two wary dogs, observing each other with mingled curiosity and animosity.

If she left her alone with Andi, would Jolene feel abandoned? Maggie hesitated, but a large hand at the small of her back propelled her through the archway. Startled, she glanced over her shoulder, encountering John's benign smile.

"Sometimes," he said when they were in the kitchen, "kids get along better without adults present."

"I'm not sure Jolene's going to learn to get along with Andi with or without adults present," she said, busying herself with the coffeemaker. "Every day there's a whole new litany of woes to listen to as soon as she gets off the bus."

Concern creased his face. "What's Andi been doing?"

"Nothing. Nothing but existing." Maggie smiled wryly. "It would have been hard enough for Jolene to deal with having a twin, but to make matters worse, Alison, who was her best friend last year, has decided she likes Andi better now. While Jolene freely admits she prefers Monica's company this year, she's being a real dog in the manger about Alison. She's jealous. Her nose is definitely out of joint, and Alison's having a ball, playing one off against the other."

"According to books I've read, little girls do that all the time. I'd have thought being one would have helped prepare you for raising one."

Maggie laughed and threw up her hands. "*Nothing* in my life prepared me to deal with something like this."

She took two mugs from a cupboard, set them on the table, and added a sugar bowl as the aroma of coffee began to fill the room. "I understand now why my poor grandmother sighed so often when I was growing up." She smiled over her shoulder as she opened the fridge for cream. "*I* have trouble coping with all this raw emotion spilling from my daughter, and Grandma was much too old to be asked to deal with it. My early adolescence must have made her last few years hell."

He gazed at her for a moment. "Were you orphaned very young, Maggie?"

"My father died when I was five." She finished pouring the cream into a small pitcher and shut the refrigerator. "My mother remarried and moved away shortly after."

His eyebrows knitted. "Without you?"

She met his gaze for a minute, then looked down. "Her husband didn't like me."

"Maggie." His tone held a note of protest.

"So my grandparents got stuck with me." She shrugged as she glanced at him again. "End of story."

"I don't think so." He caught her hand and pulled her toward him. "Tell me about it, Maggie."

"What's to tell?" She tugged her hand free, turned, and grabbed an orange from a bowl. Quickly she sliced it into wedges and divided them onto two saucers. "I'll take these to the girls."

Once more he caught her hand and held it, this time pulling her to a chair at right angles to his. The warmth of that large hand wrapped around hers reminded Maggie too strongly of the warmth of his kiss, the way his hands had felt as one locked behind her head, the other glided down her back. A stab of need as sharp as pain sliced through her. She could only hope it didn't show in her eyes, because his gaze held hers steadily, his expression caring, concerned.

"Don't run away," he said, and his smile wormed its way inside her, creating a delicious, fluttering sensation in her middle. "Sit down and talk to me."

She sat because her knees had turned to Jell-O. Oh Lord! If he looked at his patients like that, with sympathy and tenderness and compassion, she figured his waiting room would be filled twenty-four hours a day.

"Let's leave the girls alone together," he continued, rubbing his thumb over her knuckles. "They won't die of vitamin C deprivation over the next ten or fifteen minutes, and they'll do better without us while they get to know each other."

From Jolene's room a delightful blend of giggles confirmed his prediction. The less interference the better, at this stage.

John stood, reached for the coffeepot, and filled their cups. "I'm hoping for your advice," he said. "For some insight into how to deal with something that's obviously worrying Andi."

"What's that?" she asked.

"She asked me what would happen to her if she lost me and her grandparents, in addition to her mother. I didn't know until this evening she'd even thought about it. I'm not sure I handled it well. How do you reassure a seven-year-old who knows firsthand that the adults who love her can and do die?"

Maggie shook her head. "I don't think I can help. I wasn't left on my own as a small child. I was fourteen when Grandma died, and seventeen when I lost Grandpa."

"You can help," he said, "by telling me about Maggie Adair the child."

She stirred sugar into her coffee. This wasn't something she often discussed. She hardly knew where to begin. "Maggie Adair—the child," she said, continuing the third-person usage he'd begun.

"I guess to her mother, she was a sad reminder of an unhappy marriage. To her stepfather, she was a small replica of a redheaded Irishman he wanted to forget had ever been a part of his wife's life. To her grandparents—who'd been in their forties when Margaret, their only child, was born, and in their sixties when Maggie, Margaret's daughter, came along—she was a burden and a trial."

"I find that hard to believe," John said, shaking his head. He took her hand again, linking their fingers.

"It was true," she replied, sliding her hand free. She picked up her coffee mug, sipped, then set it down, keeping her hands wrapped around it. "Grandpa was nearly fifty when my mother was born, and Grandma was forty-three. They'd long since given up hope of Grandma carrying a baby to term, so my mother came as not only a great surprise but a joyously welcomed gift. They indulged her every whim, lavished gifts on her, and spoiled her so utterly, they lost control, but by the time they realized it, it was too late to undo the damage."

She switched back to third person. "When they ended up with Maggie, the result of the big mistake their daughter had made at age twenty, they were determined to do it right the second time around. No indulgences for *this* child. Even her ponies and horses were used to teach her responsibility, and the threat always existed that riding was a privilege to be withdrawn at any moment for any infraction." She grinned. "And frequently was.

"Maggie Adair knew more about parental control, guidance, and discipline than Margaret Monro ever dreamed of. Maggie had rules to obey, boundaries to respect, and restrictions and values drilled into her. It didn't hurt her a bit, of course, and her grandparents loved her. There was never any doubt in her mind of that, but they were strict. They had to be. Maggie was, to put it politely, a difficult child who broke every rule, pushed the edges of each boundary, and resisted all restriction." She paused for a moment, staring into her coffee cup, then added, "I guess you could say Maggie was an angry child."

"With good reason," John said, peeling one of her hands free and enfolding it in his. She let him retain it. His grip was warm, strong, comforting, and reminded her again of how good it had felt to lean on him, to breathe in the scent of his skin and clothing. To be held.

"Her father abandoned her in the worst way possible —irrevocably—by dying," he went on, discussing Maggie Adair the child as if she were a case history, but the warmth in his eyes made it a personal, intimate thing. "Her mother left her behind like unwanted baggage. Her stepfather rejected her too. What other emotion could have been top on her list but anger? What choice did she have but to test her grandparents to see if they could be forced into throwing her away as well?"

To Maggie's horror, her eyes burned the way they had at the tender ending of the movie. Blinking rapidly, she jerked her hand free and jumped up. "Now you're beginning to sound like Elmer Abernathy. My grandparents didn't subscribe to pop psychology any more than I do. And I fail to see how any of this can help you find words to reassure Andi."

Grabbing the saucers of orange wedges, she turned so quickly, the fruit nearly slid off. Righting them, she slowed down, crossing the kitchen with more control and a modicum of dignity that clearly said she was not running away.

Regardless of how it might look.

At the doorway to Jolene's room Maggie halted, suppressing a small sound of mingled pleasure and pain. The girls lay sprawled at opposite ends of Jolie's bed, both sound asleep, facing away from each other. Each had a leg thrown over a pile of Barbies and assorted bits of doll clothing, and the tips of the girls' toes touched. One bare foot, Andi's, one sock-clad, Jolie's, identical in size, identical in shape, as if in sleep the twins had reached out for each other and connected.

Each child clutched a Barbie. Each doll was dressed exactly the same. One had long hair, the other short, and beside Andi's lay a pair of blunt scissors and a hank of hacked-off Barbie hair.

Maggie set the dishes down on the dresser and stood for several moments gazing at the scene. Then, blinking hard and fast again, she backed out of the room and came up against a hard wall of warm male flesh.

John slid his arms around Maggie's waist, over her own arms, and pulled her back against him.

To his surprise, she let him hold her like that as together they watched their daughters. Her hair was like silk against his cheek as he rested his face on the side of her head. He drew in a deep breath laden with the delicate scent that surrounded her like a sweet aura, and let it sigh out slowly.

"Leave them to sleep awhile," he murmured. "I see this as a bonding process for them. Whatever it is, it can't hurt."

When Maggie nodded, a surge of elation swept through John. She wasn't making him leave! Half releasing her, with his right arm lying across her shoulders, he turned her from the children and steered her, not toward the kitchen, but toward the living room.

"I'll, uh, get some more coffee," she said, but he shook his head and tightened his grip on her, turning her.

"Not for me." He draped both wrists over her shoulders as she stood face-to-face with him, loosely connected.

"You were telling me about Maggie Adair," he reminded her. "Tell me more."

She laughed and tossed her head to shake her hair back from her face. "No way. Now it's your turn."

He caught a fistful of her hair, rubbing it between his fingers, and smiled. Then, out of the blue, he asked, "Does your sister have red hair too?"

"No," she replied absently, then started, her back stiffening. "How do you know I have a sister?"

"You said the other day that it takes more than an accident of birth to turn two girls into sisters, that shared blood has nothing to do with shared anything. Even parents."

"You asked if I spoke from experience, and I said no," she said in a teasing tone, but John saw the wariness in her eyes.

"You lied." He, too, kept his manner light.

She shrugged. "I do that sometimes. When—" She broke off.

John drew her down with him as he sat on the couch. "When people try to get too close?"

"Something like that, though it's not a secret that I have a sister. And a half brother." Maggie smiled. "Nothing is secret, of course, in Maples. My mother was pregnant with Katrina when my father died."

"I take it her second husband had no difficulty being a father to Katrina."

"No, nor to her brother, Kevin. I believe he's been a good father to them, but the truth is, I know more about people I've met on buses than I do my siblings."

"Why is that?"

Maggie crowded herself into a corner of the couch,

pulling up her knees and wrapping her arms around them. "I never lived with them when I was a child, nor was I so much as invited to visit. Not until my grandfather died. After that, though, I did live with them for about eight months."

"And?" He wasn't about to let her small shrug and the final-sounding tone of voice stop this story in its tracks.

"It wasn't a . . . successful experiment, nor a happy time for any of us. I guess my mother thought it was her duty to offer me a place to live, since she and her husband were selling my home out from under me."

"The house that I have now?"

She nodded. "It was supposed to come to me. They always said it would, but Grandpa must have thought he was indestructible. He never left a will, so his estate went to my mother, as his only 'living issue,' as the legal people like to call it."

John steeled himself not to respond to that small puckering of her chin that meant Maggie was suppressing some strong emotion. "She didn't even need that house," she said, and he heard the betrayal in her tone. "They already had three."

She squared her shoulders and lifted her chin. "Anyway, when I turned eighteen, I received the money I'd inherited from my grandmother. It wasn't a lot, but enough to support me while I studied accounting. I moved out of my mother's home and into my own apartment."

She fell silent, gazing out the window at the darkening sky.

"And then what?"

She glanced at him, and John got the impression she had almost forgotten his presence. "I studied, and partied, and dated, and enjoyed life for a few years until I graduated and took a job in a bank. Then, like the young, fresh-out-of-college fool I was, I lived one of the biggest clichés of all time. I married my boss, the first 'real' man who was kind to me, who gave me hugs and made me feel loved, cherished, and cared for. He was a lot older."

She flashed him a smile. "I suppose people who believe in pop psychology would say I was looking for a father figure."

John gazed at her. "And don't you suppose they'd be right?"

"Yeah, I guess so, especially in light of his having hair that had once been as red as my father's. Of course, when I went to work at his bank, he had very little hair left of any color. It didn't take me long to realize what I'd thought was the love of my life was something else entirely. But I'd made my bed, as my grandmother would have put it, so I continued to sleep in it. I hoped things would get better, that one day I'd wake up and really *believe* he loved me for myself alone."

She hesitated before adding deprecatingly, "His being my mother's banker, and knowing what she and her husband were worth, helped make me attractive to him initially."

John reached out and closed his fingers around her crossed wrists, giving her an impatient little shake. "I suspect there were other factors."

Maggie laughed to hide her sudden tension, and shifted, breaking his hold. Once before, she'd been seduced by what she had mistaken as kindness and understanding; she wasn't about to do it again. Especially not when she was experiencing such emotional turmoil and feeling so vulnerable. Not to mention aroused every time John touched her.

Swinging her feet to the floor, she stood. "Events proved that not to be the case. I was a terrible disappointment to Barry, and not only in my lack of financial expectations, which he didn't realize until we'd been married several months. But even before that, who I was, what I was, had become a constant source of conflict as he tried to mold me into the shape he wanted."

She picked up a basket of laundry that had been half hidden behind the end of the couch and dumped its contents onto the cushions. "Too bad he never knew my grandparents," she said, giving a towel such a shake, it snapped. "They could have told him I never have been easy to mold." She laid the folded towel in the empty basket. "Though it actually lasted nearly four years, I suspect our marriage was over long before either of us knew it."

"Was the adoption one of those ill-fated attempts to heal a sick marriage?"

"Maybe," she said, with a short, humorless laugh. "He'd told me originally that we'd never have children. He'd raised a family with his first wife, and had a vasectomy long before we met. He didn't want more. We'd been married about two years when I realized it wasn't working out, that I was growing more and more unhappy. When I told him I was leaving, he completely flabbergasted me by saying he thought I was just restless. He was sure a baby would change things and did I want to adopt. I think at that point he still believed my mother and stepfather could be persuaded to invest some of their money on my behalf, through him."

She laughed raggedly, her hands twisting a blue-and-white-striped tea towel. "It had cost me a lot to agree to remain childless, but I told myself if I loved him and wanted him to love me, then I'd have to make sacrifices.

His doing a one-eighty on the position of children convinced me that he loved me and would love our baby. Since what I wanted more than anything was to be loved, to be part of a close and happy family, it was easy to believe. I agreed to try again."

She shrugged and gave the tea towel a shake before folding it. "He scarcely paid Jolie any attention, except to complain about her noise and the fact that my mother and her husband had failed to make a settlement in trust for Jolie that he felt was her right as the granddaughter of a very wealthy couple."

Maggie snapped another towel, releasing its outdoors scent before she folded it neatly. "Jolene was mine alone from the day we brought her home. He took no interest. It didn't take him long to regret ever having arranged for me to have her."

"Arranged?"

"We didn't exactly have to sit on a year's long waiting list like most couples," she said, watching his hands as he began to fold a tea towel. "About three months after he first suggested it, we brought Jolene home. I guess I knew at the time that he'd used his political clout to expedite matters, but I didn't want to admit it, or to question it."

He set the towel on the stack in the basket and reached for another piece of laundry. "He was a politician too?"

She shook her head. "No, but he had friends in high places." She paused for a moment, hands idle. "Now," she went on, her voice not entirely steady, "I find myself wondering if it was that same clout that was responsible for twin sisters being separated at birth."

John thought it was entirely possible. "*You* weren't responsible for it, though," he said, feeling slick fabric glide through his fingers. He glanced down and saw he held a sheer black nightie with lace cups. He tried not to imagine how it would feel with warm, firm flesh inside it. His imagination took over a large part of his mind as his fists scrunched the delicate cloth. "And you're as good a mother as you would have been if you'd had to wait for years like everyone else."

"I hope so," she said, turning a child-size T-shirt right side out. Then, with a silent gasp, she dropped it and snatched the nightie from him, flinging it atop the stack of folded clothes.

"I'm sorry," he said, shooting to his feet. "I didn't mean to—"

"Oh, it's all right," she said, irritation peppering her tone, lending color to her cheeks. "You didn't hurt it. I was just being . . ." She shook her head and bent forward to take the last article, another towel, from the couch, tumbling her hair over her face.

"Just being what?" he asked, unable to resist the urge to slide his hand under that fall of hair and lift it back. She went perfectly still, staring straight ahead, but he felt a fine tremor coursing through her. Gently, he turned her face toward his. "Just . . . what, Maggie?" he asked again.

"Nothing. I . . ." Her gaze slid away. "Embarrassed, I guess," she said with a breathless laugh. She tried to move away. He clamped his hand over her upper arm. The feel of her warm, smooth skin under his fingers sent need stabbing through him.

"Why?" he asked, his voice soft, but verging on hoarse. "Because a man was touching your lingerie?"

She shook her head and this time met his gaze. "No," she said, just as softly. "Because *you* were touching my lingerie."

"*Maggie* . . ." Her honesty, the candidness of that steady green stare of hers, fired his blood as much as the sensations of silk under his hands. He wanted to touch a lot more than her lingerie. He drew her up to him, slid his hand down her back. She made no attempt to break free, not of his physical hold, not of his gaze. In her throat a pulse jumped and skipped. Her chest rose and fell quickly. "Maggie," he said again, filtering her hair through his fingers.

"What?" She stepped back.

"Nothing. Just—I like your name. It suits you." He lifted a hank of hair and let it fall, caressing her neck with it. "I like your hot silk hair, the way it feels so cool."

"Hot silk feels cool?"

"I know, I know. But it looks as if it should feel like fire in my hands, and it doesn't." He skimmed a thumb over her cheek. "The same as your skin, so smooth, so fine-grained—like delicate porcelain. Even when it shows the fire inside, it's cool to the touch."

"I don't feel cool," she said, bunching the towel in her hands.

His heart hammered high in his chest, yet he felt its pulsations everywhere in his body. "No?" he asked. "What do you feel?"

She swallowed. "A little bit scared," she whispered. "And a lot on fire. Wondering what will happen when . . ."

He watched the fire rise, saw it spark in her eyes, saw her response in the parting of her lips, lips he couldn't resist. He bent and brushed his over them, felt her instant response, the shudder that coursed through her. "When I do this?"

He stroked her lower lip with his tongue, seeking entrance, finding it, then backing off.

"Yes," she sighed, her eyelashes fluttering. "When you do that."

He regarded her through half-shuttered lids. "I want to do it again."

"I want you to. Kiss me, John."

SIX

She went soft as he kissed her, as if her muscles were melting. She swayed, and he gathered her close, her thighs brushing his, her breasts cushioning his chest. He splayed one hand against the back of her head, sliding his fingers through her hair as he covered her mouth in a deep kiss, taking all she offered, giving, sharing. His other hand glided down over the curve of her waist, moved on to the flare of her hip, drawing her more tightly against him, between his legs. Her nipples, hard beads, pressed into his chest.

Blood rushed through his veins, roared in his ears. He needed air, but could get none. He needed to stop, assess, take stock of what was happening to him, to her, and could not. His innate caution flew away. Her lips were soft, her mouth hot and wet and clinging, tasting of cinnamon, coffee, and woman.

Maggie . . . She held nothing back, not afraid to show him her need, not afraid to enflame his.

Still cradling her between his legs, he backed up and sat on the edge of the couch. She went to her knees on the floor, stomach pressed against his groin, his hardness against the yielding softness of her. His hand under her buttocks, he lifted her up, onto his lap, urging her closer. The towel in her hands wadded between their bodies, and he impatiently tore it away as he lifted his mouth from hers to gasp a huge gulp of air.

She threaded her fingers through his hair, her hands clasped around his head, holding him to her as her lips traced the line of his jaw. He captured her mouth in an even deeper kiss, eliciting a sweet, soft sound of welcome, and he thrust his tongue past her teeth, tangled with hers, felt its pulsing response and heard another little moan from her.

Maggie burned. Her entire body sizzled. She'd have collapsed if she hadn't been kneeling. She slid her arms around his back, nails raking over his shirt, then drew her hands down until they curved around his waist and clung. He responded with a deep, gravelly sound and a heady intensifying of their kiss.

How he could kiss! No one had ever kissed her this way, with such total abandon, such sensitivity and sensuality. His lips played over hers while his tongue did incredible things. One second his mouth was hard against hers, the next it was soft, and before she could adapt to that, it was gone, exploring her throat, her ears, her cheeks. He gasped as if completely out of oxygen, but the slightest hint on her part brought his mouth back to hers, elicited another of those grateful little growls he emitted from time to time.

She wanted more. Her breasts ached. Her body throbbed. His fingers squeezed spasmodically on her back, her bottom, her thighs, but it wasn't enough. She brought one of his hands to her breast, and he growled a ragged sound, cupping her, thumbing a rigid, burning nipple.

His mouth trailed down her neck, lips nudging aside the strap of her tank top as he pressed kisses on her shoulder, the top of her chest. "Maggie," he murmured. "Oh, heaven help me, Maggie, but you're doing things to me that I—" He broke off, his breath hot against her skin. "You're—"

"Don't talk," she whispered against his lips, smiling into his bemused eyes. "Just kiss me."

He obeyed, teasing her with small, nibbling kisses that traveled up her throat, around her ears, across her cheeks, just touching the corners of her mouth until she thought she'd go mad with need. At last he took her mouth in a hot, wet kiss, capturing her tongue, drawing it deep.

Oh God! The taste of her! John reveled in it. The feel of her against his mouth, under his hands, in his arms! He filled his hands with her hair, sending a wild cascade of color tumbling about her shoulders and his forearms, over her breasts. Impatiently he shoved the hair aside as he tilted her back again. His body burned as she writhed against him. A flush rose from the low neckline of her top, up her chest and neck. Beneath the thin fabric, her breasts stood out, proud and firm, nipples hard. He cupped her in his hands, bent and suckled her through her top, leaving wet marks, leaving her mouth slack, her eyes half shut, and her chest heaving, as he lifted his head and gazed at her.

Her eyes glittered between fluttery lashes, her cheeks glowed rosy-pink. Her skin—at last—gave off the heat he'd known it could. He felt it in her body, in the radiance of her face, even in the tips of the trembling fingers with which she stroked his cheeks.

He was going to burst. He'd never been this hard, this much in need. He leaned forward, one arm around her hips, the other hand planted square in her back, and suckled her breasts again. In response her hands came around his head, holding him, her hips moving in slow cadence, enticing him. He wanted her breasts naked in his mouth, bare against his bare chest, wanted her body wrapped around his, wanted to bury himself deep inside her, and he knew she wanted it too. As he was about to give in to her silent pleas, to his own desperate need, somewhere in the house, a door slammed hard.

Maggie stiffened in his arms, eyes going wide, mouth parted in an O of surprise. "John! Stop! The girls!"

"They're asleep," he said, groaning as he pulled her tightly to him, unable to let her go, loving the feel of her aroused nipples against him. "It was the wind."

As if to prove his words, another gust wafted a cool breeze through the open window, blowing the drapes inward, lifting Maggie's hair in a scented cloud toward John's face.

Another door slammed as she squirmed off his lap. He tried to pull her back into his arms, totally unwilling to let the magic be blown away by a rising breeze, but she snatched up the dropped towel and held it in front of her as a small voice said, "Daddy? Where are you?"

John froze as his daughter stumbled into the room. Sleepily she rubbed her eyes in the brighter light. "Whatcha doin', Dad?"

"I, uh, helping Maggie," he said quickly as Maggie nudged the laundry basket toward him. He stared at it for a moment, seeing the black nightie that had started all this. Maggie's nightgown. Maggie's body. Maggie's potent kisses. If she hadn't insisted they stop, if she hadn't moved away from him when she had, if Andi had come in two minutes earlier— He didn't like to think of it.

He felt sick and risked a glance at Maggie. Her eyes shone warmly, half amused, half troubled, but the moment their gazes connected, her expression changed. She blinked, took half a step back, and looked as stunned as if he'd slapped her.

"What's—" *What's wrong,* he'd been going to say, but Andi stepped between him and Maggie.

"How come?" she asked, picking up the towel Maggie had dropped. "You never help Mrs. Wisdom fold clothes."

"I, uh, I know I don't. I don't think she'd want me to. Mrs. Wisdom's a very independent lady."

"And so am I," Maggie said, as if reminding herself of that fact as she rose to her feet and took the towel from Andi. "Is Jolie awake too?"

Andi yawned and shook her head. Then, without preamble or warning, she said, "Miss Adair, did your mom die? My mom did. She got really sick, her hair all fell out, and then she died."

Maggie sat down quickly, her gaze focused on Andi, but not so fully that she was unaware of John's sudden, watchful stillness. "I'm so very sorry, honey," she said, pulling Andi to her, stroking her tousled hair back from her face. "I know you miss her a lot. It's bad when one of your parents dies."

Andi nodded, her gaze fixed on Maggie's. She leaned on Maggie's knee, and Maggie encircled her with her arms, loosely but comfortingly.

"My mother didn't die, but my father did when I was a little girl. He was sick too."

"Yeah." Andi nodded. "I saw there were no more pictures of him on the wall." She glanced at her father. "My dad said maybe he died. But *he's* not going to, 'cause he's healthy."

Maggie agreed solemnly after a long, speculative look at John. "He looks pretty healthy to me. I don't think he's likely to die."

Andi appeared happy to have this confirmed. "Was your mother pretty healthy?"

Again Maggie nodded. "Oh, yes. She still is."

Andi's eyes widened. "She didn't die? Not even yet?"

Maggie smiled and curved her hand around the side of Andi's face, a soft caress the child leaned into instinctively. "Not even yet, chickie. And probably won't for a long time to come."

Andi glanced up at her father, assessing age. "Is she very old?" she asked Maggie.

"Quite old," Maggie replied, thinking with nasty pleasure how her fifty-two-year-old mother would hate to hear that. "Lots older than your dad."

Andi smiled and stepped out of Maggie's embrace. "That's good." Taking John's hand, she said, "Can we go home now, Daddy?"

John bent and scooped her up, cuddling her close. That was the most she'd said about the loss of her mother since it had happened. "Sure, baby," he said, and kissed the top of her head.

He and Maggie exchanged a glance before he carried his sleepy daughter to the car, Maggie going ahead through the beginning spits of rain to open the rear door for him. When he had Andi safely buckled in and propped against a rolled blanket, he shut the door quietly.

"Thanks, Maggie," he said, and bent to take her mouth in a quick kiss. To his surprise, she turned her head away, giving him only her cheek. She tasted of rain, and herself, a flavor that made him hunger for more. "Good night."

Before she had time to respond, he stepped away and slid behind the wheel, shutting the door while he still had the will to do it.

"I don't think Jolene's mom likes me very much, Daddy," Andrea said as he tucked her into bed.

"Why do you say that, sweetheart?" he asked. "She was very nice to you."

She shrugged. "She looks at me funny. As if her eyes are sort of angry and sort of sad all at the same time."

John was amazed, though he knew he shouldn't be, at her insight. "I think Maggie *is* a little bit angry and a little bit sad, all at the same time. But not angry with you, honey, and not sad because of anything you've done. She feels bad because you aren't her little girl, too, as well as Jolene."

She stared at him. "But I'm *your* little girl!"

He laughed and tousled her hair. "Of course you are, and nothing is ever going to change that."

"It's kind of a funny situation, isn't it, Dad? I mean, me and Jolie being sisters, and you and Maggie not being our mom and dad. Like in the movie, the parents had been married and then they got back together. But you and Maggie have never been married." She smiled. "I like her a lot, Daddy. Do you like her too?"

"Yeah," he said. "I like her too."

Andi smiled again as he pulled the covers up to her chin. "Good," she said softly. "Maybe . . ." She didn't finish the thought, but looked at him speculatively.

He wanted to tell her, *Don't think about it, Andi. Don't so much as consider it,* but he said nothing, because she said nothing. He didn't want to plant ideas in her mind if they didn't exist.

Yet the idea had been securely planted in his mind, try though he did to eradicate it. It followed him into sleep that night and woke him well before dawn. Not so much the thought, but the restless emotions the thought engendered.

He lay on his back staring up at the ceiling, memories of Maggie circling in his mind. The feel of her in his arms, the taste of her mouth under his, the easy, open way she kissed, holding nothing back, her passion rising like a Fundy tide, meeting with the gale-force wind of his own to create a rip that had threatened to tear them both apart.

If the wind hadn't started slamming doors . . . But it had, and that was good.

Good? How could it be good, when he still ached like a seventeen-year-old after a virginal necking session? How could it be good to be left wanting her like this, totally unsatisfied, and with little hope of ever being satisfied?

She was there! A strange lurch of surprise half took John's breath away, though after a moment he asked himself why he hadn't expected to see her. He went to church when he could make it, so why shouldn't Maggie? He hadn't noticed her until she was past him, but even in her blue and white choir robe there was no mistaking her as she filed by with the other singers. His gaze followed her as she ascended the spiral staircase to the choir loft over the left side of the sanctuary. It remained fixed on her as she took her place in the front row, just behind the rail.

Her hair was up, wound into some kind of a twist, but little wisps escaped, catching the morning sun as it beamed through a stained glass window, giving her a copper halo. He tried not to think of the scent of her hair, the taste of her mouth, the feel of her body. Her hard nipples through her top, wet from his lips and tongue . . .

He shifted uncomfortably in his pew and casually—he hoped the action appeared casual—laid an open hymnal across the most uncomfortable portion of his anatomy. He cast a guilty glance at the elderly woman sitting next to him. She was incredibly skinny, smelled of mothballs, and wore something old and purple with feathers at the neck and cuffs. She smiled sweetly at him, seeming not to have noticed his problem, thank heaven. The thoughts filling his mind were not appropriate for church, and his physical response to those thoughts wasn't appropriate for an old lady to witness.

With difficulty, he forced himself to pay attention to the sermon. After all, that was why he'd come.

The children were still in Sunday school when church let out, so John joined in the social hour in the basement, accepting a cup of coffee and a plate of cookies from a gray-haired lady behind a long table.

Negligently Maggie returned his wave from the other side of the room where she stood laughing with the minister and another man, but before he could make his way in her direction, an elderly woman had him by the arm. "Dr. Martin, I've been wanting to meet you. Do come and sit down with me so we can chat. I'm Mrs. Baker, the Late Mayor's Widow." She pronounced it as if it were an extremely honorable title, one she prided herself in carrying. "I must say," she continued, "it's certainly been a shock to the entire community, your turning up here with an exact copy of Maggie Adair's little girl."

She eased her arthritic bulk onto a sofa, patted the

cushion beside her, and fluttered her eyelashes at him. "Do sit down and tell me all about it, Doctor." She filched a gingersnap off his plate and took a dainty nibble.

"Is it true," she asked, leaning conspiratorilly close, "that you and Maggie were . . . well"—she dropped her voice to a whisper—"lovers? And that you separated right after the girls were born?"

"Mrs. Baker—"

"Oh, it's all right," she said, patting his thigh. "You can tell me. I've been hearing so many rumors, I decided it was only fair to go right to the source and get the true story." She swallowed the rest of the cookie whole. "I always say, when in doubt, ask or risk repeating the wrong gossip."

"The 'right' gossip being better?" he asked, but she completely missed his irony.

"I tried to get the straight goods from Maggie," she said, "but sometimes there's simply no talking to that girl. She's got a spine like a steel rod, and when she gets her back up, there's no dealing with her. Got her coloring and the rest of her personality, volatile and passionate, from that redheaded reprobate who sired her, but she certainly got her stubbornness from her mother."

"Oh."

"She was rude to me, Dr. Martin, dreadfully rude. And me, an old friend of her grandmother's, rest her dear soul. So when Maggie refused to tell me the truth, I told myself, Lottie—that's my first name, Lottie—Lottie, you owe it to that young man to ask him for his side of things. I pride myself on always doing that."

John blinked and took a gulp of his coffee, fascinated. He wanted to know more about the mother of his daughter's twin sister. Where she came from, what made her tick, if anybody had ever found a way to channel all that "volatility and passion" . . .

"Doc Monro was the salt of the earth," Mrs. Baker went on, "and he never said a word against his daughter's husband, even though everyone saw trouble when that loud Irishman came breezing into town and before you know it, Margaret Monro was having to let out the waists on her skirts, and there was one of the fastest weddings this county has ever seen, and her not quite twenty at the time.

"But Michael Adair was a good father, you have to know that. He adored his little Maggie, carried her with him everywhere, those two red heads blazing all over town, until that terrible winter when the pneumonia carried him off.

"And his own wife catting around in Halifax with that rich fellow from Fredericton, New Brunswick, if what you hear can be believed, and nobody knowing if that baby she carried when he died was his or someone else's. I personally think the second girl must not have been Michael's, because there was Margaret, up and remarrying and moving off to Toronto within six months of poor Michael being in the ground. And leaving her little five-year-old daughter here for her parents to raise, and them too old and tired to do it.

"Many's the time I saw poor Julia Monro in the kiddie's playground, rubbing her aching back, she, who should have been lying down, not up pushing a swing with her granddaughter on it." John recalled the portrait of the stooped lady crippled by osteoporosis, and frowned.

"But that's all beside the point," Mrs. Baker swept on. "What I wanted to ask you is, are those two darling little girls truly twins? I must say, they both look a lot more like you than they do their mother, but it sometimes goes that way, doesn't it? I mean, take Maggie, looking the spit of her daddy, right down to those big green eyes. I—"

"John! So there you are!"

John's head jerked up. He met Maggie's laughing gaze, feeling as if she had just thrown him a life ring. He grasped at it eagerly, grasped the hand she held out to him, letting his gaze sweep over her. "Maggie."

With difficulty, he dragged his eyes off her nylon-clad legs, exposed by her pleated navy skirt, and up to the blue leather belt encircling a waist that looked ridiculously small above the flare of her hips. Her breasts thrust out pertly inside a hot-pink silk blouse that no other redhead he'd ever known would have risked wearing, even under a navy jacket. She was something else. He'd never seen her in a skirt before, and she took his breath away. Shorts, like the cutoffs she'd worn the other night, were casual, blatantly revealing. But a skirt—it flirted, teased, beguiled.

"Were you, uh—" His voice cracked and he cleared his throat. "Looking for me?"

"Of course, silly," she said, tugging on his hand, trying to get him to his feet. "Didn't you promise to let me introduce you to the choirmaster right after the service?"

"I, uh, yes. Oh, yes!" he lied quickly. "Sorry, I forgot." He set his plate and empty cup on a scarred end table and jumped up. "Mrs. Baker, forgive me. Lovely chatting with you. Excuse me, please."

"Oh, run along," she simpered, selecting another of the cookies he hadn't had a chance to eat. "I know I can't compete with the young girls. But I'll be seeing you. I'm bringing you my gallbladder on Monday morning at nine-thirty."

John managed to get turned away before his laughter exploded in an almost silent gust.

"Lord!" he whispered. "I hope she brings it in a bottle! Thanks for the rescue."

Maggie only laughed into his eyes with sparkling, silent amusement.

It wasn't until she had performed the introduction between him and the choirmaster that John realized he had held Maggie's hand tightly in his as they walked all the way across the church basement. He wondered what the congregation would make of that, and realized that he really didn't care.

"I'll leave you two to talk," she said, backing away.

"No!" John's startled exclamation both surprised and embarrassed him. "I mean, I can't talk long. Andi . . . Sunday school . . ." His voice trailed away lamely. "Will the kids come in here for refreshments when they're done?"

"Some, maybe," Maggie said. "Most of them stay in the hall. They have their own refreshment table, Kool-Aid being preferable to tea and coffee.

"How about I keep track of Andi for you?" she offered, and he jumped at it. Her suggestion meant she wasn't rushing off, that he was going to see her again. Soon. Somehow he hoped to extend their time together that day, get to know her better, have more of his multitude of questions answered.

With another of those casual little waves, she departed, saying over her shoulder, "Catch you later."

He watched her go, skirt swinging just above the backs of her knees, high heels imparting a sexy sway to her backside, and three small, bouncing curls drawing attention to the vulnerable nape of her neck.

Maggie . . .

He would surely have followed her, but Alvin, the choirmaster, all but grabbed him by the buttonholes and impressed upon him the need for a strong male lead in the choir.

Catch you later . . . If she caught him, or let him catch her, what then? What would be the point? Could he contemplate a future with her?

Future? Nodding and making automatic responses to the choirmaster, John tried to recall when he'd begun to contemplate a future even for himself, let alone one that he'd share with anybody else. Till now it had been enough to live in the present, trying hard not to think of the past, hoping that the pain would one day ebb completely. It had eased, of course, in three years, was seldom as sharp and biting as it had been at first, but it was always there, a deep ache so familiar, he'd almost come to like it.

But now, with the word *future* echoing in his head, he experienced pain of a different kind, much like the harsh, burning tingle of a limb coming to life after having been asleep. He didn't like it. He didn't like it at all. There were, however, other things he liked. Too many of them to have counted yet, and he didn't think he was anywhere near the end of the list.

High on that list of things he liked, John realized half an hour later, was looking at Maggie Adair. He liked that almost as much as he liked holding her, touching her skin, kissing her lips, breathing in her scent, absorbing her taste . . .

"You won't believe what just happened to me," he said quickly, gazing up at her after greeting both girls. He was amazed he'd remembered to speak to them. He might not have if Andi, seeing him coming, hadn't shrieked at him from a hundred feet away, telling him where she was. As if he might not have noticed. Maggie's hair stood out like a beacon, drawing his gaze from the moment he stepped out of the church and looked around.

She stood, shoeless, feet wide apart, in the center of a teeter-totter with one girl on each end. She'd shed the navy jacket that matched her skirt, and as she rocked from side to side with the board's motion, her hands on her hips seemed to narrow her waistline even more. The movement of her legs slid her skirt up and down her thighs.

"I'll believe what happened to you," she said as one long leg straightened while the other bent. "I'll even *tell* you: Alvin has talked you into joining the choir."

Andi went up; Maggie's right leg bent as her left leg straightened. John swallowed.

"You'll be doing a solo next Sunday," Maggie added as the teeter tottered and the whole, fascinating process with her legs and skirt and flexing waist repeated itself.

John stuffed his hands into his pockets to keep them out of trouble. They itched to reach up and wrap themselves around her waist and lift her down. Lift her down, pull her against him, hold her in place while he explored. With his hands, with his mouth. With every part of him that could explore a woman.

Oblivious to his inner turmoil, she smiled down at him. "Well? Am I right?"

He nodded. "Are you—" As before, he was forced to clear his throat. "Are you going to choir practice tomorrow night?"

"Yes. Of course." Then, to the girls, she said, "Okay, you two, balance evenly now. I'm getting off."

John's hands whipped out of his pockets, and he reached up and plucked her down before she could jump.

She landed lightly before him, hands wrapped around his wrists, whether to steady herself, to push him away, or because she, too, had wanted to touch, he couldn't have said. Her eyes were wide, filled with laughter, and . . . something else. His fingers tightened on her waist. Hers tightened on his wrists. His heart hammered in his chest, nearly strangling him as it forced an excess of blood into the vessels in his throat.

He pulled Maggie an inch closer. The breeze fluttered a curl just in front of her ear. He tried to breathe, failed, heard her breath rasp in, then sigh out. He watched her moisten her lips with the tip of her tongue.

He wanted her mouth under his with a desire greater than any other temptation he had ever faced. He wanted her body under his, open, welcoming, receptive. And looking at her, seeing the faint flush on her cheeks, the smoldering fire in her eyes, he knew she knew all of that, and that her desire ran as hotly as did his. Just as close to the surface. Her hands trembled on his forearms.

Could he— Should he— What if— He closed his eyes for a second. The thought of the risk he'd be taking made him feel sick as pain twisted through him. *No!*

When he looked at her again, Maggie's gaze was still on his, but something had changed, something warm had gone from her eyes. For another long, uncomfortable moment they stared at each other, then she broke away with a faint sound. She turned from his sharpened scrutiny, but not before he read in her eyes a swift and total repudiation of every one of those confused and potent emotions he had seen only seconds before.

"Time to go, Jolie," she said, using her daughter's

shoulder to steady herself as she slipped back into her pumps.

"No." John couldn't disguise the hoarseness of his voice. "I thought, maybe . . . lunch? Somewhere. Together. The four of us?"

Maggie's chin tilted as she turned back to him. Her smile was cool. Her lashes, gold tipped and thick, hid whatever her eyes might have revealed. "I think not," she said, and crouched, the breeze fluttering the hem of her skirt. She hugged Andi, who hugged her back tightly. "Bye, honey," she said. "See you soon."

Without so much as a further glance at John, she hopped over the low rail separating the playground from the sidewalk, Jolene at her side, and strode away toward her Cherokee parked at the end of the street.

The clicking of her heels sounded like quick, angry words of rejection aimed right at him. What had he done? What had he said? Or not done, not said? Women! Who could figure them out? On the short walk home with Andi chattering at his side, he resolved to forget about women in general for the rest of the day, and Maggie Adair in particular. With any luck, for the rest of his life.

Still, John found himself driving by Maggie's house late that afternoon. It was legitimate. He had an elderly patient whom Dr. Blaine had suggested he visit frequently. The man lived only half a mile from Maggie. He could use the road that led past her place as easily as he could any other.

Seeing her on the back of her bay horse, hair whipping out behind her as she rode, his heart caught in his throat and he had to pull over and stop. Long after she'd ridden out of sight, he sat there, filled with the kind of ache he'd thought he'd never feel again. It was an ache he knew had a cure, a very specific one, one with the name Maggie Adair written across it in big, bold letters.

But if he took so much as one small dose of that cure, would the side effects haunt him forever?

John continued to sit in his car, head back against the high top of the seat, fists clenched around the wheel. Presently Maggie rode into view again. He watched her and Medallion rise up and over a fence, then she slowed the horse to a walk. It picked its way toward the barn, and the two of them disappeared inside, leaving him with the feeling of being shut out, held apart from something good and special that he needed in his life.

With Maggie, would he find the emotional warmth, the personal intimacy, the human closeness he'd done without for too long?

And a future?

He wasn't even sure he could offer her that, or if he did, that she would want it with him. Because he also had something she wouldn't want—a past he could never deny.

SEVEN

Monday evening at choir practice Maggie could only hope no one else noticed her difficulty in concentrating. Her eyes strayed too often to the doorway at the top of the spiral stairs. Where was John? Had he decided not to join after all? Alvin would be more than disappointed, she knew, if that was the case. She'd seen his avid, must-have-that-singer expression the day before when John's deeply mellow voice with its perfect pitch soared above the rest of the congregation's as they sang hymns.

She glanced at the choirmaster, whose focus was on Marjorie Clark and the beautiful soprano the woman released so that it flew upward and resonated in the acoustic vault of the ceiling. Alvin didn't look disappointed, or even aware that John hadn't shown. But Alvin was getting on. Maybe he'd forgotten Maggie had all but shanghaied John for him, under the guise of rescuing him from Mrs. Baker.

Not that she cared personally, of course. She didn't need the man, or the conflicting signals he sent out. Yet, as he rushed through the door, raindrops glistening in his hair and dampening the shoulders of his jacket, the sight of him was enough to steal half a beat from her cadence. Alvin gave her a sharp look, and she felt herself flush as guiltily as a schoolgirl. She forced herself to tear her focus from John as he strode past.

Alvin swept his hands up to bring the rest of the choir in on the chorus of "Amazing Grace," and John's tones joined in, rich and powerful.

If her concentration had been off while she'd wondered if he was going to turn up, his arrival shot it right out of the air. His singing filled her, tampered with her heartbeat, interfered with her breathing. Even when he was silent, simply knowing he was somewhere behind her kept her on edge. The woman on her right nudged her when she failed to pick up on Alvin's next cue, and the woman on her left scowled, half turning away, as if to avoid Maggie's unsure notes lest they pollute her own.

Cut it out! Maggie ordered herself. *Stop thinking about him. Pay attention.* For a time, she did, but then Alvin cued in the baritones, and through all the other voices, John's was the only one she heard. Her mind went blank as her soul stilled and she absorbed the sound of his voice.

For the remainder of the practice she was next to useless.

She would have left the minute they were done, but a friend cornered her to discuss a bridal shower scheduled for Thursday evening the following week, and asked her to make cookies. That conversation carried her down the stairs to the main church level, where she might have escaped out the door and into the rainy night, had not a hand descended onto her shoulder. She froze.

"Hi." His single word sent a warm breath past her ear.

She glanced back at him. "Hi, yourself." She was

determined to keep her manner remote, or failing that, friendly but cool. She ruined the effect immediately. "You were late."

"I know. I had a baby." Grinning proudly, he added, "My first Maples baby."

His delight was so infectious, she couldn't help but smile back. "Good for you."

"It's a boy." He looked as puffed up as if he were solely responsible for the arrival of the new child. She dragged her gaze from his eyes and swept it over him. He'd removed his gray windbreaker and held it slung over one shoulder, hooked on a finger. His royal blue sweater added highlights to the slatey shade of his eyes.

"You don't look any the worse for wear."

He stretched and arched his back. "I'm not. It was an easy delivery. It just came at an inconvenient time. I didn't want to miss my first practice." Something in his eyes sent a slow, delicious shimmer through her. It tingled in her toes, made mush out of her leg muscles, and pooled hot in her middle. "I hoped you'd be here," he added as he linked their fingers. "Think we could sneak out for coffee on our own, or are we obliged to stay here?"

"Here?" Maggie blinked and looked around, realizing for the first time that they were in the church basement, where Geraldine, Alvin's wife, always had refreshments ready after choir practice. She swallowed, knowing there was a reason she should refuse, but unable at the moment to recall what it was. Before she could reply, Alvin was there, thanking John for coming, complimenting him on being in such fine form that night.

With a sly smile, he narrowed his gaze on Maggie. "Not like certain other people I could mention. I think you completely took her breath away tonight, John. The minute you walked in, Maggie's talents walked out. Maybe I'll have to get her in for a little extra practice when there are fewer . . . distractions."

Belatedly Maggie snatched her hand free of John's and floundered for a reply.

Geraldine came to her rescue. "Oh, don't plague the girl, Alvin. Everyone's entitled to an off night once in a while." Placing an arm around Maggie, she steered her away.

"Here, drink this." She handed Maggie a mug of herbal tea. "It's lemon. It'll soothe your throat. Alvin's right, you know. Even I could hear that you weren't truly on this evening. Are you sickening for something?"

"Lovesick, maybe," cackled one of the other choir members, nudging Maggie with an elbow.

Maggie steadied her lemon tea as it threatened to slosh, and managed a laugh. "Not me, Shirley."

"Why not you?" asked Rose, the organist, a septuagenarian spinster about whom fascinating rumors had circulated for many decades. "Think you're immune? Nobody's that, Maggie-me-love, especially not with a handsome new doctor in town." She smiled archly, no doubt hoping someone would ask her how she knew. Rose had undoubtedly seen a lot of new doctors come through town.

Nobody asked her, and she fell silent as Shirley took up the refrain. "It's about time you found a daddy for that little girl of yours. It's not right, the way you young people try to raise your kiddies alone. And what better solution than you and your daughter teaming up with—"

Sending Shirley a glare that would have shut up a lesser woman, Maggie set her cup down hard. Geraldine smiled blandly as she lifted the teapot. Her "More, Maggie dear?" just barely covered Shirley's continuing with "the doctor and his daughter, especially under the circumstances."

"No." Just barely, Maggie managed to remember to add, "Thank you, Geraldine. It's time for me to go. Good—"

"Oh, now don't rush away," said Rose, with a wink at Geraldine. "I think you look much too flushed. Doctor, do come and have a look at this girl. Maybe Gerry's right and she is sickening for something."

Maggie flinched away. "I am not! I—"

By the way John's eyes were dancing as he strode to her side, Maggie knew he'd been aware of the teasing she was enduring. "Let me see." He laid the backs of his fingers against her cheek, drawing them slowly over the curve of her face until they rested against her throat. "Hmm," he murmured, and his expression sent a renewed surge of heat through her, heat she saw reflected in his eyes.

As his hand turned under her chin, she jerked her head back. She'd seen that look in his eyes before, and had seen it swiftly replaced by ice and repudiation. "I'm perfectly all right." Her tone was curt. "If I need a doctor, I'll call my own. Good night, everyone. I promise to do better next week."

Without waiting for a reply, she whirled away and marched out.

John caught up with her as she was about to slam the door of her Cherokee. He caught it, held it. "What's the rush?" His expression was hidden by the glare of a streetlamp behind his head. "I asked if you'd come and have coffee with me. You never did answer."

"No," she said, wrestling for control of the door. When he refused to let it go, she challenged him with a glare. "You asked for an answer, John. I just gave you one. *No.* Now let go of my door. I'm leaving."

"Hey, cool down. Don't take your temper out on me. I wasn't the one teasing you."

"Stupid old biddies," she muttered. "Nothing better to do than gossip and speculate and pry." She raised her angry gaze to his face. "And you played along with them."

"I'm sorry. I didn't realize it was really upsetting you. Come on, Maggie. They all care about you. They're your friends. You must be used to their teasing."

"Maybe they're my friends, but—" She clamped her mouth shut.

"But I'm not, so I don't get to tease?"

"No, you're not, and no, you don't. Good night, John."

He didn't move. "I thought we were going to be friends."

"So did I."

He shifted, putting a foot up on the floor of her truck and leaning his arms on his knee. "So why aren't we, Maggie? What's wrong?"

Maggie drew a deep breath, held it for a beat, then let it out slowly. She thought about lying. She thought about pretending she didn't have a real answer. She thought about sliding out the far side of the truck and running away. But none of those options would move her any further along the road to understanding this man, or being understood by him. Suddenly she knew it was important that she have both.

"All right," she said, "since you ask: I think it's pointless for us to spend time together. I'm attracted to you and I believe you're attracted to me, but you look guilty every time you kiss me, or touch me, or . . . want me. I don't care for the feeling that gives me—as if *I'm* doing something wrong."

He stepped back and let out a long breath. "I see." They both remained silent for several seconds, then John ran a hand through his wet hair. "Okay. I did ask, didn't I?"

Maggie nodded. "Yes, you did." She noticed he didn't deny her accusation. "To the best of my knowledge, we're both adults, both free to do what we wish, and with whom. *I* have no encumbrances. I suspect you still do, John, and they're making you uncomfortable. So until you unload them, unless you unload them, I think it's best if you and I are simply acquaintances."

She turned on the ignition, and the Cherokee's engine roared to life. "I know we'll be thrown together as the parents of two children with an extraordinary connection, but we don't have to let that force us into something we don't want."

"But I do want—" He broke off and set his lips firmly shut as he shook his head in what she took to be self-disgust.

"I know what you want, John," she said evenly, putting the truck in gear. "But it's also very plain to me how much you'd rather not want it. Good night."

He released a loud puff of air. "Good night, Maggie." He closed her door for her, and Maggie drove away, wipers smearing the moisture on the windshield, making it difficult to see.

John watched until Maggie's taillights winked out around the corner, then began walking home. Rain splattered up off the sidewalk, drizzled down through the leaves on the trees, and created misty halos around every street lamp along the way.

He'd wanted to explain, but no words had come. He hated thinking he was so transparent to her, that his uncertainties had hurt her. It wasn't fair to her. He wished he'd had an explanation to offer her, but how could he, when he didn't really have one for himself?

A question came from nowhere. *Do you believe Laura would object?*

No! The answer was immediate and adamant.

Even if he had believed that, loyalty to a dead woman —regardless of how deeply he'd loved her, would always love her for all she'd been to him and given to him— simply didn't make sense. If he was using her memory as a means to keep a barrier between him and Maggie, then he was doing all three of them an injustice. Besides, he hadn't been celibate in the years since her death. So it wasn't that.

Then what was it? This entire situation with Maggie was different in every way from those earlier itches he'd scratched with other women.

Different how?

He not only wanted her as a woman, he liked her as a person. He liked talking to her, liked listening to her. He liked the openness of her gaze, the candid way she said what she felt, how she gave freely of both physical and emotional affection. He liked the fire of her temper, the texture of her skin, the smell of her hair.

He liked, too, the tenderness she'd extended to his daughter, the instinctive way she reached out and touched Andi, comforted her, and answered her questions in language a seven-year-old could easily understand.

It was easy to like Maggie.

It would be just as easy to fall in love with her.

He slipped on an exposed tree root and nearly went down on one knee.

Once more he thought of intimacy, belonging, a home. All things he needed, all things he'd been thinking of more and more frequently since Maggie had come into his life. He wasn't the only one whose life lacked those qualities. Andi needed a mother, and the old ladies of the choir were right. Who would be a more logical choice than the mother of her twin?

But what if the entire attraction they felt for each other was nothing more than the result of propinquity, the fact that their daughters were sisters? What if they tried to make it together and failed?

John shuddered, not liking the questions or the way they made him feel. The fact was, though, he was acting as if he were half paralyzed by fear. Acting? Hell, he *was* terrified at the thought of leaping into the unknown. He was afraid to take a chance lest it all be snatched away. If he let himself love Maggie, if she and he and the children created a family out of the separate bits and pieces they were, and screwed it up, he'd be risking too much. He knew better than most how quickly, how irrevocably, things could go wrong. It didn't require an error in judgment. Death could sweep in and wipe away a lifetime's dreams and hopes and plans, so there was more at stake than his own heart and sanity.

There were two children involved, making his fear even more valid. Certainly, adults could be expected to survive the pain when a serious relationship failed, but children were a different matter. Andi and her happiness were his responsibility. He *had* to think about all the ramifications. If there were to be a second devastating loss, and *he* didn't make it through, what would happen to Andi? She needed a mother, but she needed him too. She'd need him for many years to come. She worried about his dying.

She was too young to know that there was more than one kind of death.

With a shiver that had little to do with the September rain soaking his clothes, he realized he was home. He inserted the key into the lock and let himself in. Weariness washed over him, and a strong need for sleep that he doubted would come with any ease that night. As he'd tell any patient, things would look a lot different in the morning. For a troubled patient, he might prescribe a sedative.

For himself, though, he did not, and his night's sleep, and the ones that followed it, were anything but good. He still had more questions than answers.

One question, disturbed him more deeply than all the others. What of his past, and his chances with Maggie once she knew about it? It wasn't a question he wanted to hear. Nor did he want to contemplate any of the possible answers.

The rest of the week was busy for Maggie, with one new client added to her accounting list, riding lessons nearly every afternoon, and household tasks taking up what remaining spare minutes she had. Thursday she realized most of those tasks were make-work projects she'd devised to keep herself from noticing that John had taken her at her word. Of course, they weren't successful. He was on her mind much too often.

One minute she'd be busy berating herself for telling him they were better off as nothing more than acquaintances. The next, she was arguing with herself, saying that she'd been right to lay it on the line. They couldn't be friends if they weren't open with each other, and they couldn't be anything more than that, despite the heady kisses they'd shared, if he couldn't forget the past.

Saturday morning she and Jolene shopped for a birthday present for another second grader, then had dinner with friends in the evening. They were up early for church on Sunday morning, and Maggie's heart was beating much too quickly as she drove into town.

She wasn't sure if she was relieved when John didn't appear. Maybe relief *could* emulate great emptiness.

After dropping Jolene at the birthday party, Maggie worked hard on fall cleanup in the garden, then enjoyed an hour just for herself. Such times were rare, and she was nowhere near ready to get out of her bubble bath when she heard the slamming of a car door, followed by Jolene's running footsteps up the steps and across the porch.

"Mom! Come and see what I got for you!" The shrill voice shattered whatever peace remained, and Maggie rose reluctantly to wrap herself in a towel. "Mom! Where are you?"

"I'm here, honey," she said, and stepped out into the hall, dripping suds all over. She froze in mid-step, gaping at John, who stood equally still, staring at her with dark, hungry eyes.

She wanted to move, wanted to escape, yet there she stood, naked but for a few square feet of soggy terry cloth and some bubbles sliding down her legs. Bubbles his gaze followed all the way to the floor before he looked upward again as if seeking more. Didn't he even have the decency to look away?

No. He stared. Openly, blatantly, voraciously, and not in the least guiltily, as Maggie hitched her towel a little higher over her breasts, wondering desperately how much she was exposing below its bottom edge. For what seemed like hours, they stared at each other before she came to her senses and backed through the bathroom door again, slamming it shut and leaning on it, breathing hard.

Seconds later she heard Jolene say, "Bye, John. Thank you for driving me home." The screen door slammed, then Jolene knocked on the bathroom door, obviously still excited about whatever she'd brought for her mother.

"Just a minute, babe," Maggie said, ashamed of her shaky voice and glad no one but she could see her trembling hands. She sank onto the edge of the tub, because her knees were completely boneless. He was gone? Just like that, he'd left? He'd gobbled her up with his eyes, then bolted? It mattered little that she had fled first; she'd had good reason. Couldn't he have waited even five minutes for her to get dressed? No. Apparently not. Quickly she dragged on a robe.

"Did you have a good time at Lori's party?" she asked, emerging into the hall.

Jolene's reply came from the kitchen. "It was okay." She waved at a plastic container on the table as Maggie entered. "Look! Lori's mom sent you a *huge* piece of cake."

Maggie opened the container and took a swipe of chocolate icing with one finger, licking it off in appreciation. "That was nice of her." Then, with a sharp glance at her daughter, she said, "I hope you didn't hint that I might like some, sweetie. That wouldn't have been good manners." The size of the slab suggested Lori's mom had considered a seven-year-old's appetite for cake as well as an adult's.

That offended Jolene. "Mom! I got good manners. *Andi* doesn't, though," she added with disdain. "She was the one who said that if Lori's mom was giving John cake, she should give you some as well, 'cause if single dads deserve special treats, then single moms do too. I think it's just as rude to ask for something for somebody else's mom."

Maggie raised her eyebrows and smiled at her daughter's purse-lipped disapproval. She wasn't at all surprised to learn that Andi was a budding feminist, or that Andi had earned herself another black mark in Jolene's book of offenses. "It's not nearly as rude," she said mildly, then asked, "Who gave you permission to use Dr. Martin's first name?"

"He asked me to, Mom. He said under the circumstances, he thought it would be best."

"*What* circumstances?"

Jolene frowned as if it were a stupid question. "Me and Andi being sisters."

"Oh. Of course." Maggie sighed silently. She figured those were the circumstances he'd meant too. What had she expected him to do, say, *You should use my first name because your mother and I have shared some extremely arousing moments and I think our families are going to become inextricably intertwined?*

She cleared her throat. "Did you and Andi get along all right at the party?"

Jolie's face puckered. "She brought the same blouse we got for Lori only in a different color."

"It shows she has good taste, honey, and there isn't a huge selection in Maples. I'm sure Andi didn't do it on purpose to annoy you."

Jolene's eyes expressed her doubts.

Two weeks of knowing she had a twin sister had done little to soften her attitude.

Monday she was infuriated to learn that Andi was the older twin. Those twelve minutes burned in her heart as a personal affront.

"It's not fair that Andi came to live here!" she complained, tears shimmering. "She wants to play with me all the time and now both Monica and Alison are mad at me because of her and I haven't got any friends at all." The tears spilled over. "I *hate* her!"

"I'm sorry, sweetie," Maggie said. "I know it's hard for you. But I think Andi just wants to be your friend too. I'm sure she didn't mean to cause trouble between you and the others." As she hugged and rocked her, Maggie knew there was no point in telling Jolene that friendships, especially among seven-year-olds, were often in a state of flux.

"She only wants to be my friend because we got horses. Monica said so. Andi wants to come and ride, but her dad says he won't bring her unless you invite her, 'cause he's not coming here again without an invitation from you." She pulled away from her mother's embrace and sent her an accusing glare. "I think he was embarrassed when you came out of the bathroom yesterday with no clothes on."

Maggie's insides quivered. *He* was embarrassed!

As she readied herself for choir practice after dinner that night, Maggie's thoughts continued to center on John. He hadn't looked embarrassed, seeing her in nothing but a towel. And why, come to think of it, had he come in on Sunday? It certainly hadn't been to speak to her, nor to visit for a few minutes, not the way he'd whipped on out again in five seconds flat.

She stared at herself in the mirror as she outlined her lips with a bright, sassy pink shade. It still pleased her to recall that there hadn't been a hint of guilt in the way he stared at her Sunday. There hadn't been anything in his expression but pure admiration. Well, that, along with some good old-fashioned lust.

Maybe he'd been too shocked to feel guilty—and maybe not.

Her heartbeat accelerated. What if he'd gotten over whatever was bothering him about their mutual attraction?

In the mirror her eyebrows arched up as she recapped her lipstick. *Whatever?*

Who was she trying to kid? She took a swipe at her lashes with her mascara wand. In light of his continuing to wear his wedding ring several years after his wife's death, it didn't take a lot of imagination to figure out what kind of pebble he had in his shoe.

She frowned. Had his saying that he wouldn't come to her house again without an invitation from her meant he'd like one? If so, in what capacity? That of Andi's father, or that of a man interested in a woman?

And did it matter? If he wanted to tell himself it was merely the first, hadn't he shown enough inadvertent interest in her that the second capacity might develop if given a chance? She added one little spritz of perfume, though she normally didn't bother just for choir practice.

"Maybe we should have Andi and her father over for dinner one evening," she suggested to Jolene as she emerged from the bathroom.

One evening. Right. That should be vague enough not to speed up her pulse to escape velocity and put her hormones in an uproar. Except it did. The not-so-sensible part of her demanded, *What evening? When? Choose one, Maggie, fast. Do it now! Pin him down. Ask him tonight at choir practice.*

The idea made her insides quiver. He'd asked her and Jolene to join him and Andi for lunch; she'd refused. He'd asked her out—just the two of them—for coffee. She'd rejected that suggestion, too, and told him why. What made her think he wouldn't turn the tables on her, to say nothing of his back, if she asked him out?

Still, nothing ventured . . . "What do you think, Jolie? Should we ask them?"

"I don't know, Mom." Jolene looked trapped.

Her daughter's reluctance deflated Maggie's eagerness. "You might find you like Andi better if you see her more often away from school, honey, without other kids pulling you this way and that. You did seem to get along with her the night they came and watched the movie with us. I heard you laughing together."

She and John had gotten along together pretty well that night too. At least until his guilt came into the room on his daughter's heels, just as it had the following Sunday after he'd all but undressed her with his eyes, then snatched her down from the teeter-totter.

Jolene said nothing, and Maggie had to let it go at that because Stephanie, her baby-sitter, pulled up at that moment.

Maggie sighed as she drove toward town. She wished that she could forget John Martin, and that Jolene could find a way to accept Andi. Maybe then she could return to the quiet, peaceful state of emotional lethargy she'd enjoyed right up till the day after Labor Day.

John arrived early for choir practice and stood with scarcely controlled impatience waiting for the rest of the group to assemble. Where was Maggie? Would she come? Would her face turn pink when she saw him? Would she look away in confusion and embarrassment as the sight of him reminded her of the moment she'd stepped out of her bathroom all but nude, to find him in her hallway? He suppressed a grin.

No. Not Maggie. He might suffer momentary embarrassment if his body responded the way it did each time he thought of those bubbles sliding down sleek, wet skin, but Maggie would brazen it out, meet his gaze squarely, daring him to make a comment. Would he ever get over the sexy sight of her? How was he supposed to get through choir practice with his tongue as dry as an old glove?

He heard her laughter before she came into view, but even the advance warning didn't help. He still lost his breath as her bright hair caught the light and threw it toward him.

"*Me* run against *Masterson*?" she was saying incredulously to the man at her side, a tall, gray-haired guy who had his arm draped over her shoulders.

The mayor. Right. John recalled seeing him in the choir. A childless, fiftyish widower with a hefty bank balance and several business properties around town.

"You've got to be kidding, Charlie," Maggie went on. Not for so much as an instant did she look toward John, so intent was she on her discussion with the other man.

"I'm not kidding and you know it," the mayor said. "I also know you've been thinking about it. We've all heard how you threatened Elmer that day your little girl got beaten up."

"I didn't threaten him. I simply said that if I ran, and if I won, I'd see some of his policies changed."

"Which means you at least gave the idea some thought."

"Some, yes. But now I know Masterson's running again? Not a chance, Charlie, I couldn't win against him."

"Trust me. You could. And you will." The mayor, a tenor, if John remembered right, squeezed her shoulders, then let her go. For the first time since the pair had entered, John unclenched both his fists and his jaw.

Alvin strode in, looking like Albert Einstein on a bad hair day.

"We'll talk about it again after practice," John heard Charlie say before leaving Maggie's side. She shook her head, but didn't argue anymore. Alvin called them all together and began outlining plans for the choir's involvement in the church Christmas concert.

Charlie glommed on to Maggie the minute Alvin dismissed them, keeping at her all the way down the stairs to the basement. There, he was joined by several other choir members, plus Rose, the organist, all of whom seemed to think Maggie should accept the challenge.

John poured himself a cup of coffee, then filled another one, stirred four lumps of sugar into it, and carried it over to Maggie. He tried to appear casual and relaxed, though he felt anything but. For an instant his gaze and Maggie's clashed as he handed her the cup. He read questions in her eyes before she hid behind her lashes and stared down into her coffee. "Thanks," she murmured.

"Ah, doctor," Charlie said. John sensed the mayor wasn't happy to have him join the circle, but was willing to use him if it would help. "Many of us who've known

Maggie all her life feel she should run for the school board. Maybe your powers of persuasion will work where ours have failed. Will you talk to the girl? She is so stubborn."

Breathing deeply because she smelled so good, John stood close beside her. "Maggie strikes me as a woman with a mind of her own. Why would I want to try to convince her to do something she doesn't want to do? Surely those of you who've known her all her life know better than to try."

A woman from the alto section answered John. "We need her and plenty others like her, parents with a vested interest in education, if we're ever going to regain the basics that have been chipped away from our school system, year after year, school board after school board. Why, there's nothing left but fluff and frills and kids who can scarcely read when they leave seventh grade."

"Just a slight exaggeration, wouldn't you say, Ethel?" Maggie said with a smile. "But you're right in principle. We do need to return to the fundamentals of education. However, that doesn't mean I'm willing to run." She turned to a rotund man with a red face half hidden behind a bushy blond beard. "How about you, Sven? You're a good public speaker, and you have six kids in the system from kindergarten to high school. Surely that gives you even more of a vested interest than I have."

"But Maggie," Charlie began, only to be cut off by someone else eagerly addressing Sven. John grinned in admiration at the neat way Maggie eased herself out of the circle now that the focus was off her. It wasn't that simple for him. He was forced to stop and respond to three people who spoke to him as he tried to follow her, and he didn't catch her until she was halfway across the parking lot.

"Maggie, wait up. I owe you an apology."

Her eyebrows shot up as she turned to look at him. "Whatever for? Championing me in there? I didn't need it, of course, but I'm glad to know you recognize me as a woman with a mind of my own."

"Not that. For walking in on you the way I did yesterday. For embarrassing you."

She slipped her elbow free of his clasp. "I wasn't embarrassed, John," she said, but the color in her cheeks belied the statement. "Jolene thinks *you* were, though."

He shook his head. "Jolene's wrong. I was lots of things. Enthralled. Captivated." He smiled as they came up to the side of her Cherokee. "Turned on, but never, never embarrassed."

She shrugged. "All right. I didn't suppose you were. Lord knows you must see enough women every day in various states of undress, not to be embarrassed by a little incident like that."

"Yes," he agreed as the car beside them backed out. "I do see a variety of women in, as you put it, various states of undress, but they don't turn me on, Maggie. You, however, do."

"You don't have to say things like that." She wrinkled her nose and squinted as headlights flashed across her face. "I guess I owe you an apology, too, for what I said last week."

"No, you don't. You were right. Sometimes what I'm beginning to feel for you makes me feel guilty because . . ." He didn't finish it. "But I never intended *you* to feel you were doing something wrong."

"But you feel you were?"

Another couple of cars left. Someone called out a goodnight. Maggie waved, never taking her gaze from his face. John let out a long breath as he stared at her. "I didn't know until you said it, about me looking guilty, that it showed."

"It does." She didn't add, *and I don't like it*, but John felt as if she had.

Maggie wished he would deny feeling guilty. She wished the conversation had never started. She wished he would go. The parking lot was empty but for them.

When he said nothing further, she got into her truck. The engine didn't start. It didn't so much as click. She jiggled the key, jiggled the wheel, and tried again to no avail. Frowning, she pumped the gas and gave it another useless attempt.

"Damn," she said in frustration. "It's under warranty and I just had it serviced."

"Never mind," John said, his voice taut. "I'll drive you home and you can call the dealership in the morning."

There wasn't, as far as she could see, much choice. For either of them.

As they walked toward his house he stopped under a tree, drawing her to a halt where a lamp cast diffused light through the branches. "Maggie . . ."

His hand wrapped warmly around hers. Their gazes locked. For a moment he said nothing further. He simply touched her cheek, sliding her wind-tossed hair back behind her ear. "Do you think you and I *can* be friends?" His smile was crooked, his eyes wistful, his caress tender. It sent a delicious shiver right through her and made her want to lean into him.

Keeping her spine straight, she studied him in return. "I think we could be, John. If that's what we both want."

He nodded, then after a moment, his gaze slid away, following a car as it passed. Her gaze followed the turn of his head. He had a wonderful profile: strong jaw, square chin, and hawklike nose. Not handsome, but certainly rugged and attractive. His lower lip gleamed. He licked it as if sensing her stare, maybe disturbed by it. Which was only right. Simply gazing at his lips, remembering the way his mouth had felt on hers, disturbed her half to death.

They walked on, soon reaching his house. When they were both seated in his car, he started the engine, then sat there gripping the wheel, staring out the windshield. At length he said, "I'm not sure I can make you understand what's going on with me, because I'm not sure I do, either. Not fully." He turned and looked at her, his expression unreadable in the green glow of the dash lights, but his tone was strained. "I'm not used to analyzing my feelings. Feelings just are. You have to accept them, go with them, only . . . I've got some I want, really badly, to go with, and others I'd like to forget about, but can't. They . . . conflict."

He gave a self-conscious shrug as if he didn't know where to take it from there.

"You loved your wife very much," Maggie said, to help him out. "Why don't you tell me about her?"

EIGHT

"Is that what—" John clamped his teeth shut on the question, not quite sure if he was glad or not that Maggie assumed his ambivalence had to do with his marriage and the loss of his wife.

As he supposed it did, at least in part. He thought he'd sorted all of that out in his own mind, but maybe he hadn't. He backed out of the drive, swung onto the street, and accelerated smoothly. The tires hummed as they spun on pavement, whined as they crossed a metal-decked bridge, and thumped over an uneven patch. On the radio Michael Bolton crooned a song of heartbreak and longing. John felt cocooned in the darkness with the soulful voice, his own unhappy thoughts, and Maggie.

"What I had with Laura was pretty special," he said at last, clearly startling Maggie. Her head jerked toward him. "First love," he added. "I keep wondering if something so potent, so all-consuming, can ever be more than a once-in-a-lifetime event. If so, how fair would it be to offer another woman something less, or to accept something less myself?"

What the hell was he doing? he asked himself. Why

hadn't he said "offer *you*?" Because he was a coward. It was easier, less risky, to keep this on an impersonal basis, make it a hypothetical discussion.

"I don't know, John," she said. "Maybe with another woman it wouldn't have to be less. Maybe it would simply be . . . different."

"Maybe," he said, but he knew he was right. What he'd felt for and with Laura wasn't the same as what was happening here. This was totally different, more painful, and a hell of a lot scarier because there were more people involved. With Laura, he'd known her for a long time before he realized he was in love with her, and she'd fallen in love with him knowing everything there was to know about him, his past, everything.

Maggie didn't know, and it wasn't fair that he keep it from her.

So tell her, idiot.

And if I do, while what she feels for me can still be classified as "an attraction," I risk killing it before it's born.

Her voice cut through his misery, giving him something to focus on besides his own indecision. "Where did you meet Laura?"

He started to reply, cleared his throat, then managed to speak. "Her parents owned the stable where I worked. I think I told you the job came with an apartment. But apart from some very basic furnishings, it was an empty shell of a place, and I didn't have a clue what to do with it."

A soft laugh escaped him. "Enter Laura. Fair-haired and blue-eyed, she reminded me of a perfect princess out of a storybook.

"She was only fourteen, but she took pity on me. Took charge of me and my life, dragging stuff out of her parents' attic and fixing my place up for me. Her parents laughed at her, referred to her attempts as 'Laura playing house.' "

He chuckled again. This was easier by far than going even deeper into his past. He was almost giddily glad Maggie hadn't said instead, *Tell me about your mother.*

"But she always said she wasn't playing," he continued. "She was making a home for me because I didn't have one and . . . I let her because I didn't want to disappoint her."

He flicked on the turn signal and pulled into Maggie's driveway, beside what he assumed must be the baby-sitter's car. "No one ever wanted to disappoint Laura. Even when I tried to pretend she was a bothersome, pesky kid, beneath my eighteen-year-old notice, I'd have died myself rather than hurt her feelings. Everyone who knew her wanted to make her happy because she spread so much sunshine around her. People of all ages adored her as a child."

He draped his forearm over the wheel and turned to face Maggie. "And then she grew up. Almost overnight, it seemed, and it was no different. She was tall." He measured Maggie with a glance. "Almost as tall as you, but . . . delicate. At least, she looked delicate, as if she hadn't been meant to survive long in this kind of world." His voice broke momentarily. Maggie took his hand, squeezing it on the seat between them.

He stared down at their hands for a second, wrapped his fingers around hers, then cleared his throat again and continued. "I had to wait for her to grow up. I married her ten years after I met her, when I was interning. We'd been married only a couple of months when she got sick."

He stared out the windshield. "It was cancer. It meant a hysterectomy. She was devastated—we both were. We'd planned a big family. Once we were over the shock, and when we were assured that they'd gotten the entire tumor, we applied to adopt and, in time, got Andi. Life was good.

"Then the cancer returned. They should have taken her ovaries in the beginning, but she was so young, and it seemed a straightforward case. It was a very small tumor, they said, neatly encapsulated. There was no way it should have spread, but it did."

Maggie clenched her teeth as John went on, his grip tightening on hers. "They tried Tamoxifen, but—"A spasm of pain creased his face. "At least it was fast. Three months from the recurrence until she was . . . gone. She's been dead nearly three years."

Her throat ached from the sorrow she saw in his face. "I'm sorry."

"Yeah. Me too. I—" He broke off as his beeper sounded, and looked relieved as he turned on the dome light and checked the LED display.

"Come in if you need to," Maggie said, "and use the phone."

"It's okay. I have one here."

For the first time Maggie noticed the phone clipped under his dash. "Oh, okay. I'll leave you to it. Thanks for the ride, John." She reached for the door handle. Before she could leave the car, he slid after her, cupping a hand around the back of her neck, turning her toward him.

"Maggie . . ." His Adam's apple bobbed. "Thanks for the friendship."

"You're welcome." Impulsively she leaned closer and kissed him, a brief, friendly kiss, but before she could back away, he made a ragged sound and took control of it. His lips moved over hers, hard and warm, as his fingers tightened in her hair, and he tilted her head back.

Before she knew it had happened, she'd willingly re-linquished command and let him draw her against his chest. It felt wonderful. It felt right. She stroked her hand down his cheek, eliciting a soft, growling murmur, then he deepened the kiss until it went hot and wild and needful as they both strained closer. Her fingers slid through his hair as his tangled in hers. His mouth devoured hers; his free hand slipped inside her jacket, and cupped her breast, molding it.

She groaned deep in her throat as her flesh swelled under his caress, her nipples hardening until they ached. He shifted, leaning back behind the wheel, and pulled her onto him, drawing her up his body until she fit between his legs. They pressed intimately together, breath coming quickly, jaggedly, and stared at each other.

"Maggie . . . oh Lord, Maggie," he gasped. He encircled her head with his hands before taking her mouth again in an even more devastating kiss that dragged a response from her like she'd never known. It had no beginning, no ending, only a burning, aching need to give it form and substance.

She moved against him, with him, lifted up when he caught her shoulders and tried to turn her to a more comfortable position, but a sudden, startling blare of sound made them both freeze. The sound went on and on even as they both blinked in sudden brilliance of the porch light as Stephanie, the baby-sitter, turned it on.

Quickly, his face a picture of consternation, John set her upright, putting her away from him, thereby removing her elbow from the horn. In the sudden silence his mouth opened, then closed, then opened again as Stephanie continued to stare at them. After what seemed like an hour she went back inside, closed the door, and turned off the light.

Maggie felt laughter rising up in her. She tried to hold it back, but it filled her chest, her throat, and broke free. "Oh, John, if you could have seen your face!" she spluttered. "You looked—" She bit her lip. She put a hand over her mouth. She chewed on the inside of her cheek, but she was beyond control. "You looked exactly like Gilgamesh the day I caught him with one of my hens in his mouth." Collapsing forward against her knees, she shook with spasm after spasm of mirth.

Moments later she realized John had joined in, and his laughter, blending with hers, only made her laugh harder. She wrapped her arms around her middle, leaned against the seat back, and laughed until she was weak. When the paroxysms finally tapered off, she pushed her hair out of her eyes, wiping her wet face with her palms.

John, she saw, was doing the same, his breathing as choppy as hers. "That was—"He smothered another chuckle as it threatened to get out of hand. "That was crazy. But fun." He shook his head as he stared at her. "Was it . . . was it really that funny?"

"Well, no, but—"She bit her lip, met his gaze again, and once more they were gone, laughing like lunatics, whooping and howling and gasping until exhaustion overcame them.

"Ooh," Maggie said, prodding her aching stomach with her fingertips. "Oh! I *hurt*. I haven't done that for ages. I can't remember the last time I laughed like that."

"Neither can I." John touched her cheek with the backs of his fingers. "Maggie?"

She said nothing, only looked at him as she sucked in a breath whose tremulousness was not caused entirely by the aftermath of laughter.

"Did I look guilty?" he asked.

She nodded. "Not—"

Not in the same way, she'd been going to say, but he smiled and slid his hand into her hair, effectively cutting off her oxygen supply. "I didn't feel it," he said. "I only felt—"

"Felt what?" she asked when he failed to finish.

He seemed to be searching for words. "Good," he said at length, then leaned forward and brushed a quick, soft kiss over her mouth. "Damn good. The way laughing with you made me feel." He tapped her nose with a finger as if she were one of the children. "I'll be in touch."

And that, Maggie supposed as she alighted from his car, was better than nothing. She stood on her porch and watched him drive out of sight.

Be in touch when? she wondered for the next few days.

Not the next day, as she'd half expected. And not Wednesday either.

Thursday she reluctantly took her plate of cookies and a gift of a silky nightgown and went off to the bridal shower. She was late getting home and rushed in the door bursting with apologies for Stephanie, who had a school-night curfew. Stephanie left in such a rush, Maggie forgot to ask if there'd been any messages.

She didn't suppose there had been anyway.

Friday afternoon during her dressage lesson Jolene volunteered the information that Andi had kicked Rodney Watson and Miss Larkin had caught her doing it.

From her perch o Ghost's back, Jolene looked solemnly down at her mother, who held the reins. "Rodney cried and lay down on the ground and held on to his knees. He rolled over and over and yowled really loud. I think he was faking."

Maggie said that she wouldn't be surprised, because often bullies hollered louder than anyone else when they weren't really hurt.

Jolene looked worried. "Andi's in a lot of trouble over that."

"What did Rodney do?" Maggie asked.

"He pulled my hair and tried to tie me up with the skipping rope, then Andi came and kicked him and he stopped. She said if he tried to hurt her sister again, he was going to be in worse trouble."

"Well!" Maggie used her crop against Ghost's chest to slow the horse's gait. "I see. Maybe Rodney will be a little nicer now that he knows you have a sister who's willing to fight on your behalf."

With a swift change of subject, she added, "But now I suggest you concentrate if you and Ghost want to be ready for the junior gymkhana next spring."

"Yeah. Okay." They made one more circuit of the paddock before Jolene spoke again.

"Mom?" Jolene's brow was furrowed. "Is it okay to kick a boy in the balls if he's hurting you?"

Maggie, walking backward, missed a step and fell flat on her backside. Maybe Rodney hadn't been faking, after all, she thought, when he rolled around and yowled. She was still convinced, though, that he'd deserved some sort of retaliation for what he'd done to Jolene, and felt an entirely misplaced and inappropriate grin of delight spread across her face as pride in Andi surged up. It was all she could do not to laugh as she scrambled to her feet, but she somehow managed to sound and look stern as she said, "*Testicles* is the right word for that part of a boy's body, Jolene, but I don't want you to go around saying it all the time. It's for use in private conversations between you and me and only when we're discussing body parts."

They were cleaning up after their workout when the subject arose again.

"It's no fair," Jolene said, sounding amazingly like her sister.

"What's not fair?"

"That Andi got three detentions for kicking Rodney and he didn't get anything when he stole her brand-new Power Ranger eraser and her mom's 'gagement ring. If her dad ever finds out that ring is gone, she's *toast*! She wasn't supposed to take it to school. She's not supposed to have it to keep till she's all grown up, but she took it the first day for good luck and Rodney swiped it out of her pencil box."

"Engagement ring?"

"Yes. Andi says it's blue and has diamonds all around it and is really, really pretty."

Maggie stared at Jolene, jaw hanging as she recalled the small rubber man and the Crackerjack ring Rodney Watson had thrust into her hand the first day of school.

"Oh my goodness!" she gasped, and raced to the Cherokee. She dug through the gum wrappers and popsicle sticks in her truck's trash container until she found the eraser and the ring. Thank God she was a slob and didn't dump the small plastic trash can until it literally overflowed!

Jolene followed her. "What's the matter?"

"Look." Maggie held out her hand. "All this time, since the first day of school, they've been sitting in my car."

Jolene's eyes went round. "Ooh! We gotta take them to her! Right now. Boy, is she gonna be surprised!"

Maggie hid *her* surprise at Jolene's eagerness and bit

down on a surge of the same that welled up in her chest. "We can do that if you like," she said casually, and Jolene nodded emphatically, a big grin on her face.

As they left the house Maggie suggested dinner out. Jolene voted for fish and chips, and Maggie agreed. Why not? Her daughter's capitulation to the inevitable, if that's what was happening, was surely something to celebrate.

It was the prospect of not having to cook or clean up that put them both in such a lighthearted mood, she decided as they drove into town, both singing along with the radio. She also decided that they were going to have to get out more often. Jolene didn't normally behave quite so effervescently. And neither, when it came right down to it, did she.

John's heart slammed to a stop as Maggie's truck did the same right behind his car, which he had been about to back out of the driveway. As he opened his door Maggie jumped from her Cherokee.

Perfect! We can all have dinner together. The thought was in his mind, plans made, picture forming of the four of them together around a table, before he was so much as aware it was going to. About to offer the invitation, he saw how serious her face was. She flicked him only a quick smile and a word of greeting. It was Andi whom she addressed.

"I have something for you," she said, holding out her closed fist. Andi, clearly mystified, hesitated before she opened her hand under it.

Maggie dropped her gifts, and for a heartbeat, John thought Andi might cry. She squeezed her eyes shut, scrunched up her face, then opened her eyes again to stare into her half-cupped hand. Her finger prodded whatever it was Maggie had given her.

"Where did you *get* them?" she exclaimed, closing her fist just as John, still no wiser, saw a flash of silver, a glint of blue.

"Rodney Watson gave them to me the first day of school," Maggie explained. "I guess he hadn't figured out that you weren't really Jolene, and was afraid he'd be next on my list."

Andi's eyes remained wide as she nodded. Maggie went on. "The problem was, when Rodney gave me your things, I didn't realize they were important. Then I forgot all about it until today when Jolene told me you'd gotten in trouble for kicking Rodney in the testicles."

John felt his jaw drop. "She did *what*?" he demanded, and saw a look of total dismay cross Maggie's face.

"She kicked Rodney 'cause he was hurting me," Jolene supplied, but that scarcely registered on John. He glared at Andi. When was she going to learn? She had to stop fighting at school!

"I was going to tell you, Dad," she said defensively.

"When?" he asked, narrowing his gaze on her. "*After* we got back from having our hamburgers? Do you honestly believe, Andrea Jane, that I'd have done anything but ground you again if I'd known you were fighting at school today?"

Her chin tilted defiantly. "But I got a punishment there. I have to sit at the isolation desk for three recesses, all by myself and I can't talk to anybody, so I don't see why I have to be punished at home, too, for the same thing. It's no fair, Dad, and anyway, Rodney started it. He made me so mad! He kicked me under the table *all morning* when the teacher wasn't looking, and she wouldn't listen when I told her about it. Then at lunchtime, when I found him hurting Jolie, it felt like he was hurting me, and I got mad all over again and *I* kicked *him*. Hard. Right where it hurts."

John ran a hand into his hair. "Okay," he said tautly. "Back inside. We have to talk about this."

Turning to Maggie, he managed a smile and a rueful shake of his head. "Forgive me, but this isn't something I feel can wait."

"I understand," she said. "And we stopped by only to drop off Andi's things." She flicked a regretful glance at Andi, then continued, speaking to John. "I wouldn't have said anything, but I was sure Elm—the principal—would have been on the phone to you about the, er, incident, within minutes of its happening."

"He probably was, but I've been so busy I have a list this long"—he held his arms wide—"of calls to return."

"We're going out for fish and chips," Jolene said into the ensuing silence, turning her big, serious eyes to John again. She slipped a hand into his. "We wanted you to come with us, John." He knew by the startled stare Maggie turned on her daughter that it was the first she'd heard of it.

His urge to say to hell with discipline came suddenly and strongly, but he fought it. "I . . . uh, no, I'm afraid not, Jolie."

"Oh." The disappointment in her eyes nearly wrung him dry. He was glad when she looked down. "Okay," she said, then swept her gaze back up, using her lashes with such inborn feminine skill, he was taken aback—and almost turned to marshmallow. "But Mom said we should ask you and Andi for dinner sometime, and Andi was only trying to help me. Rodney always does mean stuff and he never gets caught 'cause he's so sneaky. All the kids were glad that Andi kicked him in the—" She glanced at her mother, then looked quickly away, not finishing the sentence.

"I'm not supposed to say that word. He's a real bad bully, but his dad's rich and he always gets away with stuff at school 'cause Mr. Abernathy plays golf with him." John assumed the "him" referred to Rodney's rich father. He supposed a man *could* get rich owning a diaper service, a funeral home, and a hardware store.

Jolene drew a deep breath, then went on. "That's why my mom's running for school board. 'Cause Mr. Abernathy's a dink."

John hooted with laughter and Maggie stared at her daughter.

"Jolene! That's another word you're not allowed to say, and *I* never *once* said it! Nor did I say for sure I was running for school trustee. I was considering it, but now I probably won't. But if I do, it'll be only because I'm interested in education and want to do my part to make sure our tax dollars are well spent and all the children get everything they need. It would have nothing to do with any kind of personal vendetta."

She glared at John when he made a snorting sound that she knew was a derisive laugh. "Now come on," she said, reaching for Jolene's hand. "If we don't hurry, Mr. Little will sell all his fish and chips and we'll have to go to bed hungry."

Andi said in a small voice, "Daddy? Are we going to have to go to bed hungry? I mean, Mrs. Wisdom went out for the evening because you said we were gonna grab ourselves a burger, so she didn't cook us anything."

John's exasperation was audible in his sharp sigh. "Andi, we've never gone—"

"I'll save you some of my french fries and a piece of fish," Jolene said, unexpectedly reaching out to Andi.

"Mr. Little always gives me too much. We can drop it off before we go home. Okay, Mom?"

Maggie blinked and bit her lip. "Jolie, I think John and Andi can make their own plans."

"But Mom!" Jolene protested, her eyes beginning to shine with a film of tears. "She's my *sister*! I can't let her go to bed hungry."

John wiped a hand down over his face. Maggie heard the rasp of beard under his palm. It sent odd, hot little shivers down her arms and legs and tightened her up inside. "Oh, dear Lord," he muttered. "Why didn't I just stay in Hamilton?"

"Because you're like a salmon, Dad," Andi said. "Your homing instinct got too strong. That's what you said." She went on to tell Jolene about salmon coming home to spawn, then looked at her father and asked, "Have you spawned yet, Daddy?"

Maggie laughed aloud and with great enjoyment at the expression on John's face. She felt justified, considering how he'd snorted at her discomfiture.

"I have utterly no desire to spawn," he said to Andi, but she wasn't listening.

She looked at Jolene. "Bring me cod or halibut, okay, Jo? I don't like salmon."

Jolene's nose wrinkled in derision. "Dummy. They never give you salmon with fish and chips. Don't you know anything?"

Andi set her shoulders back. "I know lots of things you don't know. You're the dummy. You didn't even know how to kick a boy in the—" She glanced at Maggie and said loftily, "Testicles."

Maggie couldn't help herself. She crouched and hugged both girls, hiding her laughter against their shoulders. Under cover of the embrace, she felt Andi bury the ring deeply in her jeans pocket.

"I'm sure there are lots of things you'll be able to teach each other, but not tonight," she said, breaking apart from them but maintaining a hold on their hands. "Tonight Andi's grounded again, and for good reason: fighting dirty."

She focused on Andi. "I'm sure your dad has explained how much damage you can do to a boy kicking him there. It's a kind of fighting you should use only when you really believe your life might be in danger or you're about to be r—"

She clamped her mouth shut. "When you're in real danger," she continued after a moment. "Then, it's perfectly all right. Then, it's a good thing to do."

Standing, she let go of Andi's hand, stricken by a terrible reluctance to do so.

"Come on, chickie. Let's go," she said to Jolene, speaking through a sudden thickness in her throat. She didn't want to go. Not without Andi. She'd been looking forward to spending time with both girls—and John— even before she realized she had, even before Jolene suggested it. But she had no option. Andi was John's child, and her discipline was his responsibility. And John—she had to face it—while he might want to be with her, didn't *want* to want it.

"Wait." John's voice turned her. "I never did explain to Andi how much damage that kind of kick could do, so in a way, this is partly my fault. And Andi *was* defending her sister. Fish and chips sounds good to me. I take it you know the best place in town?"

At the sight of two little girls' beaming faces and linked hands, Maggie felt her heart lift like a balloon in a breeze. "Not in town," she said. "Out of town. Climb in. We're on our way to Digby."

John hesitated for only a moment before reaching for Maggie's door and opening it for her. "Great," he said. "I haven't been to Digby in years."

As he settled in the passenger seat John closed his eyes and rubbed a hand over his face.

"You look tired," Maggie said.

"Bushed. Really wiped. It's been a horrendous week. I've hardly had an hour to myself, let alone one for Andi. It's no wonder she's been acting up at school again. How have you been?"

"Busy too." Maggie tried to keep her elation under control, but it simmered and tickled inside. His failure to call wasn't necessarily the brush-off she'd thought.

"So you're still considering running for the school board?"

She shrugged, flicking him a sidelong glance. "If I did, would you vote for me?"

He pretended to consider, chewing on one corner of his lip. "I'd need to know more about you."

From the backseat Andi piped up, "I'll vote for you, Miss Adair. After you win, are you going to fire Mr. Abernathy? Jolie's right. He is a dink."

John spun to stare over his shoulder. "Andrea Jane, you aren't allowed to say that word either."

Maggie angled the rearview mirror so she could see the children. "If I run, and if I win, I'll only be one member of the board, and I'm sure there's no question of anyone's getting fired. Mr. Abernathy does a good job in many ways and is very popular with quite a number of parents and students."

"Not me," said one twin.

"Me neither," her sister agreed in an identical voice.

Determined to change the subject, Maggie twisted the mirror back to its proper position and said to John, "What made your week so horrendous?"

"Andrea Jane," he said, eliciting a screech of denial from the backseat.

After that, conversation was general and laughter-filled, with both girls chipping in freely. Maggie was delighted to hear Jolene holding her own, not sitting back shyly and letting Andi have everything her way, as she was wont to do with her other friends. The only awkward moment came when John asked during a pause, "What was it you gave Andi back at the house?"

She thought for a minute, then gave him a bland smile. "Just . . . something she values. She took it to school the first day for luck, or maybe for comfort, or courage. It's something I'm certain she'll be more careful with in the future. I'd rather not say more." In the rear-view mirror she caught Andi's intensely grateful gaze and winked at her.

John turned and looked over his shoulder, narrowing his eyes. "Andi? Is this something I *need* to know about?"

It was Andi's turn to ponder the question, then she said, "No, Dad. Miss Adair's right. I'll be more careful from now on. I promise, Miss Adair!"

With another grin and wink into the mirror, Maggie said, "If you want to call me by my first name, honey, it's okay."

John grinned and said, "Gee, thanks, honey. I'd be honored."

Maggie laughed, but it gave her a pleasantly tingling sensation inside to hear him call her that, if only in jest.

In no time, it seemed, she was pulling into a parking spot at the head of the pier where Mr. Little's fish and chips stand had been in business as long as she could remember.

"I'm glad I came," John said as they finished up their dinners. He was. Very glad. He'd enjoyed the light, amusing conversation he and Maggie had kept up as they ate, enjoyed sharing the odd french fry with the ever vigilant sea gulls, and enjoyed listening to the girls talking, arguing, and giggling together.

He and Maggie had chosen a spot at one edge of the pier, where they sat with their feet dangling. The girls had taken their newspaper-wrapped dinners to the other side, close enough for their parents to watch them, but far enough away to give both pairs a feeling of privacy.

"You're entirely welcome," Maggie said. Her eyes glittered green and bright, and her cheeks glowed pink from the remains of sunset still staining the sky. John couldn't think of a single place he'd rather be, or a single person he'd rather have shared a meal with. It was hard to hang on to any of the reasons he'd once dragged out to remind himself why spending time with Maggie Adair was a bad idea. "Though technically," she added, "Jolene was the one who invited you."

"But she said you'd thought about asking us over for dinner," he reminded her.

She shrugged. "I thought about it. She wasn't keen on the idea, so I let it drop."

"I see." Their gazes remained locked for several seconds. He looked away first.

When he glanced back at her, she was searching the bottom of her folded-newspaper container for the crisp, broken remnants of fries, which she tossed to the gulls.

Lifting her gaze to his, she said, "I can't tell you how

glad I am to see this breakthrough in Jolene's relationship with Andi. I think she's all over her unhappiness about the situation."

"And you?"

Her eyes widened. "Me?"

"You weren't happy about it at first."

She shrugged. "I guess I felt threatened. She's all I have. I was being . . . selfish. I didn't want to have to share her, not even with her own sister, and then there was the instinctive way she responded to you. I was jealous. I feel bad about that, such a fraud. Because even as I was experiencing those feelings myself, I was busy telling her that love isn't like a pie that gets cut into smaller and smaller pieces when it's shared, that it grows bigger and bigger to fit around everyone we have in our hearts."

Some quality in his silence made Maggie glance at him again. His dark profile had a set look about it, his chin jutting, his lips compressed, his eyebrows drawn down as he stared straight out over the water. She bit her lip. Dammit! Did John think she'd aimed that comment right at him and the guilt he still hadn't mastered? Did he think she was suggesting that he should try to find room for *her* in his heart alongside Laura?

Desperately she cast around for something to say, but before an idea broke free of the jumble in her brain, he was on his feet, half turned away. "I need another cola," he said. "Can I get you one?" He strode off without waiting for her reply.

Maggie stared after him, then realized she hadn't so much as looked at the children in far too long. She turned to see them . . . gone.

NINE

Maggie leapt to her feet, eyes searching the gathering dusk. She ran to the far end of the pier and scanned the darkening water, fear in her heart, her mouth dry, her palms damp, her knees weak. Nothing! She ran to the other side and there they were, wandering hand in hand along the floating dock far, far down a steeply sloped ramp, checking out the boats and their floodlit decks.

Even as she watched, a man on one of the boats spoke to them, then reached out a hand and helped Jolene aboard. Maggie knew it was her daughter by the long hair blowing in the wind. He reached inside the cabin, got something, and offered it to her. She accepted. Whatever it was, she put it in her mouth, then turned to speak to her twin. Andi steadfastly shook her head, her hands behind her back.

The man disappeared into the cabin of the boat, and the next thing Maggie saw was a beckoning arm extended out of the door and Andi climbing aboard the boat.

With a hoarse cry, she launched herself down the ramp at a dead run, her feet thudding, her heart ham-

mering as she raced along the float, calling the girls'
names into the wind.

As Maggie approached the boat, Jolene wheeled,
looking guilty, her mouth pursed around a stick of black
licorice. Andi jumped half a foot before scrambling off
the boat, dragging her sister with her.

"Jolene Adair," Maggie yelled, grabbing both children and pinning them in front of her, one hand on a
shoulder of each. "What in the world do you think you
were doing? How many times have I told you not to—"
She snatched the licorice and flung it away.

"Lady, lady, please," the man called from the boat,
"don't be mad at the kids. It was my fault. I was only
trying to be friendly. I like kids. I have granddaughters. I
didn't mean—"

She completely ignored the man as she continued to
go at the children. "How could you be so stupid? So
irresponsible, so— How many times have you been told?
Oh! What's the point in even talking to you? Obviously,
words are lost!"

She grabbed two small hands and dragged the girls
along with her. "We're going home right now, and that's
it for you for the rest of the weekend. No treats, no
privileges, and no more dinners out with your sister until
I'm convinced that you can remember how to behave
yourself and not risk your lives in stupid, reckless behavior."

"Me too?" asked the child on her right, and Maggie
looked down into Andi's eyes, where defiance had been
replaced by awe.

"Yes, you too," she said without thinking it through,
though if she had, she doubted the answer would have
been any different. "You both knew better, but you went
aboard that boat anyway, so it's clear you both need

plenty of time to think about what you did. And I don't much care if your father agrees or not. I'll park in your driveway if I have to see that you do what I say. Is that clear?"

Andi nodded, her eyes enormous. "Yes, ma'am," she said.

"Her father does agree," John said, startling Maggie. She had been too intent on the girls to see that he had joined them, out of breath, face flushed as if he, too, had run the full length of the ramp and float. "He agrees with everything you've said. That *was* a stupid, irresponsible stunt, Andrea Jane, and I expected better of you as well. Now, Maggie's right. It's time we went home."

They each took the hand of their respective child and marched them up to the pier.

"To think I moved away from a big city mainly because I was becoming afraid for Andi," John said, fifteen minutes into the drive home. The girls had sat silently in the backseat, then fallen asleep, leaning on each other. "I thought the dangers there were getting too great to ignore. Yet they exist everywhere, don't they?"

Maggie recognized it as a rhetorical question. "Is that why you left Hamilton and came back to Maples?" she asked.

He nodded, then shrugged. "I wanted a small-town practice, anyway. That it was Maples was more accident than design. I was visiting my in-laws in Halifax last July and heard that one of the doctors up the valley was retiring."

He gave his head a rueful shake. "I guess maybe it wasn't quite as much an accident as I like to think. Actually, my mother-in-law was the one who told me. She was heartbroken when Laura and I moved to Hamilton, Ontario, when Andi was only a month old. She's been after me to come back to Nova Scotia for a long time.

"When she said the practice was in Maples and pointed out that it wasn't very far from Halifax, I called Dr. Blaine without so much as a second thought and made an offer. He interviewed me, accepted me as suitable to care for his patients, and here I am.

"I thought it would be the right move for Andi and me both, give me more time to spend with her. Though this past week hasn't been great, generally, I have had more time. Without a mother, she needs all of her father that she can get.

"For whatever that's worth," he added with a wry grin. "I feel like I'm floundering most of the time, as if when I do something right, it's by chance more than anything, and that I make more than my share of mistakes."

"One thing you didn't make a mistake about is those two needing each other. I'm glad you made me see it. And glad Jolene came around too."

He smiled. "So am I."

A few miles farther along the road he asked, "Does Jolene spend much time with her father?"

Maggie shook her head. "None at all. When we split up, he made it clear that was the way he wanted it. He pays support, but most of that I'm socking away for her future."

"How does she feel about not seeing him?"

Maggie frowned. "She hardly knew him. She was only a year old when she and I left and came back to Maples, so I don't think she misses *him*, as a person, though I know she envies kids who have dads. Still, the two of us have always done just fine on our own."

"Yes." John swallowed hard. "I can see that."

The remainder of the drive was made in silence, and almost in silence Maggie dropped off John and Andi at home. He touched her cheek as he stooped to look in her window. "Hey, Maggie?" When she cocked her head in reply, he said, "Thanks again. Good night. See you soon."

After he spilled his sleeping child into her bed, John tugged off her jeans, not bothering with her sweatshirt. He pulled up the covers, then scooped up her jeans to stuff them into the laundry. Automatically he checked her pockets, and as his fingers closed over something cold and metallic, he remembered why Maggie had shown up at his house in the first place.

He knew exactly what he'd see before he withdrew the ring from Andi's pocket. The stone caught the light from the hallway, bouncing blue fire into his eyes. His fist closed around it for a second, then, carefully, he dropped it back into the pocket it had come from. Smoothing out Andi's jeans, he laid them on the foot of her bed for her to find in the morning.

He recalled Maggie's saying ". . . for luck, or maybe for comfort, or courage." He bent and stroked Andi's hair back from her face. His poor baby. She must have felt he was abandoning her in a strange place among strange people, that first day of school. Needing comfort, needing her mother, she'd taken Laura's ring as a talisman.

He kissed her gently, then went outside, feeling restless and cooped up in the house. He sat on the steps leading down from the back porch, listening to the quiet of the night, drawing in the scent of the ripening plums on the tree at the end of the yard.

Maggie's tree, he thought, remembering a story a

patient had told him the other day. Maggie . . . She was the sassiest, sexiest, most exasperating and exciting woman he had ever met, and he couldn't keep her out of his mind. *I didn't want to have to share her,* she'd said that evening. *Not even with her own sister.* Had Maggie been glad when her ex-husband wanted no contact with Jolene? Would she resent it if her daughter transferred some of her love and dependence to someone else? *I was jealous of the instinctive way she turned to you.*

He went to bed and eventually slept, only to waken from a dream in which Maggie was sliding down a long, steep hill toward a raging sea creaming around jagged rocks. As hard as he tried, as far as he reached, she kept sliding, just out of his reach, and he knew he was losing her. . . . Losing her *too.*

He lay in bed with his heart hammering, sweat drenching him, and a coppery taste in his mouth. The horror failed to recede, and he flung his overheated body out of bed, dragging on shorts and a tank top. Sleep would elude him for the rest of the night, he knew, and he'd rather not lie there and think.

After tugging on gym socks and his sturdiest running shoes, he left the house and jogged down the sidewalk, determined to outrun his disturbing thoughts.

He changed his pace as he wound his way up a hilly road that took on greater and greater familiarity the closer he came to what he realized had been his destination all along. Perhaps even his ultimate destination since his return to Maples. Was he, as he'd jokingly told his daughter, truly like a salmon, swimming desperately upstream?

Dawn had lightened the sky before he finally stopped, stepping off the side of the road. He stood, hands on knees, sweat pouring freely down his face. He breathed slowly and deeply until he felt his heart rate returning to normal. Then, rubbing his arms and shoulders briskly, he sat on an outcropping of rock, looking down into the one little corner of the Annapolis Valley that he had thought never to see again.

He discovered he could view it with an almost dispassionate eye.

The house was still there, in much greater disrepair than he'd remembered, but after twenty years that wasn't surprising. It looked as if the front porch had caved in and maybe some windows were broken. A few bricks from the kitchen chimney lay on the roof, leaving the flue looking like a death's-head grimace filled with rotting teeth.

Appropriate.

From his vantage point his gaze searched the thick grass and weeds in the side yard for the wooden cross he had made one dismal day, but he didn't see it. Likely it would long since have rotted and fallen, as the house was rotting and falling. The fence had collapsed in several spots that he could see, and probably others that he couldn't, since it ran well back into the woodlot where it abutted the boundary of Kejimkujik National Park. The dog run, surrounding the house like a moat, was empty.

Of course it was empty.

Still, he shivered and rubbed the tips of his fingers over the scars high on his thigh, tracing the welts and punctures that had twisted muscle and marred skin since he was nine years old.

Doc Monro had stitched him up, shot him full of antibiotics, and given him a bottle of pills to take home with him. He'd seemed to understand without being told that it would do no good to call John's mother, or to take his stepfather to task for keeping dangerous animals.

He'd seemed, also, to sense John's fear that somehow, even though the teacher had promised confidentiality, Jack Porter would learn that the teacher had taken him for medical treatment.

For many years he'd remembered his first impressions of the doctor's house. Above the tall double doors, a stained glass window spilled a pool of multihued light onto a polished floor. He'd felt he was entering a palace or a holy place. The smell of the house as he walked through it to the offices at the back had lingered long in his mind. Beeswax, he now knew, and the aromas of cleanliness and good cooking. Things outside his experience.

He'd also remembered the old man's kindness, and had returned four years later when he came to realize the desperation of his mother's plight. The help he'd sought from Doc Monro on that second visit had not been forthcoming. Not because the doctor hadn't cared, but because, as he explained, he could only help John's mother if she herself asked for help. Until then his hands were tied.

But he had tried to help John. He had offered him a way out, a place to go, a different life. *Hope.* For a few minutes he'd been tempted. He'd sat beside the doctor's big, highly polished desk, looking at the reflection of a lamp in the deep varnish, seeing the light glimmer and waver at even the slightest motion in his part. He'd blinked back the tears that, at thirteen, he'd been too manly to shed. He could leave, the doctor said, and John knew it was true. He could.

But he also knew that his mother could not.

Now he determinedly threw off the memories of that day's desolation and stood, stretching, preparing to leave.

A light mist rose from the pond, with a glimmer of

blue water beneath it. A willow with autumn-gold fronds hung low over the water, and he was oddly pleased to see a mallard swimming across the still surface. Life went on.

It could have been a beautiful place, had anyone cared to look after it. But in his lifetime, no one had.

In his lifetime, no one would.

He paid the taxes faithfully every year, but beyond that he ignored it.

Maybe, someday, Andi would want to sell it. Maybe, someday, it would be worth a lot of money to her. But never to him. Any money it brought would be, to him, filthy, untouchable. By the time he died, though, perhaps the taint would be gone.

He didn't think he'd return that way again.

Yet as he began the long, slow jog home the image of the empty fields stretched away in his mind, and over them rode a woman on a red horse. Its black mane and tail fluttered in the breeze, and her long red hair streamed out behind her as she streaked toward the house, where smoke rose lazily from an intact chimney.

He blinked it away. Fantasy. It was a scene that had never been. It was a scene that never would be.

Maggie, too, was sleepless much of that Friday night.

John's face superimposed itself on her inner eye, and when she awoke far too early, it was still there, along with the sound of his voice, as if she'd been dreaming of him.

She told herself severely she had no time for dreams, and spent Saturday morning cleaning house and planting bulbs to bloom in the spring. During the afternoon she conducted riding lessons. That night was a repeat of the previous one, mostly sleepless, and when she dozed, she dreamed of John again.

But Sunday she stood enraptured, listening to his strong baritone soar upward. Goose bumps rose on her arms. Even after his solo, when she and the rest of the choir took up the refrain, his was the only voice she could hear. He was paged midway through the service, though. Without his voice, the singing sounded flat in her ears.

She and Jolene left church immediately after the service, and on Monday evening when she was about to leave for choir practice, her wretched truck refused to start again. She ground her back teeth together and vowed mayhem come morning when she called the dealership. It wouldn't be the first practice she'd ever missed, but it rankled because she'd wanted, more desperately than she'd realized to see John, to hear him sing.

All through the week that followed, his was the only voice she really heard, both waking and sleeping. She heard it in the back of her mind every time Jolene mentioned Andi, which was on every second breath. The girls' bonding now seemed unbreakable.

She heard it on the wind when she rode Medallion hard, hoping to leave it behind. She heard it in the lonely sound of a loon out on Fisher Lake at night as the fog rolled in. *Call him*, she told herself. *You're no timid miss. Just give the man a call.*

She reached for the phone, then drew back her hand. She'd never chased a man in her life and could see no reason to start now. He'd said he'd call, and he hadn't. He'd said, "See you soon," but it hadn't happened. It was clear to her that he didn't have the same aching yearning for her company that she had for his.

The next morning, Saturday, she gave in to Jolie's

begging that the girls be allowed to have dinner together, followed by a sleepover.

"Okay," she said. "If Andi's dad says it's all right with him, then it's all right with me. He can drop her off any time in the afternoon and pick her up at church on Sunday." That was the answer, she told herself. She would start referring to him—thinking of him—as "Andi's dad." That way she'd get over him sooner.

Yeah, sure. In the six years since her divorce, though she'd had a couple of relationships, neither of those men had made her feel like this. Which was likely why both relationships had been of such short duration. What this was, wasn't something she was going to get over anytime soon. But she would get over it. Of that, she was determined.

John dropped Andi off about two, while Maggie was grooming Ghost. She waved at him and he left without looking as disappointed as she felt. He'd probably had no intention of staying for so much as a brief conversation.

Andi's information confirmed that. "Dad's going golfing with another doctor." Since she knew that Mrs. Wisdom took most weekends off, Maggie was sure he was glad of an evening free of child-care. Late in the day, though, shortly after she'd lit the barbecue, he showed up.

Maggie stopped what she was doing and simply gazed at him. He looked as if he'd just stepped out of the shower. She was certain, even at the distance that separated them, that his hair was damp and his face was freshly shaved. Her hand itched to stroke it, to see how smooth he'd feel. She wondered if he would be wearing aftershave, if its scent would turn her on. Of course it would. Everything about the man turned her on.

He'd been what Levi Strauss had in mind when he

invented jeans. His navy Miami Dolphins sweatshirt, with the sleeves pushed up to expose his muscular, brown forearms, emphasized the breadth of his shoulders and the depth of his chest. He carried a large brown shopping bag in one hand and a smaller one tucked under the other arm, and wore a curious, indecipherable expression on his face.

"Hi," he said from the other side of the gate.

Maggie had to struggle to find her voice. "Hi, yourself." The barbecue tools, which she had been about to take inside and scrub, dangled loosely from her hands.

To John, her response sounded almost like a query—and certainly not much like a welcome.

He reached over and unlatched the gate, swinging it open and stepping through as Maggie continued to stand motionless, watchful, he thought. Waiting. For what?

"Where are the kids?" he asked.

She approached him slowly, her expression giving little away. "Chasing down the bunnies, rattling cans of rabbit food, hoping to entice them back to their hutches." She placed the long fork and tongs onto the table with what he thought was undue care, considering their less than pristine condition.

She wasn't in much better shape, wearing a lopsided ponytail, charcoal smudges on her denim shorts, apple leaves in her hair, and one stuck to the loose crochet of her white top, just above her left breast. It drew his eyes like a magnet. He could see the outline of her bra through the fabric, and the pink curve of her breasts over the edge of the cups. His throat went dry as he tried to swallow, tried to think of something sensible to say.

She beat him to it. "I understood you were golfing."

Relief at having a topic to discuss made him light-headed. "I was. My partner was called to the hospital."

"Mmm. Tough luck."

Was she glad to see him or not? he wondered. With Maggie, it was hard to tell. He'd known her for a month. He'd seen her at church, at choir practice, had dinner with her once, and spent other time in her company. In her arms. Yet he couldn't tell what she was thinking because he didn't know her well enough.

That was why he was there. He suspected that getting to know Maggie properly might be one of the most rewarding tasks of his lifetime—or something he might not survive. At any rate, he was there to do just that. As long as she'd cooperate. But something in her closed expression hinted at resistance, at barely concealed anger. Her actions during the past week also led him to think she was angry.

He held out the larger of his two packages toward her. "I heard via the grapevine about a redheaded girl who—among many other things—once sat in a plum tree and fought off the neighbors with a shotgun. I thought that might be indicative of a strong liking for Italian prune plums. I brought you some so that *I* wouldn't have to fight *you* off with a shotgun if you realized the tree was still in the backyard of Doc Monro's house, and producing like crazy."

"A base canard," she said briskly with only a glimmer of a smile. "It was crows I was repelling, not neighbors, and it was a BB gun. Besides, I was only about nine years old, and my judgment hadn't yet properly developed."

Suddenly she grinned impudently, laughing as she accepted the bag. "*Now* I would use a shotgun."

Poking her nose into the bag, she drew in a long breath of the plums' scent. "Oh Lord," she murmured, "that smells like home!"

"I waited until I was sure they were just right," he said.

She lifted her face and gave him a genuine smile. "Thank you, John." Her eyes shone, and as her lips parted on his name for just an instant, he thought they trembled. His heart slammed hard into his ribs. He nearly reached for her, but she hitched the bag onto one hip, took out a plum, and buffed the bloom off on the front of her white sweater. "Let's see if you're as good a judge of plums as I am."

She took half of it in one bite, white teeth neatly severing it so it pulled away from the pit. John swallowed hard as he watched juice spurt. She licked it off her lips, chewed, and swallowed, her eyes closed, long sweeps of gilt-tipped lashes making coppery arcs on her cheeks. "Mmm. Great." She opened her eyes and smiled at him again. "Another few days and they'd be too ripe. I like them only when they're firm and tart, just like this."

She took the stone between her teeth and gave it a little tug. It came free with a soft, sucking sound. She dropped it from her teeth to the palm of her hand and flung it over her shoulder into the garden. Then, turning, she walked back to the table and the smoking barbecue, carrying the bag on one hip, her long, beautifully tapered thighs swinging beneath the baggy legs of her shorts.

He would have followed her if she'd been stepping off the edge of an abyss.

Maggie tried not to stare as John pulled a package of steaks and a bottle of white wine from the smaller bag and set them on the picnic table. "I know it's supposed to be red wine with red meat, but I like white better. I also know I wasn't invited," he went on, his gaze searching hers, "but I came anyway."

He handed her the wine. "Thought maybe I could buy my way in."

Maggie stepped back, examining the label on the bottle. "You bought your way in here with the plums," she said, lifting her gaze to his. "With this, you could probably buy your way in anywhere in town."

He met her gaze, held it. "There's nowhere else in town I want to be, Maggie."

All she said was, "Nice choice," and he could only assume she was referring to the wine. She still didn't say he was welcome, but neither did she say he was not.

"Daddy!" Andi spotted him and tore across the grassy expanse. Flinging herself on him, she wrestled him to the ground. He tossed Maggie the steaks, saying "Fridge, please," as Jolene piled on and the three of them rolled and tussled, adding grass stains to grass stains on knees, elbows, and clothing, and sending gales of laughter into the apple trees and beyond.

He stood minutes later, his hair mussed, his clothes awry, but grinning with such delight while a child dangled from each of his biceps, bare feet walking up his sides, that Maggie's chest ached with inexpressible emotion.

Quickly she turned away, rushing inside to put the wine and meat in the refrigerator to keep cool.

She scrubbed baking potatoes, wrapped them in paper towels and set them into the microwave, ready to cook when the time was right, then began to toss a salad.

"The coals are hot," John said behind her, and she jerked around. He lounged in the doorway, looking tousled, relaxed, and at ease. She wondered how long he'd been standing there watching her work. He carried the grimy barbecue tools she'd forgotten. Quickly she grabbed them and took them to the sink to scrub.

"The steaks are in the fridge," she said over her shoulder. "Help yourself."

He didn't move. "You act like you're mad at me, Maggie."

She flung up her head and blurted, "*I'm* not the one who's been doing the avoiding," then could have used the Brillo pad on her tongue.

"Is that the way it seems to you?" he asked, finally shouldering himself erect and coming the rest of the way in. He opened the fridge, took out the steaks, and set them on the counter beside the tools she'd just dried. After washing his hands, he lifted the hem of her terry cloth apron and, without so much as a by-your-leave, dried them.

"You rushed away from church on Sunday just as I arrived back," he said, "and didn't stop though I called your name. I saw you at the hardware store Monday, but you hopped in your car and left before I could get near you, then you didn't show up at choir practice. You ignored me again yesterday as you were leaving the bank and I was arriving."

"I said hello." Maggie hated the defensive note in her voice.

"And kept right on rushing."

"I was in a hurry. I had to pick up my truck at the dealership."

He dropped his lashes halfway over his eyes. "Of course. A pressing engagement."

She flushed. She knew as well as he did that her truck could have waited five minutes, ten, even until after lunch, if she'd waited around so that maybe he'd ask if she wanted to join him. She didn't even know if he took the time for lunch or grabbed a snack on the fly between patients.

He filched her paring knife and punctured the clear shrink-wrap that surrounded the meat. After peeling it back, he leaned across in front of her to grab the tall wooden pepper mill from a shelf near the stove. He ground a liberal dose of black pepper over both steaks. "Got any garlic?"

She handed him a bulb and he broke off two cloves, crushed them under the heel of his hand, and popped them free of their skins. Deftly he slit them both in half, rubbing the cut surfaces over the meat. When one side was finished, he flipped the steaks over and repeated, pepper, then garlic, working two-handed.

She stood frozen, watching the ease with which his large hands handled the small cloves. His nails were scrubbed clean and cut short, his fingertips spatulate, the backs of his knuckles and hands darkened with sprinkles of hair. Sinews moved under his skin in response to the motion in his wrists.

Hands you can trust.

She started, wondering where the thought had come from, and turned away quickly to rinse her own hands under the tap.

"Did you miss me?" he asked, and she whirled. Though he had a teasing smile on his lips, his eyes belied his easy manner.

"Not unduly. I've been as busy as you obviously have." She turned away and checked, quite unnecessarily, the wrapping on the potatoes. "Tell me when the steaks are half done, and I'll bring you the girls' wieners, then turn the potatoes on."

"Right," John said. As he carried the steaks out to the barbecue, he found himself thinking that Maggie Adair could turn on more than a potato. He could visualize her turning on turnips. Limp heads of lettuce. Ice cubes. Even the thought of ice cubes didn't cool his blood.

He pushed aside those thoughts and concentrated on barbecuing the steak to perfection. That was something he could do well. What he couldn't do well was explain to Maggie why he had, as she accused, been avoiding her. Or the convoluted thought processes that had brought him there that day.

With their dinner assembled, they sat at the picnic table in the twilight, John and Maggie on one side with their steaks, the girls on the other with their hot dogs.

The chablis was dry, with a good crispness; the meat was tender; the potatoes, topped with melting butter and chopped chives fresh from Maggie's garden, were exactly the way John liked them. Conversation was general, mostly involving the children and their doings.

A family meal, a pleasant time with Maggie and her daughter, him and his daughter. Friends together over dinner, a preliminary to further times together. The beginning of a courtship? Maybe. And maybe not.

Maggie's polite, friendly remoteness frustrated John. And it wasn't with the eyes of a mere friend that he watched her walk away to get the dessert.

He glanced up at her with a smile when she set a large slice of her famous apple pie before him. "Ah, that's what I was hoping for tonight. One quick trip to heaven."

To his amazed delight, since he had meant no double entendre, her face colored. After a brief, startled smile in return, she refused to meet his gaze. He noticed her hands trembling as she scooped ice cream onto the girls' portions of pie, then shoved the container toward him, letting him do his own.

"Maggie? Is something wrong?" he asked, when she set her plate away, her dessert only half eaten.

"Why, no," she said, her tone and expression bland as she finally met his gaze. "I'm not used to eating so much meat at one meal. It filled me up."

Then, obviously to change the subject, she mentioned an antique stethoscope her grandfather had been given by one of his professors, and offered to show it to him later.

While they were doing the kitchen cleanup and the girls were playing a game at the kitchen table, a knock sounded on the back door.

It was the mayor, who raised his eyebrows at the sight of John with a tea towel draped over his shoulder, but said nothing to indicate he thought it strange.

"I'd like to talk to you for a few minutes, Maggie," he said without preamble. "You, too, Doctor, if you're interested in what happens to this community."

John nodded as Maggie said, "Sure, Charlie." She poured three cups of coffee and shooed the girls away to play their board game in the dining room instead.

"Three eighth graders were arrested at school this afternoon," Charlie said before so much as taking a sip. "They were caught making angel dust in the science lab. An investigation uncovered a quantity of that, and marijuana as well, in their lockers. Seems they've been supplying a growing number of other kids and making a killing."

Maggie stared at Charlie as she absorbed his announcement.

"Killing," she finally repeated, her fists clenched on the table. "Oh God, isn't that the truth? Dammit, when are they going to figure out the danger of what they're doing, understand that drugs can mean death and that death is final? I'd have thought what happened to Peter

Flynn last year would have scared them, but it seems not."

To John, she said, "One of the best and brightest boys in high school dropped a tab of acid last year, supposedly for the first time, and committed suicide that same night."

She ran a hand through her hair, casting a glance at the girls visible through the archway. "Eighth graders!" she groaned. "Drugs used to be a problem in senior high and college, not in the earlier years."

"And you know what's really disgusting?" Charlie asked. "The parents of two of those kids are suing the principal and the school board for violating their children's rights by forcing open their lockers!"

"Somebody should sue the parents for having failed their kids," Maggie exploded, shoving her chair back and pacing across the kitchen. "What kind of schools are our kids attending? If they're making acid and angel dust and whatever else they learn the chemical composition of in junior high, what will be available in elementary school next year, or the year after?"

Her frown deepened. "What's available for them now that we don't know about?"

John knew it was lame, but he said, "All we can do is street-proof them to the best of our abilities."

"Street-proof? That's not enough. We've got to clean up our schools. We've got to clean up our communities and our attitudes."

She strode back, her hair swirling. "And we've got to get drugs and drug dealers out of our children's lives. Dammit, they are the scum of the earth, a scourge, a plague, and it's getting worse, not better." She glared at the two men as if it were all their fault.

"And the only way we're going to change that is get

in there and do it ourselves." She smacked one fist into the opposite palm. "All right, Charlie, you win. It doesn't take an astrophysicist to figure out why you came *here* with that information. I'm filing my candidacy first thing Monday morning."

She leaned her fists on the table. "By heaven, I'll take on Masterson and all the rest of those permissive idiots with their belief that they can fix every problem by throwing more money at it, and make kids healthy and happy by providing them with more *things*."

Charlie stood and applauded loudly, bringing the girls back to the kitchen at a run. They stared as he swept Maggie into a bear hug and spun her around the room. "Brava! You can do it, Maggie. You can beat him. With that kind of passion, you'll ace the all-candidates' meeting. Hell, you could beat anyone with that kind of passion. I knew you'd make a superb politician."

He danced her around until they were both reeling and the girls were demanding to know what was going on.

Maggie staggered as Charlie released her, and caught the back of John's chair. "I'm running for school board," she told the children. "It's official now."

"Oh. Is that all?"

"Yes," Maggie answered her daughter. "That's all."

Suddenly, as she said the words, doubts assailed her and she sank back onto her chair, wrapping her suddenly unsteady hands around her coffee mug. The girls, losing interest, flitted away.

"I recognize that look," Charlie said. "Don't you dare chicken out on me now. You know you can do it."

"Oh Lord!" Maggie stared from John's expressionless face to Charlie's eager one. "You're wrong, Charlie. I'm not a politician. I'm just a woman. A mother."

Charlie leaned toward her. "A mother with a passion to keep her daughter and all other children safe from—what was it you said?—a scourge, a plague. And you're right, Maggie. That's exactly what drug dealers are. We must eradicate them. And who better than you to spearhead the campaign? You have a personal reason to hate drug dealers and the addicts they create for their own profit. There's your platform, Maggie. Stopping permissive attitudes in the schools, taking us back to a system where values and rules and order are respected, and drug dealers are not welcome. Who better to do it than you, whose own grandfather was killed by addicts who might have had their first taste of drugs in one of the very schools you're now determined to protect?"

Charlie *was* a politician, Maggie thought. She could learn from him. Slowly she nodded.

"And one more thing," Charlie said, rising, his expression that of a man who had saved the best for last. "Guess who's the father of one of the kids arrested?"

Maggie stared. "Masterson?"

"You got it. And he's one of those screaming lawsuit. Someone asked him how he accounted for the fact that his son had deposited over fifteen thousand dollars in a savings account in the past four months, and he said the boy has a paper route and mows lawns. Sweetheart, you're a shoo-in, but for all that, you have work to do. The minute you file, the papers are going to want interviews."

"Then I guess I better get to work."

"Atta girl," Charlie clapped his hands once more. "Want some help?"

Maggie's head was suddenly spinning almost as fast as it had when Charlie had whirled her around. "No. No, I don't think so. What I need to do is some deep thinking. But thanks for the offer."

"Right, then. I'll let you get on with it."

John, too, rose to his feet. Maggie realized how quiet he'd been the past few minutes, and shot a swift glance at him. His face was set into almost grim lines, as if he were trying to hide something. What? Anger? Disappointment? Whatever it was, she didn't need to be psychic to recognize that he wasn't as enthusiastic about her entry into politics as Charlie was.

John pretended not to see the questioning look Maggie cast in his direction. "And I'll get out of your hair too," he said, striding across the kitchen and through the archway to the dining room. There, he kissed both girls good night, then hugged Andi tightly.

"You're going to be okay?" he asked. Andi wasn't used to sleeping away from home, except, on rare occasions, at her grandparents' home. "If you miss me, honey, you can call. If you want me to come and get you, I will. Anytime. Remember."

Her return hug was little more than cursory, and she didn't even try to hide her impatience. "Da-*ad*! I'll be *fine*. I mean, I'm with Maggie and Jo. What could go wrong?"

He felt a little sheepish. "Well, I suppose you could miss me."

"In other words, *you'll* miss *me*," she said with such a grown-up look that he heard Maggie snicker in the background. He couldn't help laughing as he hugged Andi again. "You bet I will. But you have fun. And be good for Maggie, or else."

Andi looked momentarily solemn. "Yeah," she said with a glance at Maggie. "I'll be good." Leaning confidingly toward him, she murmured, "Maggie doesn't like brats."

To Maggie's surprise, following bedtime, the children settled down after only a couple of hours of giggling, loud thumps and crashes, and innocent responses of "Nothing!" to questions as to what they were doing. As long as she didn't hear glass shatter, she supposed, or hear shrieks of pain or calls for tourniquets, they were, in truth, doing "nothing." She left them to it and tried to sort out her thoughts, tried to write a speech, tried to work up a profile that might satisfy the reporters.

At eleven, drawn by a sudden silence, she checked on the girls. Each lay sprawled atop one of the twin beds in Jolie's room. Toys, books, and candy wrappers—*candy wrappers?*—littered the room.

The little monsters. She could only hope they'd brushed their teeth again after the illicit snack. The thought brought a smile to her lips as she straightened limbs and pulled up covers. Of course they hadn't. They were seven years old and didn't believe in cavities.

Maggie took a quick bath, brushed her own teeth, and slid between her sheets, only to lie there and listen to an owl hooting the eternal question: "Whoo-oo kno-ows? Who-oo kno-ows?" No one answered. There was no one to answer. No one but Maggie, and the lonely, sleepless night, and neither had any answers that she could hear. Besides, she wasn't even certain what the question was anymore.

Rising, she pulled on a fleecy track suit and wandered out to the front porch. She wrapped herself in a quilt; the nights were growing cool now that it was October. She slid back into a corner of the swing, curling her feet under her. From a mile away, Gilgamesh barked, then another dog, more distant. Two friends trading comments on the beauty of the night, or enemies warning each other off? At any rate, the barking dogs somehow added to her sense of isolation.

Across the fields, over toward the river, a light burned in a distant house. Someone else, aching, yearning, sleepless like herself? Or someone awake with a sick child? Would they call John, and if they did, would he go to them?

Of course he would. He'd be one of those rare doctors who made house calls. She knew that without ever having had to be told it was so. Did Mrs. Wisdom wait up for him to make him a hot drink or offer a snack in case he was hungry?

She remembered Grandma doing that, remembered her bustling and worrying and scolding, trying to make Grandpa take things a little easier as he grew old. The love her grandparents had shared over sixty years of marriage had always left her feeling set apart from them. She knew they'd cared for her, but most of their devotion had been, rightly she supposed, reserved for each other, right up to the night her grandmother died at the age of seventy-nine.

That night Maggie had been the one waiting up when Grandpa came home to tell her that Grandma had slipped away quietly without regaining the consciousness she had lost the week before. He'd kissed Maggie tenderly, tucked her into bed, and left her to her slow, silent tears. Maggie knew he must have shed his own, though she never saw them.

She'd tried to offer her grandfather the same kind of devoted care his wife had given him. After Julia's death, when he went out on night calls, which, since he was eighty at that time, was rarely, she was the one who got up at the sound of his return. She faithfully made him a hot drink and buttered toast, with sugar and cinnamon sprinkled on it just the way he liked it. But he'd never managed to eat it all. He'd shoved his plate away, leave his tea half sipped, and send her off to bed.

He had missed her grandmother too much to be consoled with Maggie's poor offerings.

Had the perfect, irreplaceable Laura waited up for John? Maggie groaned as the errant thought intruded. What would it be like, being loved so much you were irreplaceable?

She buried her face in her hands. Oh Lord! Why did she care so deeply? And dammit, why couldn't she keep thoughts of John Martin out of her head for more than two minutes at a stretch?

That was one answer she did know. She couldn't stop thinking about him because she wanted him with an intensity that made her ache inside. He was the only man she had ever wanted so badly that it had swiftly begun to feel like an obsession.

Obsession? Oddly, that sounded less threatening than love. She liked the idea that this was nothing more than an obsession, more akin to lust and infatuation— either of which she was sure she could overcome given time. She groaned and shoved her hair back behind her ears. Maybe, like the measles, it was something that would run its course and leave her immune to further attacks. She could only hope.

The sweep of headlights brought her quickly erect, and she swung her feet to the porch floor. It didn't take the light of the moon revealing the shape and size of the vehicle to tell her the car belonged to John. She knew it viscerally before she noted such details. Nevertheless, for the first time in her life she truly understood the cliché about a woman's heart standing still.

When it resumed beating, she had to steel herself not to gasp at the pain of its slow, heavy thudding. All she could do was press her fist to her breastbone and hope she wasn't about to die. Nope. This wasn't lust. It wasn't mere obsession. She was deeply, irretrievably in love with the man.

TEN

"Hello," she said when John stepped out of the car close to the bottom of the steps. Even the single word reflected the condition of her pulse, which had gone from ponderous to skittish. She glided to the edge of the porch and stood watching him.

"Hello, Maggie." His words were a low rumble of sound. "I saw your lights on and wondered if everything was all right. Still planning your campaign strategy?"

She shook her head. "I've written a draft of a speech, but after that my mind caved in."

"I know what that's like. Did Andi go to sleep okay?"

She heard the worry, the loneliness in his tone, and empathized. Another weekend, she knew, Jolene would want to sleep at Andi's house, and she'd be left alone, worrying that maybe Jolie missed her but was ashamed to say so.

"Everything's fine, John." She smiled. "I promised I'd call if there were problems."

"I know, but—" He shrugged. "I'm here now. Could you . . . could you stand a bit of company if it's not too late?"

She stepped back at the same time as he moved forwrd. "Yes," she said, wondering how she managed the cool tone, but proud of it. "Of course."

"Good." He ascended the steps, coming to a halt with one shoulder on a post that held up the sagging porch roof. "So could I."

She continued to wait, wordless, merely gazing at him. He cleared his throat. "A bit cold for communing with nature, isn't it? There'll likely be frost by morning."

Maggie shrugged. He might be right, but the moon was bright and the sky was filled with a dazzle of stars. She could think of no better place for wondering about a man, for wishing things were different, for dreaming dreams she was only now beginning to fully acknowledge. "I have a quilt."

"Then sit down and wrap up again," he said in a tone almost tender, as if he knew that her bare feet were half frozen, and cared about that. The love inside her swelled to huge proportions, nearly choking her.

She didn't move. He shifted, shouldered his way off the post. Hands in the pockets of his bomber jacket, he stepped closer.

"Would you, er, like to come in?" she asked in a rush. "To check on Andi?"

John thought about the warm intimacy of Maggie's home, the kid clutter, the books, the drawn drapes, the cushiony softness of her couch where he'd held her weeks ago, where their bodies had flared into passionate response to each other much too soon after they'd met. He wasn't there for that tonight any more than he had been the night it happened.

This time he needed to talk to her. To find the courage to tell her all the things that might cost him not only her friendship but any chance of a future too.

"I'm sure Andi's okay," he said. "And I'd rather stay out here."

"Fine. Have a seat." She perched her bottom on the wide porch railing and gestured him toward the swing. Wicker squeaked under him as he sat. He gave the swing a push with one foot and said, "When I saw you out here, I wondered for a minute if you were standing guard over your bag of plums. I was glad not to see a shotgun blast come flying across the porch."

She laughed. "If you insist on listening to gossip, you're going to get screwed-up stories every time. I told you, it was a BB gun." Her quick smile flashed. "You know, you're as bad as my grandpa was for collecting stories. He knew everything there was to know about everyone in town. Of course, he never repeated it, but people always told him things."

She gave him a quizzical look. "I guess that goes with the territory?"

"Maybe. But I've learned these past few weeks, Maggie, what a well-loved man your grandfather was. He and his wife commanded as much love and respect in the community as you do."

"*I* do?" She laughed. "It must be residual family respect then, more a reflection of what my grandparents earned than anything I've ever done myself. I was the kid with the BB gun, remember, the kid who broke more windows than any other kid in town, the one who soaped more of them on Halloween as well, and bloodied more noses than her fair share. You want to hear horror stories about me, just ask Frank and Dora Murchison. They used to live next door to us, and I think I was solely responsible for their selling a home they loved and moving out to the country."

"You're also the kid who dragged Mrs. Barnes's spaniel out of the lake when it got tangled in the weeds and would have drowned. The kid who collected more money for UNICEF three years in a row than anyone else because of your relentless pursuit of pennies."

Maggie groaned. "They're *still* talking about that? People used to cross the street when they saw me coming. They were sick to death of hearing about how those pennies were going to wear holes in their pockets, and about how, in saving their pockets, they could also help starving children in South America. I earned almost as many enemies as I did pennies, believe me. Boy! People must be pretty hard up for stuff to talk about."

John laughed as he stretched his legs out before him, crossing his ankles and stuffing his fists into his jacket pockets. "No one who's told me about it sounds like an enemy. I've heard more about you, about your flaming hair and temper flying all over town on missions of one sort or another, about your 'causes' and about your big heart, since I came here than I have about any other single person."

Maggie wrinkled her nose. "I guess they talk to you about me because of the connection between our kids."

"I guess they talk to me about you because I let them," he said, leaning forward, arms on his knees, staring up at her. "Because I encourage them to, even if I do it subtly by not changing the subject."

"Why?" she asked softly. "What makes you so interested in my childhood?"

He stood and crossed over to her. "Because," he said, running one finger down the curve of her cheek.

"If Andi gave you an answer like that," she said, "you'd never accept it."

"It's the best one I can come up with." He transferred his silken touch to her hair, one finger sliding under it, curving around her ear. Deep inside, her body pulsed hard, hurting, then began to melt.

"I figure I should know a lot more than I do about you," he said, "since you're the woman I dream about at night. As well as during the day. I find myself drifting off into thoughts of you when I should be writing up patients' charts. I welcome any of the old ladies—and old men—who are willing to sit in my office and gossip about you, to let drop little tidbits about your childhood."

He drew in an unsteady breath. "I gobble up information about you as if it were food and I were starving. You're in my mind, Maggie. In my blood. Day and night."

She tried to speak, couldn't, and compressed her lips and swallowed.

"It kills me," he whispered, his fingertips stroking over her chin. "You do that little thing with your mouth, as if you're trying not to cry, and your chin puckers. When you do that, Maggie, I have to kiss you. I . . . have . . . to . . ."

The last three words were whispered against her mouth, and she parted her lips, breath shuddering in as she tasted him. The sound she made was close to a sob, and he gathered her into his arms, holding her tightly, pressing his hands to her back, one sliding down over her hip, urging her closer to him.

"I never cry," she said against his neck when he let his lips trail off her without really having kissed her. With supreme effort, she pushed him away. "So there's no need for a kiss to make it better."

Was that what this was all about? she wondered. He felt sorry for her, because he knew her feelings were different from his, deeper?

You're in my mind, Maggie. In my blood.

But not in his heart. She jumped off the railing and turned her back on him. He put his hands over hers as he stood behind her. She glanced down at their hands, at his darker skin against the paler shade of hers. He had such big hands.

Hands you can trust. But not emotions. She slid hers out from under his and slipped aside, closing her heart to the aching he created in it.

Capturing her, he encircled her face with his hands. "Don't take yourself away from me, Maggie," he said. "I need to know you."

"Then ask the gossips. Talk to ten of them, and you'll get ten different versions of my childhood."

"It's not just your childhood. Present-day stuff comes into it as well."

"There can't be much to tell about that," she said tartly. "My life is totally uninteresting. I work. I raise my child and volunteer two mornings a week at the school library. My social life is next to nonexistent and—"

"And that's where they're all hoping I come in."

She made an impatient sound and slipped away from him again. "Oh, for Pete's sake! Pay it no mind. It's just because of our children being twin sisters. And I'm single. There's nothing people of a certain age hate more than a single woman. Unless it's a single *father*."

"Nobody in this town hates you, Maggie. Everyone loves you."

"Good," she said crisply. "Maybe they'll vote for me."

"I certainly will," he said as he sat down and set the swing in motion again. He refused to permit her sneaky attempt at changing the subject. The subject of the moment was Maggie Adair, delectable woman, not Maggie

Adair, budding politician. He wanted it that way whether she did or not. Maybe if she talked about herself for him, he'd find a way to bring himself to tell her about his past. Without his having done that, he knew, what was happening between them could go no further.

"One of the things I've learned about you by listening," he said, "is that your grandparents once owned this swing, that it belonged on their front porch, that you and your grandmother used to share it on summer evenings. When you were a little girl, she read to you. When you were a teenager and her eyesight was failing, you read to her."

Maggie stared at him in disbelief. "Where did you get that one?"

"Mrs. Baker. She also said that it was sold along with everything else when the contents of the house were auctioned off on your mother's orders. I know that the sight of it on Frank and Dora Murchison's porch when you attended one of their garage sales shortly after your return made you cry."

With another brusque sound, she turned her back, gripping the railing. "That's not true," she said, her voice cracking. "I told you, John, I never cry. I haven't cried in maybe—five, six years. I gave it up for Lent once," she added facetiously, swiveling to look at him over her shoulder, "and never took it up again. It was a bad habit, anyway."

He stood again and moved in behind her, planting his hands on either side of her.

Maggie stiffened as his arms formed barriers beside her. She felt the heat of him against her back, though he didn't touch her. His breath stirred the hair at the nape of her neck when he continued. "I also know that Frank swiped a five-dollar price tag off something else and slapped it on the swing so you could have it back and save face."

She whirled within the circle of his arms and stared at him. Immediately she wished she hadn't. His scent surrounded her, along with his heat, his nearness. "You mean they didn't *want* to sell it?"

"I mean they didn't plan to sell it until they saw how much you wanted it. They wanted you to have it, but they were also determined to preserve your pride, so they couldn't just offer to give it to you. You wouldn't have taken it, according to Frank."

"He was right." Maggie's teeth made a sharp clicking sound. "I've a good mind to give it back to them."

"No. Don't do that." He brought one hand up and touched her cheek. "It would only hurt them."

Though the moving of that one hand had left her an avenue of escape, Maggie didn't take it. Still looking into his eyes, she nodded. "I know." She made a moue of self-disgust. "That was just a spurt of the famous Adair temper venting off."

"I like that temper of yours," he said, stroking her cheek again with the back of his fingers. "It makes your eyes glitter and your cheeks go pink." He repeated the gesture, and Maggie's eyelids felt heavy, as if they wanted to close.

She forced them to stay open.

"John . . . Why are you doing this?"

She saw him swallow. "I'm not sure, Maggie. I just can't . . . *not* do it. I see you and I want to be close to you. I get close to you and I want to touch you. I touch you and I want to touch you more."

His hand turned, cradled her cheek, his fingers sliding over her ear and into her hair. The base of his thumb pressed gently under her chin, tilting her head back, and her eyelids grew too heavy to stay open. They sank shut as his head came down and his mouth covered hers.

It was a brief kiss, but powerful for all that. His firm lips parted hers for just an instant. His tongue traced the shape of her mouth, hot and hard, evocative, and Maggie felt a shudder of need course through her.

He lifted his head and looked into her eyes, his own eyes dark and brooding. "I want you," he said.

She said nothing, could say nothing, but knew, too, that her eyes must be repeating the phrase back to him.

"I don't do . . . casual sex," she managed to whisper finally, giving him notice of how much more she wanted than a brief fling.

"I know." She watched his throat work. "I do know that, Maggie. This will be anything but casual."

"Then what will it be?"

He pulled in a ragged breath and drew her tightly against him. "Good," he replied. "It will be very, very good, Maggie. And very, very important. That's if you're saying it will be at all."

For answer, she slid her arms around his neck and pulled his head down to her.

His tongue thrust into her mouth, hard and deep, making up for all the kisses they had both wanted over the days and weeks they had known each other, kisses they had mostly denied themselves and each other. She welcomed John's kiss, held him as tightly as he held her, sliding her hands inside his jacket, raking her nails over his back.

He tunneled his fingers through her hair, loosening it, lifting it, letting it fall around her shoulders. "Darling . . ." He raised his head and looked at her, then bent and ran his lips lightly over her cheeks, her eyelids, her throat. He stroked her skin from earlobe to collarbone with trembling fingertips, then buried his face against her neck. She burned where he had touched her, burned hotter where he hadn't.

He tilted her back, slipped both hands around her waist, and pushed up her sweatshirt. The baggy top rose easily, and his hands whispered over her skin, drawing a shaky gasp from her as they curved around her breasts. In the cool night air her nipples puckered, hardened, and she cried out softly at the warmth of his mouth as he covered the tip of her breast with a kiss.

"John . . ." Her voice was a trembling sigh. Her fingers shook as they ran through his hair, holding his head to her. "Please . . . stop."

Reluctantly he lifted his head. "Ah, Maggie, you don't mean that," he said, his voice a ragged rumble.

"I think we should go inside." She slid her hands around the back of his neck. "Where it's warm. Where we can lock the door."

He scooped her up, teeth flashing in a relieved grin. "Show me where."

She opened doors for him, closing them again as he turned to permit her to do so. In her room he set her slowly, very slowly, on her feet, leaning against the inside of her bedroom door while she reached around him and twisted the lock in the knob. Illuminated only by the moonlight shining through parted drapes, his eyes were dark, mysterious, fathomless, yet they seemed to see into every secret corner of her heart.

"Maggie, we need to talk. I need to talk." His mouth cut a straight, solemn line above his square chin.

"Not now." She traced his mouth with a fingertip, hearing his respiration speed up, watching his fists clench. His lips parted and he drew her finger inside, sucking gently until she shuddered and slipped it free.

He cradled her face in his hands, kissed her again, then stepped back.

"Yes," he said. "Now."

Something in his tone frightened her, and she shook her head. Talk was not what they needed now. *This* was. Quivering, she reached for the bottom of her sweatshirt and drew it up, tugging it off over her head and tossing it on the floor. He groaned.

She saw his eyes gleam as his gaze swept over her, saw how his focus lingered on the swelling curves of her breasts, and suddenly she felt raw and exposed. With a soft cry, she reached for him, burrowing against his chest, her arms clinging around his waist. "Just hold me," she said. "Don't talk. And don't look. I'm—" Words failed her. What was she going to say? *My breasts aren't big enough to balance the pear shape of my butt?* That would sound like fishing!

"Maggie!" He tried to tilt her face up. She refused to budge. "Are you *shy*?" he asked, incredulous.

She shook her head.

"Then let me look at you," he said softly. "Let me touch you."

Trembling, she stepped back. He traced the shape of her breasts with both hands, fondling them, molding them, lifting them, then pressing them together. He closed his eyes for a moment, and when he opened them, he smiled at her. "Lord, you're pretty." Bending, he licked her nipples, suckled them, his touch exquisitely light. She caught at his shoulders to steady herself, digging in her fingers when he tugged harder. Overwhelmed by sensations, feeling stifled by her own heartbeats, she jerked back from him, half turning away, bringing her arm up over her breasts.

"I'm sorry," he said, hooking a hand behind her neck

and resting his forehead against hers. "Don't you like that?"

She shook her head, then realized that was the wrong response and nodded. She held herself in as tight a rein as she could muster, willing some of the need to subside, struggling against the power of it. "I'm not used to it. It's been a . . . while."

"Ah," he said. "Talk to me. I need you to tell me what you like. And what you don't."

Maggie opened her mouth to speak, but no words came and she closed it again. He traced the line of her spine with a thumbnail; her back arched. He kissed her shoulder, and she let her head fall back. He nibbled at the side of her neck, eliciting a small groan of pleasure. He hooked his thumbs in the waistband of her sweatpants and slid them down so slowly, the action was a long, arousing caress. She clutched his shoulders again when he crouched and lifted each of her feet in turn, sliding the elastic cuffs of her pants over her feet. Then, sitting back on his haunches, he gazed up at her.

She was naked! Clad in nothing but moonlight. Totally exposed to his interested gaze, and suddenly, ridiculously, she felt even more like a terrified virgin, unsure of herself, unsure of her appeal, her confidence shot as she mentally catalogued her physical deficits. She was thirty-one years old and parts of her *sagged*. Maggie squeezed her eyes shut and froze in place as if in doing so she could hide herself from John.

"Maggie, look at me." His voice told her he had stood.

She shook her head. Her eyelids felt glued shut. She wanted to wrap her arms around herself, use her hands to cover her body, but she couldn't move. She wanted to weep, and she wanted to hide, and she wanted, desperately, for John to hold her again, to make her feel all the things she'd felt only moments before, instead of just . . . inadequate.

As if he knew that, he cradled her close, stroking her hair, sliding one hand down her back and curving his palm over her buttocks. When her trembling abated, he walked her backward to the bed and leaned down, still holding her, to pull back the covers. Lifting her, he laid her down and mercifully drew the sheet up over her. Then, and only then, could she open her eyes and look at him.

He stepped back from the bed and quickly slipped out of his own clothing. Maggie lay rigid, and a small sound escaped her as he turned back to her, his erection proud and tall before him. Slowly, carefully, holding her gaze with his, he rolled a condom onto himself, then sat beside her.

He pulled the sheet back, exposing her breasts again, then bent and kissed them before drawing the sheet down past her waist. His hands molded her shape, then continued their downward journey, sliding the cover with them, to her thighs, her legs, her feet, until she lay bare before him.

His breath rasped in and out. His hands shook from the strength of his restraint as he glided them up her body until he cupped her breasts again.

She gasped and shivered. Slowly, so slowly she thought she might die from the waiting, the wanting, his hands slid back down her body, pausing at her waist, encircling it, then skimming over her lower abdomen to the junction of her thighs. He raked his nails through the curly hair there, drawing a shuddering sigh from her. One hand pressed on her left knee, moving it aside. The other lifted her right one, and to her surprise, he bent and kissed it almost reverently.

She quivered at the sensation of his lips on her inner thigh as he kissed his way back up to her abdomen. Then, lifting his head, he glided his hands back up over her stomach until he cupped her breasts. He lifted them, raked his thumbnails over her nipples, and, at her immediate response, bent to take one of them in his mouth.

So tenderly did he suck on her that she released another little sob of pleasure and cradled his head in her hands, arching her back to feed him more of herself.

"John . . ." she murmured.

He lifted his head, his stroking thumb and forefinger replacing his tugging mouth. Through the glazed desire in his eyes, she saw an instant alertness gleam. "What is it, darling? Don't you like that? Do you want me to stop?"

"No," she gasped. "I want you *never* to stop. I only wanted to say your name out loud."

And she wanted him to say *her* name, too, so she'd know he was aware of exactly who she was. She wanted to be more than some faceless "darling," a pale shape on the moonlit bed. She wanted no fantasy, no ghost in his mind while he made love to her. But he didn't say her name, only made an inarticulate sound against her breast.

Her breath shuddered out as she cupped his cheek. The smooth, freshly shaved skin he'd displayed at six that evening was now roughened by the beginnings of a beard. She loved the feel of it under her palm. She formed her hand to match the shape of his face, then let it glide over his throat and down to his chest. She splayed her hand over his chest, her fingers tangling in the curly hair there.

She broadened the scope of her exploration and

grazed one of his nipples with her nails, tugged gently on it with finger and thumb, then harder as it beaded in response. He drew in a sharp breath, lifting half away from her. She stopped at once. "No?" she asked.

"Yes . . ." he whispered, replacing her hand on his chest. "Oh, yes! Whatever you want to do."

"Good." She raised up to a sitting position and placed her mouth over his nipple, eliciting another pleasured sound from him. He cupped the back of her head and pressed her mouth to him. When at last he closed his fist in her hair and tilted her face up, she smiled and said, "I'm glad you like that. When you were doing the same to me, I could feel it in every fiber of my body. I want to make you feel good too."

Suddenly her voice trembled with the passion of words she could not withhold. "I want to give you so much!"

I want to make you forget . . . She squeezed her eyes shut. She hated the swiftness with which that thought arose. The sensations between her and John belonged to them and them alone. She wanted to believe that. She wanted it so badly she did believe it. She must!

"You do," he said, and took her lips in a deep, arousing kiss. He cradled her breast, fingering the nipple, tugging it as she had tugged his, while his tongue tangled with hers.

When they broke apart to gasp for breath, his voice was unsteady. "Already I feel you've given me more than I deserve. I want to give you more pleasure than you've ever known."

Maggie looked into his eyes while she traced the shape of his mouth with one thumb. "I'll take whatever you can give," she said, capitulating to the dictates of her own needs, knowing in her heart that if all he ever offered her was this one night, then that was what she'd accept.

"And I'll give whatever you can take," he vowed, and lowered his head to suck her other nipple into his mouth, his hand stroking a path down her body, between her legs to her dewy sex.

She thought he already had given her more than she could take, until he laid her back down, leaning over her again. She stroked his face and asked for his kisses with silent, unmistakable pleading. Tenderness flooded her, and love such as she had never known, making her ache deep inside with unfulfilled longings she could not voice.

When she said, "I want you to make love to me a million times," she knew she was speaking of only a small part of what she wanted from him.

"I will," he said, his mouth caressing her throat, her shoulder. "I am. You are so sweet. I can't taste you enough."

She shivered as his lips traced the upper curve of her breast. "Just *hurry!*"

"Never," he murmured.

She moaned as need grew with each touch of his lips. She sighed his name at each sweep of his tongue around and around her nipples, each tantalizing caress of his fingers as they parted her flesh and slid inside her. She gasped each time she thought he would finally give her what she wanted, and groaned when he stopped, teasingly, discovering a different erogenous zone to torment, making her wait for what she knew was to come.

Then, with a soft groan, he knelt over her, his knees straddling her hips. She placed her palms on his chest, feeling his muscles quiver, feeling the rapid hammering of his heart. Her fingers curved, nails raking lightly through the mat of hair, finding his nipples and teasing them to even harder erectness. He shuddered, his glittering gaze on her face, his lips pressed tightly together. For a moment he squeezed his eyes shut as her hands tracked down his body, over his stomach, which rippled and spasmed under her touch. They opened wide again, shining darkly, when she curled her fingers around his shaft, moving her hand up and down in an evocative stroking.

"Stop!" he exclaimed, and grabbed her hand away. He held it against the mattress as he lowered himself fully atop her, covering her burning body with the hardness of his. He rolled to his back, carrying her with him, inserting his legs between hers in an action so swift and so deft, she scarcely knew he had done it until she was kneeling over him.

He cupped her breasts, molded her waist, her hips, her thighs, and she dropped her head down to kiss him. Her mouth seemed to enflame him, because he captured her head and held her to him, deepening the kiss, turning it into a rapid, irresistible seduction. Then, somehow, she was on her back again, his hand sliding over her belly, between her legs, seeking, finding, testing her readiness, making her gasp and writhe and call out his name.

"Please, John!" she said. "Oh, please. Now! Hurry!"

"Yes. Oh, yes, hard and fast this time!" He grasped her knees, lifted them, parted them, pulling her to him.

His body trembled against hers as she held him, stroked her hands up and down his back as he lifted her hips, his sex nudging at hers. She moved. He moved. And then, with a groan, he was in her, hard, hot, filling her. His tongue filled her mouth, too, his scent filled her nostrils, his guttural moan of pleasure filled her ears. She arched, lifting to him, accepting his deep plunges, rising to each one, taking him in, moving against him. Faster, faster, he drove into her. Deeper, deeper, she took him in. Higher, higher, spiraled the burning ache at her core until it consumed her whole being. She had to tear her mouth free of his to drag in breath and sob his name. She dug her fingers into his back, lifted her hips high, twisting back and forth, straining for release, pumping as she wrapped her legs around his waist, then going rigid as the sensations piled one on top of the other.

Over her, John arched his back, rising up on trembling arms as his hips thrust one last, powerful time. Timeless moments passed as they stared at each other, breath abated, hearts stopped, minds linked, mouths parted in two soundless cries as they sensed the magnificence of what was coming.

With a massive shudder, he buried his face in the pillow beside her, muffling his shout as everything they had sought together rose to a climax that roared over them like a tidal wave, leaving them limp and exhausted in its wake.

"Sweet . . ." John murmured some time later, stroking her back, her shoulders, her arms, running his hand into her hair, each new touch arousing another quivering aftershock as she spasmed around him. "Maggie," he murmured, and her heart lifted. "My beautiful flame."

She exulted in the knowledge that he knew who she was. He knew whom it was he held. He knew it was she who had responded so wildly to his caresses. When she discovered she could speak, she whispered, "John. Oh, John, I—"

As if he knew what she was about to say, as if he didn't want to hear it, he covered her mouth in a kiss, cutting off her words.

Presently he lifted his head and she could only gaze at him, awed by the depth of the tenderness she had sensed in that kiss. She was sure she had felt him returning her unspoken declaration of love, love he didn't want to express verbally any more than he wanted her to. She knew there was nothing she could say that he didn't already know, and knew, too, that if he wasn't ready to hear it, she'd have to let it go.

What she wasn't going to do, though, she thought fiercely, was let *him* go.

She enfolded him in her arms, tried to hold him, tried to tell him without words how much she loved him, how much more she had to give than what he'd already taken.

Whatever it was he'd been so intent to discuss, she didn't learn. Their talk was slow, interspersed by kisses, and only of inconsequential things. The girls' antics that evening. Events at the hospital during the past week; things that worried John, happy results of patient care that pleased him. Then they spoke of the riding lessons Andi was determined to have.

"I gave her one this afternoon," Maggie said. "She's a natural, just like Jolene."

He slid a finger down her arm, lifted her hand, and kissed her palm. "Not surprisingly," he said. "All right. Give her lessons. We'll set up a schedule that suits you. How do the other families pay? Weekly, monthly?"

"Monthly," Maggie said, rolling to her side, half propped against his chest. "But *Andi* doesn't pay."

He flipped her onto her back and rose up over her, face thunderous with a dark scowl. "Andi pays like everyone else."

"John . . ."

"Maggie, don't argue with me over this. If you do, it'll make it a lot harder for me to ask you to take on my office bookkeeping as I plan to do. At the same rate as your other clients," he added quickly.

"But—"

"But nothing." His tone was flat. "Dammit, do you think I like seeing you live like this? This house is going to fall down around you if you don't soon put some money into maintenance. Since it's money I've already figured out you don't have, I can see you need more work."

She laughed as she rolled away from him and sat up, her legs folded under her, sheet drawn across her lap. "Hey, come on. My finances are not your responsibility, John. I'm doing just fine, thank you, and I do not need charity, even if it's disguised as a job offer. Don't forget, school trustees get paid a stipend, and when I win my election, my time is going to be extremely limited with that task to fulfill as well. Quite frankly, I'll only have time to teach Andi when I'm working with Jolie, so she won't be getting my individual attention. Hence, I'll be giving her nothing you need pay for."

She forestalled the argument she could see rising up in him and swept on. "And another client for my accounting business is out of the question at the moment, at least until I get a faster computer system and a more powerful program."

"When will that be?" he asked.

She smiled and slid off the bed. "When I can afford it." Forgetting the shyness that had assailed her at first, she strode to the closet and dragged out her robe. After tugging it on, she opened the door and crossed the hall to the bathroom.

When she emerged, John, dressed in jeans unbuttoned and only half zipped, lounged in her bedroom doorway. He slipped his hands around her waist and drew her against him. "Maggie Adair, you frustrate the hell out of me. You know that?"

"Why?" she whispered.

"Because you won't let me—give to you."

"You give me everything I want," she said.

Her words stung deeply. John turned quickly to hide the hurt, but couldn't prevent the sharp thud with which he shut the bathroom door.

You give me everything I want. Right. In other words, all she wanted from him was sex. He snorted.

And why wouldn't that be all she wanted? Wasn't that all he'd looked for with women for the past three years? And found. Women had the same rights, the same needs, the same desires as men. Trouble was, he knew he wanted more than that from Maggie. And he'd thought —he'd been damned sure—she did too.

If he hadn't cut her off, wouldn't she have said she was in love with him?

He scrubbed his hands as if for surgery.

He couldn't let her say the words, couldn't let her make it that real, not until she knew the truth about him. He managed not to groan aloud. He shouldn't have let her distract him, should have insisted on the conversation he'd gone there to have. He should insist on it now, but it wasn't only late, he suspected it was too late. Now that he'd made her his, how could he contemplate telling her something that might mean she'd despise him?

He stared at his face in the mirror, berating himself for cowardice. "What the hell have you gotten yourself into, Martin?" he muttered. The answer wasn't in the mirror, so he turned from it.

It wasn't in Maggie's eyes, either, when he found her sitting on the side of her bed, apparently waiting for him. The glow of the bedside lamp turned her hair to fire, the shadows it cast rendering her expression unreadable. But there was no mistaking the tenderness of her gesture as she reached both arms out to him.

He knelt before her, burying his face in her lap, sighing as her hands massaged his back and shoulders. "Stay," she whispered. "Come back to bed with me and stay."

"I want to," he said, lifting his head. "I want that so badly, Maggie, but—"

She nodded. "Okay. I understand. You have patients who might need you, and you'd rather not give your service this number."

He rose and stood before her, trying to read what her lashes hid from him. How had he ever thought of this woman as open and uncomplicated? "That's not why I'm leaving! Dammit, do you think I'm ashamed of being here with you? I'm not, Maggie. I'm proud that you took me into your bed, made such beautiful love with me. But I don't want anyone asking you arch little questions about something that's personal and private and between us two alone."

He put on a falsetto. "Maggie dear! Was someone ill at your house on Saturday night? I hear the doctor's car was seen leaving your driveway at daybreak."

Maggie stood, chin tilted, hands on hips. "I could handle that," she said with what she meant to be an insouciant smile that didn't quite make the grade. "Remember me? I'm Maggie Adair, BB-gun-totin' rebel, law unto herself."

"You're also Maggie Adair, mother of Jolene, who might not understand if people start talking about you. And Maggie Adair, candidate for the position of school trustee."

Maggie closed her eyes and nodded. "Right," she

said. She opened her eyes again, hoping her pain didn't show. What had she expected him to say, *You're also Maggie Adair, the woman I love, the woman I mean to marry?*

Suddenly she knew what she had told herself, told him, about being happy to accept whatever he could offer, had been a lie. She wanted more than his body, more than the physical pleasure he could give her. She wanted it all. Everything Laura had had—and more. His face told her nothing. She wished she could recapture the sense of tenderness she'd experienced in his embrace, the belief that he cared about her, that she was important to him as a person, that he'd known exactly who he held— every minute of the time they'd been making love.

But had he? Was she all that important to him? How could she be? She wasn't the woman he really wanted. He didn't want volatile, he wanted serene. He didn't want flawed, he wanted perfect. He didn't want Maggie, he wanted Laura.

The irreplaceable Laura.

She reached out and handed him his shirt. "On your horse, cowboy," she said, hoping her lighthearted tone hid her raging case of insecurity. She didn't like the feeling, didn't like herself for permitting such weakness.

"Good night, Maggie," he said when he was fully dressed and they stood together at her front door. "Sleep well."

She fought down a sudden, choking thickness in her throat and struggled against the urge to fling herself on him and beg him to love her, really love her, not just for one night, but for all time. Instead she gave him a carefree smile as she opened the door and he stepped through. She closed it without waiting to see him leave. Somehow it was easier that way.

A little.

Overnight the clear sky had clouded over, and periodic rain showers spattered on the windshield as Maggie drove into town the next morning. She dropped the girls at the Sunday school room, and had already donned her choir robe when John arrived at the church. He had the harried look of a man who had overslept.

He gave her a grin and a quick wave as he trotted past. Even such minimal attention made her heart and stomach perform weird stunts, and the very special smile he turned toward her ten minutes later made it nearly impossible for her to walk sedately through the sanctuary and up the spiral staircase.

How could she possibly keep her emotions under control when he smiled at her like that, rakish and promising? Church was far too public a place to look at a woman that way. Her biggest prayer, to her shame, was that church would be over soon and she could speak to him, maybe touch him, or at the very least, stand near him and breathe his scent.

She shifted restlessly during the sermon, trying to concentrate, but failing. If this was love, it was a totally different kind of love from any she had ever known before. It had taken over her mind, her life, her entire being. *Obsession*. Yes.

It was the longest sermon Reverend Crosby had ever preached, Maggie was sure, but eventually it was over. The collection plate made its rounds as she and the others sang a song of thanksgiving, and then she was free! She whipped off her robe, tidied her hair, and nearly flew from the church, dashed across the lawn to collect the girls. She had them both in hand when John joined them.

For several moments there was pandemonium as the

children told him about their "real fun" sleepover and extracted a promise from John that they could do it again the following weekend at Andi's house.

When they finally began to run down, he spoke to Maggie over their heads. "How about all my girls coming home with me for lunch? I told Mrs. Wisdom I planned to invite you, so I'm sure she'll have prepared something extra special."

My girls? Maggie couldn't have been more thrilled if he'd dropped to one knee and proposed. Such is love, she thought, clutching at the smallest crumbs. Odd, though, how those crumbs, once consumed, left an aching, empty void that wanted greater substance to fill it.

She drew a deep, steadying breath and nodded. "Leave your car here," John said, taking both girls by the hands. "If it's raining in earnest later, I'll drive you back to it."

Maggie entered "Doc Monro's" house with mild trepidation, but there were no bad feelings, only a sense of curiosity over the changes she saw after an absence of fourteen years. The wallpaper above the shoulder-high wainscoting in the hall was different, the chandelier had been replaced by a less ornate one, and the cut-glass doorknobs had been exchanged for bronze.

After introducing her and Jolene to their plump, sixtyish housekeeper, who was clearly overwhelmed and delighted by the sight of Andi with her twin, the Martins gave their guests a tour.

The tall mullioned windows still let in too little light, and though there were less dense and dusty draperies at their sides, the rooms retained their gloomy atmosphere. Brighter, more modern furniture helped, but only minimally, and even the children's lilting voices seemed lost in the high ceilings of the six-bedroom house.

Both Jolene and Andi asked a dozen questions a minute, it seemed. As Maggie answered them, telling them how it had been when she was a little girl growing up in that house, she felt the last vestiges of resentment against her mother for having sold it drain away.

The memories she retained were good ones, and this house would never have done for her and Jolene. Its large, dim rooms wouldn't have adapted to their clutter, and Maggie would have felt obliged to give it more care than she'd have wanted to. But she enjoyed showing them the room that had been hers, and was now Andi's, complete with playroom attached. Across the hall from that was the room where Maggie, too impatient to wait to get to the hospital, had been delivered by her grandfather. It was obvious by the masculine appearance of it, and the large four-poster, that this was John's room.

Maggie stroked her hand up and down one of the posts, taking sensual pleasure in the feel of smooth, polished wood. She breathed deeply of the scent that she imagined arose from John's pillows. She wanted to lie down on his bedding, bury her face in it, spread herself over its surface and cling with all her might. But his hand, an impersonal touch in the small of her back, moved her through the doorway in the girls' wake.

The master suite, which had been her grandparents', was Mrs. Wisdom's private domain, so they only peeked in the door before trooping back downstairs to the main floor.

"I don't need that much space," John said of the large bedroom, dressing room, private bath, and sitting room the corner suite afforded. "I've spread most of my 'toys' around my offices."

The doctor's office, examining room, and the waiting room had been modernized, Maggie saw with pleasure.

Fitted with comfortable furniture and bright lights, they looked less formidable than before. Many of John's antique surgical instruments and laboratory vessels filled glass cases spotted throughout the rooms. It would be an interesting place to wait for an appointment, with plenty of conversation starters all around.

As fascinating as Maggie found it, the girls soon tired of it and wandered off into the main part of the house again. As their voices receded John continued telling Maggie how the last occupant had converted the solarium to increase the space for his offices, and had even had a new, larger bathroom installed, which was much more convenient.

"Marble countertops," he said proudly, opening the door and standing back so she could enter. Maggie, not madly interested in plumbing, would merely have peeked in, but John placed a hand in the middle of her back and propelled her through the door. He followed her in, shutting and locking the door.

Startled, she turned, a question on her lips, but he had other notions of what her lips should be doing. Swiftly he dragged her into his arms. "Maggie . . ." He breathed her name. "Oh, Maggie." He filled his hands with her hair, sending pins flying as he kissed her until they were both breathless.

"Well!" she said shakily when she could speak. "Am I to assume you missed me over the past twelve hours?"

"*Missed* you?" He stared at her. "Is that what you call this kind of visceral ache? And it's been one hell of a lot longer than twelve hours. Hasn't it?"

She glanced at her watch and shook her head. Smiling, she fiddled with his shirt buttons. "Slightly less, I believe."

"God, Maggie!" he groaned, dragging her even

closer. "How can you be so cool? So unaffected? Every time we entered a bedroom upstairs, I wanted to throw the girls out, throw you down, and ravish you! Seeing you in my bedroom, watching you rub your hand up and down that post, made me as hard as I was all morning in church. Thank God for roomy choir robes, or everyone would have known what you do to me."

Would that be so bad? she wanted to ask, but he'd taken her mouth again in another of those mind-blowing kisses he dispensed.

"It wasn't fair, the way you smiled at me as you walked past," she whispered at length.

He lifted his head, glaring at her. "You think it was fair, the way you stood there so prim and proper, your hands folded like an angel at prayer, and stripped me with your eyes?"

"I didn't!"

"Did too."

"Did you bring me in here to argue?" she challenged. He grinned, kissed her earlobe, then her throat, then her mouth.

"I brought you in here because I couldn't keep my hands to myself and I didn't want to embarrass you in front of the children."

Maggie sighed. "Speaking of whom . . ." The girls' voices, calling them, rang through the old house.

Running her hands over her hair, she unlocked the door, holding her finger to her lips, and slipped out.

"I'm here, girls," she said brightly. "I was, um, combing my hair."

Jolene stared at her. "It still looks pretty messy, Mom."

Maggie shrugged. "You know me. Raggedy Ann's my middle name." To Andi's question as to her father's whereabouts, Maggie shrugged again. "I'm sure he'll turn up. Did Mrs. Wisdom send you to find us? Is lunch ready?"

Since he missed choir practice the following night, Maggie didn't see John until he dropped by at lunchtime on Tuesday. He walked through her door, kissing her before saying so much as a word, and before she knew it, she'd dragged him into her bedroom, where she ravished his body with his full compliance.

Wednesday he was there minutes after the school bus pulled out with Jolene on board. Maggie was still in her robe and nightgown, and her hair was a mess. It was a worse mess by the time he had to leave. He grinned, tousling it as he sat on her bed, where she still lay among the tumbled covers.

"Raggedy Ann, you are. Do you know how hard I had to work not to laugh out loud when you came up with that feeble excuse for having been in the bathroom?"

She sat up and gave him a push. "That's all the thanks I get for protecting your virtue? For keeping you pure in your daughter's eyes?"

"Maggie . . ." He bit his lip, looked down at her hands still wrapped around his arms, and heaved a huge sigh before pulling her into a rough embrace. He held her so tightly, she felt vertebrae snapping and popping. "Oh, Maggie! I—" He bit the word off and buried his face in her hair.

She broke free. "What?" she asked, staring into his pale, set face.

He refused to meet her gaze, shook his head, and let her go. "Nothing," he said. "Nothing."

Right, Maggie thought late Friday afternoon. Nothing. Nothing at all. Which was what she'd heard from John for two long days and even longer nights. She hadn't sat moping, though. She'd been interviewed by two local newspapers and taped a segment in the community TV studio. The all-candidates' session was scheduled for the first Tuesday in November, and she had lots of boning up on issues to keep her occupied.

John phoned early on Saturday morning, before she was even out of bed.

"Hi," he said, and it was all he had to say for every wild, tumultous emotion to sweep back over her, filling her with a yearning that had no end. She clutched the receiver in a sweaty hand and listened to his voice, a low, intimate rumble in her ear.

"I'm sorry I haven't called, haven't been around for a couple of days," he said. "I've tried to call, but there was never time. I've shuttled back and forth between here and Halifax like a milk truck driver. I've made what seems like a dozen trips. I haven't been home or slept more than a catnap or two in longer than I can remember."

"Anything you can talk about?"

"To you, yes," he said around a huge yawn, and a thrill coursed through her. "First," he went on, "a preemie that I fought for twenty-four hours to keep from being born, came sliding into the world despite my efforts. We had to medevac him and his mom to the neonatal unit in Halifax, and for the next twelve hours I didn't feel I could leave him. Then there was another patient with three strokes in as many hours. It took most of yesterday to get him halfway stabilized, then I had to deal with an emergency appendectomy that really blew things apart for me, so I couldn't call you."

Maggie could hear the weariness emanating from him. "It's okay. I understand," she said.

"I knew you would. You couldn't have been raised in a GP's home without knowing the routine. I only wish Andi understood. She's pretty ticked off that I'm on my way to bed."

He groaned as if he had just laid down and stretched out, and Maggie was about to tell him not to worry, that Andi would forgive him, when he went on. "But there's more," he said. "That emergency appendectomy happens to have been Dr. Petronius, with whom I'd arranged to share weekend duties. Mrs. Wisdom has plans for tonight, so I can't have Jolie over. I hate to disappoint the girls, but . . ." She could almost see his shrug.

"Jolie will understand that, John. Don't worry. I'll explain it to her and—" She broke off. "Wait a minute. What about Andi? She'd better come here, in case you're called out."

"Maggie . . . darling." There was a world of gratitude in his tone.

Something in her took flight. For the first time when he wasn't making love to her, he'd used an endearment.

"Thank you," he went on. "I was going to get a teenager to come and sleep in, but Andi'll leap at your offer, so I accept it gratefully on her behalf." He yawned loudly.

"Hey, you get some sleep. I'll come and get Andi in an hour or so. Just stay awake long enough to tell her and Mrs. Wisdom it's okay for her to come."

"Right," he said. Then, "Maggie?"

Her heart did that terrible stopping trick again. "Yes, John?"

Silence. She could hear him breathing. She heard

what sounded like a long, drawn-out sigh. "Nothing, Maggie. Thanks again. See you Sunday, I hope."

Sunday. Maggie could only hope too.

She woke Sunday morning from a restless night and opened her eyes to see two identical faces grinning down at her, surrounded by tousled brown hair. Her heart filled as her eyes did the same, and she reached up to gather the girls into a swift hug.

Jolene resisted, pushing back, concerned. "Mom? Why are you crying?"

Maggie squeezed her eyes shut. "I'm not," she said. "I don't cry."

Ah, but it was close! Too close. Even as she showered and dressed, she found herself fighting a ragged feeling in her chest and throat. As hard as she swallowed, it wouldn't go away.

It returned tenfold when she saw John outside the church.

He wore a charcoal suit and a white shirt, and his hair was damp as if he had just showered. His cheeks and chin had that freshly shaved look about them, and she wanted, with an intensity that scared her, to slide her palm along his jawline, to step in close and smell his aftershave. Yet she stopped five feet from him, as he came to a halt. His eyes were shadowed, and she wondered if he'd managed to get any more sleep than she had the previous night.

Both girls ran to him, and he, as he always did when the opportunity presented itself, as *she* always did, dropped down to their level and cuddled one in each arm, holding them close.

His gaze met hers as she approached more slowly.

"Hi," he said over their heads. His eyes searched

hers. Seeking what? Answers? To which questions? If he wanted them from her, he certainly wasn't offering any in return.

To judge by what his face gave away, their lovemaking over the past week might never have been. For a crazy moment she wondered if maybe it had been a particularly graphic dream on her part. Only the guarded stillness, the way he purposely hid whatever he might be feeling or thinking, told her it had all been real. That, and certain feelings in her own body, which ached and pulsed where it had not for a long time, but with such pleasurable surges she thought her knees must be visibly trembling.

Seeing him brought it all back, and she knew it was something she would never give up, not willingly. She'd fight for it if she had to. Fight for the loving they'd shared, and the love they could share in the future, with each other, with their children, with whatever more children their loving might produce.

She wanted him, she wanted *them* as a couple and everything else that went with that. She searched his gaze again, seeking the faintest clue that he felt the same, that there was a chance that he knew it had been more for him than sex. Again she saw nothing she could rely on, only doubts and concerns all mixed up with caring and hunger.

She swallowed. "Hi," she said. "How are you?"

"I'm fine." His gaze raked her from the top of her carefully arranged hair to the tips of the neat, unadorned navy pumps she usually wore to church.

She felt his gaze almost as a physical touch as he took in the wide white belt around the waist of her blue dress, her blue-and-gray-striped jacket, her nylon-clad legs.

His eyes raked upward, back to hers, and the hunger had grown to all but eclipse the doubts.

"Maggie," he said softly, raggedly, and she knew he was remembering the way it had been between them. "How . . . how are you?"

She smiled at him as he crouched there, holding his daughter and hers, sisters, twins, needing each other, each needing a mother, each needing a father, and she did what she knew she had to do.

With a hundred people milling around them, with his daughter and hers between them, she stood looking down at him and said quietly, but very clearly, not trying to hide her words from anyone, "John, you and I have to get married."

ELEVEN

In the silence following her pronouncement, John rose slowly to his feet. Maggie sensed people backing away, but not far, almost as if they were forming a circle around her and John and the children, an avid audience waiting to see what would happen next. Who would throw the first punch? Who would win and who would lose?

Every vestige of color drained from John's face as he stood. His right hand left Jolene's shoulder, raised up to the knot of his red-and-black-striped tie. He continued to hold Maggie's gaze as he took a step back, then another, another. Both girls turned to look at him.

His eyes were still pinned to Maggie's face. She saw the shock in them, the stunned, disbelieving, dumbfounded expression not even he was able to hide. Mingled with that was a deep, abiding yearning that knew no bounds, but also . . . denial. Rejection.

She swayed, caught herself, and tilted up her chin. She continued to watch him. He opened his mouth as if to speak, but no sound emerged. He shut his eyes for a second, then opened them again. His expression hadn't changed. Then he turned and strode away, leaving her, the girls, and half the congregation to stare after him.

It was Mrs. Baker who saved the day just as the bell in the steeple began to toll.

"Well, now," she said briskly, clapping her hands in front of Jolene and Andi, both of whom looked as stunned as John had. "I see your Sunday school teacher waiting for you over there, girls. Run along. Your mother will be waiting for you when you're done."

Without argument, almost as if they were relieved to be told what to do, both girls left, running across the grass.

Mrs. Baker took Maggie's arm and steered her into the church. There was no question of her donning her robe and ascending to the choir loft. Maggie felt like royalty at the funeral of a loved one as the crowd parted respectfully to permit her passage. No one made eye contact with her. No one said a word to either her or her escort, but as she sat in a pew, her elbow still in Mrs. Baker's firm clutch, she suppressed an urge to laugh hysterically.

After a few minutes of total hush a buzz of whispers began as a gentle susurration. It grew and swelled in volume until it formed a virtual storm of sound, breaking against the walls of the church, as a sea breaks against a shore, until the minister's arrival quelled it in mid-wave.

Because she was in church, Maggie closed her eyes and prayed.

John's hands gripped the wheel too tightly as he drove. He relaxed them with a conscious will, then released the wheel with one hand and flung off the tie that threatened to choke him. He undid the top two buttons of his shirt, but still he felt too hot, constricted, as if there were no air in the car. He cranked down the window, listening to the wind rush in.

John, we have to get married.

Because he had used birth control only once?

He rammed a hand through his hair, saw a corner coming up fast, and slammed on the brakes, listening with perverse satisfaction as tires whined on pavement.

He didn't know where he was going until he got there, and when he arrived, he realized how appropriate it was. Because how could he even begin to contemplate the future when he had never really confronted the past?

This time he didn't stop on the hill overlooking the farm. This time he drove right onto the property. The driveway was rutted, weed choked, as was the yard when he reached it. The car lurched as he drove across the grass, oblivious to whatever tire-destroying objects might be hidden. He had an objective now, and drove on until he reached it.

There, he sat in the car, his forehead on the steering wheel, listening to the silence, the ticking of metal as the engine cooled, the soft whisper of the wind. At last he alighted from the car and walked to the edge of the pond, gazing across its surface to the trees around its far edge. Weeping willows, fronds dipping to dimple the water; stately, golden Lombardy poplars behind them like an honor guard.

His parents had planted one of each for the first three years of their marriage, then three of each after he was born. Trees, with roots to grow deep to bind the soil as they believed their own roots would grow throughout their lives to bind them to their new home.

The trees remained. The lives had been destroyed.

The weedy grass was dry, brittle, seeds flying up in

clouds around his knees as he walked around the pond. Lily pads floated, turning brown around the edges as they were wont to do when the nights grew cool. Soon they'd be gone.

Just under the surface one blossom, nearly spent, still floated.

He remembered a face, just under the surface, floating. Hair had floated around it, wavering faintly, the way weeds now wavered faintly, disturbed by the motion of light wind on shallow water. That day, with the sun shining hot on his head and shoulders, one of the first things that had struck him was how young the face under the surface of the water looked. How at peace.

For the first time in his memory he had gazed upon the sweet smile he'd infrequently glimpsed in the one picture she had saved, hidden from Jack Porter as carefully as she had ever hidden anything—even a stolen fix.

He drew that faded black-and-white photo from his billfold, staring at it as he had not for many years, searching for . . . something. He didn't know what. A bridal veil floated around the girl's face, and happiness beamed in her smile, in the shining gaze she turned to the man at her side.

That man stared down into her eyes, clearly enraptured, oblivious of all but his new wife and a future he must have seen as extending before them forever. Slowly John returned the picture to its proper slot. Was anything forever?

"But if it's not," he said, "why do we ever try?"

Ten minutes later he rose and placed his wallet back in his breast pocket, next to his heart, where he always carried it.

He waded through the deep grass, searching, his eyes scanning, looking for landmarks, for clues. Slowly, as memories asserted themselves, he found them, found the grave. To his surprise, the cross he had carved from a solid slab of maple remained where he had placed it twenty years before. It stood crooked, and he straightened it with a gentle hand, pressing it more deeply into the hard-baked, untended soil.

Twenty years ago . . . or yesterday, the day he'd placed that small urn under the soil and planted the cross above it?

Funny, but he hadn't even known if she'd have wanted a cross. He had never been taken to church in his memory, nor sent to Sunday school. There had been no funeral to mark his mother's passing, just a coroner's inquiry, the conclusion of which was "death by misadventure." Not suicide.

And not murder.

Oh, no.

He stood and strode away. In the house the room that had been his was empty, bare, as he'd left it. If he hadn't, Jack Porter, out on bail and glad to be rid of him once and for all, would have taken everything that had been his and destroyed it.

Jack had been a master at destroying things.

People.

How many people had he destroyed besides poor, dead Cynthia Martin, whose face had looked peaceful only in death?

John completed his tour, then left the place as he had found it, open to the elements, devoid of anything of value, even memories.

The barn was half falling, redolent of old hay and still, to his shock, the marijuana that had once been baled there. Or was that merely memory having its way?

As if it had been waiting, as if no one had wanted it—

and why should they in this day of modern machinery?—the scythe still hung where it always had when it hadn't been in John's callused hands. He lifted it down and waded back into the grass to clear the area around his mother's grave.

He worked with as much care and attention as he ever had in clearing the runway where Jack Porter had landed his small plane, night after night, bringing in shipment after shipment, while John lit the lights to guide him.

And how many lives had John destroyed, too, in helping?

There was no answer to that question, either.

The memory of Maggie's words sent a stab of pain through him. *Scum. A plague.*

As if someone might want to use it again someday, when he was done, John hung the scythe back in its place in the barn.

Maggie sensed John's arrival in the murmur that preceded him through the church. Not so much the murmur of voices, but the sound of feet shifting, heads turning, hair brushing collars, bodies swiveling in response to his measured tread. She didn't look up when he slid into the pew beside her. She only stood in response to the request from the organist and took her hymnal from the back of the pew in front of her. She noticed idly that her hands shook as she opened it to the required page. Noticed, just as idly, that John's, when he slid it under hers to steady her, trembled as well.

She opened her mouth to sing as the organ cued the congregation, but no sound came. John had enough for both of them, his tones rising clear and joyful toward the vaulted ceiling. Maggie closed her eyes and just listened.

When the hymn was over, she would have remained standing but for John's touch on her shoulder, his gently guiding her back down.

He took her right hand in his left, his fingers wrapped around hers. She could have pulled free had she chosen. She let their fingers remain linked, staring at his hand, frowning. It was filthy. Burrs and grass seeds clung to his trousers; dust coated his shoes. For heaven's sake, where had he been? What had he been doing?

As if reading in her eyes the question she nearly blurted out, he tapped her lips with one of those grimy fingers. It was then that she realized his wedding band was gone. She went very still inside. If it hadn't been for the slow, almost sickening sense of falling, she'd have thought she was calm. When John leaned across in front of her as the last hymn began, she leaned back instinctively. Her heart hammered as his arm pressed against her breasts, as if it had every right to be there.

To Mrs. Baker, he whispered something Maggie didn't hear. The Late Mayor's Widow looked startled, then beamed. "My, how you two make this town buzz!" She leaned closer to John, crushing Maggie in the process. "I haven't had this much fun since the dear Late Mayor died."

John grinned like a conspirator. "How'd you like to have a little more fun, Mrs. Baker?"

She nodded eagerly, the feather on her hat bobbing over her left eyebrow.

"Go to the church hall when the children have finished and take our two girls to my house. Mrs. Wisdom is there. Tell the girls that their parents need a little private time to discuss the details of their wedding."

He leaned even closer. "But don't tell anyone else!"

She pressed her fingers to her lips. "Ohh!" Her eyes gleamed. "I won't, doctor. You can trust me."

As the congregation began to file out, Mrs. Baker hugged a stunned, still-speechless Maggie, then gave the pair of them a shove toward a side door. "Run. I'll hold the others at bay."

John grabbed Maggie's hand and ran. Her heels rapped sharply on the tiles, his made flat thuds, and their passage out the door, then across the parking lot, left a hundred heads turned. Maggie had found her voice, but lost most of her breath by the time they reached John's car.

"What have you been doing?" she puffed as he stuffed her through the passenger door. He shut it on her next question: "Where have you been?" He slid behind the wheel and rammed the key into the ignition with the swiftness of a man accustomed to having to hurry, and twisted it.

"John, you look like you've been burying bodies!" she said as he started the engine. "What makes you think the girls will go with Mrs. Baker?"

He put the car in gear and began to pull out from the curb. "Has anybody ever told Mrs. Baker no?"

Maggie grabbed the wheel and held it still. "Dammit, where are we going?"

He took her hand off the wheel and placed it, not particularly gently, on her lap. Gripping the steering wheel in both hands, he faced her. She saw his face was white again, grim, gaunt with tension. She easily read the warning in his eyes.

"Maggie," he said, "we can talk here if you insist. But I want you to know that the minute we're finished talking, I'm going to strip you out of your clothes and make love to you. We can do that here, too, if you want. Or we can go somewhere else, somewhere private. The choice is yours."

She looked at the pale strip of skin on the third finger of his left hand, then back up at his eyes. He gazed steadily, soberly, at her. She knew he meant every word he had said. She met that gaze, searched it for some time, then said quietly, "Somewhere else is fine with me too."

He took his foot off the brake and peeled out, leaving a strip of rubber and an even more astounded congregation all turning as one to stare after the new doctor's car.

"What is this place?" Maggie asked as John stopped the car beside a pond whose surface was half hidden by shed willow fronds and dying lily pads, and which was surrounded by long, dry grass.

"Come with me and I'll tell you," he said, alighting and opening the back door. He removed his jacket, flung it into the backseat, then took out a blanket and draped it over his arm. Maggie got out of the car and looked around, shading her eyes as she gazed across the wide, untended fields toward distant fences.

"Are we trespassing?" she asked.

He shook his head. "I own this place. This is where I grew up."

Her green eyes grew shadowed as she gazed at the remnants of barbed wire lying in coils, giving the place the appearance of an abandoned POW camp. The shattered windows, the half-collapsed barn, didn't detract from that impression, John knew. But he'd wanted her to see it this way. Maybe then she'd be better able to understand.

Under a willow near the water, where the grass was

still green and soft, he spread the blanket and sat, reaching up a hand to pull her down beside him.

For a long time he didn't speak, didn't touch her. He just stared at the pond. The wind had died; not a ruffle marred its smooth surface. A water strider danced across it, hopped on a lily pad, then hopped off the other side. A bumblebee, drowsy with the cool of the autumn day, tumbled into the water from a blade of grass. John cupped his hands under it and lifted it out, setting it in the sun to dry and warm.

He wiped his hands on the blanket, removing most of the water and all of the dirt.

"John?" Maggie touched the back of his cool, damp hand, her finger tracing the faded mark where his wedding ring had been. "Where is it?"

"Over there." He gestured toward the only mowed area in the shaggy grass, near the battered house, where a cross stood on a low knoll. "I left it with my mother. I think she'd have liked that. I think Laura would too. And I think they'd have both liked you." He took her hand, extended her index finger and laid it over the pale ring mark, like a bandage over a wound.

"Let me tell you about the way I grew up."

He pointed out the trees, the willows and poplars, his parents had planted. The first one of each species on their wedding day, and one more of each on every subsequent anniversary. "Roots," his mother had once said, "to bind the soil, and to bind us to it. To each other." The farm was to have been John's heritage. Neither of his parents had family, and they were determined to create one not only for themselves but for their children.

"You have brothers and sisters?" Maggie asked.

"No. I was the only one." A muscle clenched in his jaw. "That's why she stayed, why she felt it was important to stay. For me. I was three years old when my father was killed. She was badly injured in the same accident. Her pain was terrible. She became addicted to the medications she needed to keep her comfortable the first few months. Her doctors thought they had weaned her off it, but when the pain continued and they wouldn't give her more, telling her it was all in her head, she found a source.

"Or rather," he added bitterly, "the source found her."

He broke off a willow frond and ran it slowly between finger and thumb, staring at it as if it were vital that he smooth the leaves just so. "Jack Porter."

He glanced up at her. "The neighbors who were caring for me and the place while she was in the hospital hired him as a handyman. After she was released, he made himself . . . indispensable to her.

"By the time she knew what he was, when she saw that it had never been his intention to farm the property with her, to replant each year the crops she and my father had planted, she was helpless to act. And at first he did work the farm as it should be worked. His sideline was just a personal pot plantation he had back there in the woodlot. But that soon grew into a major cash crop that supported the three of us easily and meant little work for him in comparison to the financial return."

"John, this isn't necessary," Maggie said, but he shook his head.

"It's necessary. You have to know. For a long time I believed he was my father. I was enrolled in school under his name. When I was a kid in Maples, I was Johnny Porter, the weird kid from the other side of town. I was permitted no friends. If I'd had any, I might have wanted to visit them, might have dropped indiscreet comments. I would have wanted them to visit me, and of course that couldn't happen.

"To avoid detection of his illicit activities, and to keep casual visitors away, Jack Porter surrounded the farm with barbed wire and pit bulls; ostensibly, dog breeding was his livelihood. But he built an airstrip so he could land his plane and began importing more than just the heroin he'd supplied my mother with since the beginning.

"She was so badly addicted by then, there was no hope for recovery. Or so she believed."

He raised his head again and looked at Maggie. "I went to your grandfather once, asking him to help her. He'd stitched me up when I was nine and two of Jack's pit bulls attacked me."

"And the authorities never made him destroy them?" Maggie asked, staring at him aghast. "My grandfather didn't?"

He shook his head. "The 'authorities' never knew. I wouldn't even have been taken to a doctor if my teacher hadn't investigated after seeing me limping around school, and noticed I had a high fever. I told her a strange dog had bitten me, and that if she told anyone, my stepfather would find out and be angry at me for touching someone else's dog.

"She'd seen enough bruises on me to know it was true. She asked me, not for the first time, if I was being hurt at home. I always denied it. If I told, Jack would have taken away my mother's 'medicine.' I'd seen him do that more than a few times. I lied to your grandfather too."

Maggie tossed her head back and glared at the willow fronds fluttering above her before glaring even harder at John. "That was so damned dumb, John Martin! He could have helped. He could have gotten you out of that situation."

"But not my mother," he said evenly. "I was thirteen when I asked him to help her. He said she'd have to ask for help herself, but he could get me into a foster home that very day. I'd never have to go back, he said, not even for my things. But I knew I had to go back, and I suspect he knew it, too, because she was there and if I didn't, Jack would punish her. By then, you see, he needed me. He'd put me to work.

"I was becoming proficient with a scythe, keeping the airstrip open for him. I set up the lights at night for him to land. We couldn't leave them out, of course, for risk of detection. I was his . . . valued assistant, Maggie. I was as guilty as he."

"No!" Her denial was swift and emphatic as she jumped to her feet. "You were a kid, John! You didn't have any choice!"

He continued to sit, his arms draped over his bent knees, large hands hanging loosely. He looked so . . . relaxed, sounded so casual about the whole thing, Maggie wanted to shake him. Where the hell were his emotions? Didn't he care about the wrongs that had been done to him?

"I had choices," he said. "I simply didn't make the right ones. Maybe if I had left, then she'd have followed. If she'd seen that my birthday trees, regardless of how deep their roots might run, hadn't bound me to the farm, then she might have managed to escape as well. I had that all figured out by the time I was thirteen, but I was scared, too scared to take the freedom your grandfather offered me. So I told myself, and him, that I had a responsibility to her and that if I left, I'd be failing her."

Looking at his obdurate face, Maggie could see it

would be pointless to argue. He blamed himself, and she didn't know how to make him see it differently.

"Then what happened?" she asked, gripping a branch of the tree in both hands, looking down at him from between her upraised arms. "Obviously, you left."

In a few spare words he told her about finding his mother drowned in the pond the week he'd graduated from high school, about hitchhiking into town for help, and about how he'd failed to be there to light the lamps for Jack to land that night.

But the police had formed a reception party. What they'd caught Jack Porter with had been enough to send him away. He'd been sentenced to eight years in prison, but had died after only six months.

John had gone back to the farm to bury his mother's ashes and carve a cross for her. After convincing himself that was what she'd have wanted, he'd sold off several acres of property on the lake shore to help finance his education, and he hadn't set foot on the place until today.

"Why today?" Maggie asked.

"I'm not really sure," he said, rising to his feet, standing half-turned from her, one shoulder on the trunk of the tree. "I guess I wanted to see if I could do it."

He gestured at the hill where the road ran and told her about the morning he'd jogged out there and looked at the farm from a distance. "As I was leaving, I had sort of a vision, Maggie. Of you and Medallion, riding across the fields. At the time, I told myself it was a crazy notion, that I was losing touch with reality."

She went very still. "And now?" she asked. "Has anything changed?"

John swallowed twice before he could say, "I'm not really sure of that, either. What you said this morning, that shook me up. Badly. Because it's an idea I've been fighting myself for a long time."

"Why?" Her chin tilted. Shadows played over her face, hiding her expression from him. "Why have you been fighting it? Because I'm not—" He saw the difficulty she had, saw the courage with which she battled it and won. "Not Laura?"

"No. Not that. Maybe at first. I worked through that, though. Laura's gone, Maggie. The man who was her husband probably no longer exists, either. But you . . ."

He almost smiled. "You're special. You're so strong, so confident of what you want, I'm afraid for you. Because what you want might not be good enough for you."

She stared at him. "You?" She let go of the branch she'd been clinging to and stood, hands on her hips. "You're what I want, John. Why wouldn't you be good enough for me?"

He jammed a hand into his hair. "Dammit, Maggie, didn't you hear a word I've said since we came here? Don't you think I'll understand if you decide, when you've had some time to think it over, that you can't be with me?"

"What?"

"Maggie, you have to think about it. You have to realize that many of the things I did were wrong, and some of the things I didn't do were even more wrong. I want you to see me for what I am. I want you to look at the reality of me. Then if you don't want to go through with what you said at church this morning, you have only to say so. I promise I'll understand."

"Good God!" she cried. "I know what you are! You're a physician, John, a healer. And a good man. A man good enough for any woman in the world." She glared at him, fury sparking in her eyes. "Except maybe me!

"You say you want me, John. And you make love to me so beautifully, I have to believe it, but you're still afraid. I can see it in your eyes, feel it in your kisses, sense it in your words. If you loved me, if you wanted me as much as I want you, you'd be willing to fight for me. You'd never have said what you just did, that you'd *understand* if I couldn't be with you.

"Pah!" she said, color flaring in her cheeks. "What a namby-pamby, wishy-washy phrase that was, John Martin! If you wanted me with you, really, truly wanted me with you in every sense of the word, you'd have told me that you are as I find you and that if I'm not damned glad to have you exactly as you are, then *I* don't deserve *you*. And until you get over apologizing to me and the world for what somebody else did to you, then *you* don't deserve *me*!"

She spun away and left him, her shoes, her shoulder bag, and his wide-open mouth behind.

She was halfway back to the car before he caught her around the waist with one long arm. Without a word, he scooped her up, swung her over his shoulder, and headed back to the blanket under the willow tree.

He dumped her down on her back and knelt over her, one hand on her shoulder, the other on her knee to keep her there.

"You're crying," he said, staring at her in disbelief. "You never cry, Maggie."

"I know." Maggie tried to compose herself and heard him utter a soft curse as he drew her up into his embrace, pressing her face to his shoulder. Her tears burned her eyes, wet his shirt, and her shoulders shook as she sobbed.

"Please, please stop crying," John begged. "Maggie, darling, you're tearing me apart."

He released her as she flung her head back, her tear-streaked face blotchy and red, but her eyes glittered like emeralds in their shimmer of tears. "I can't stop crying!" She wrapped her hands, her long, beautiful, expressive hands, around his face, tenderly, lovingly. "I don't know if I'll ever be able to stop. I'm crying for that little boy who can't remember his father. For the kid who needed a teacher to take him for stitches because his mother couldn't and his stepfather wouldn't. I'm crying for the child terrified of dogs, terrorized by dogs, for the boy forced to labor for a vile and vicious man doing a vile and vicious thing. I'm crying for the teenager who went to my grandfather for help for his mother and was offered only escape for himself. I'm crying for the young man who had to bury his mother's ashes all alone. But mostly I'm crying for the grown man who doesn't have sense enough to cry for himself!"

"I've cried, Maggie."

"For your mother," she said, walking two steps away from him on her knees, holding a hand up to fend him off as he reached for her. "For Laura. As you should have. But not for you, John. Not for the boy who grew up as you did, hurting and alone, for the boy who still, deep down inside, hates himself for what he was forced to do, who blames himself for his mother's death, and probably for his wife's. I'm crying for the life he could have had, the life he should have and never will, because he's been turned off love, made afraid of it, made to doubt it and question it and avoid it."

She wiped her face with the back of one hand. "And I'm crying for me, John," she said. "For loving you, for wanting you, for having to turn down the future you just offered me, the future you offered our two daughters. I don't want a man who feels he has to apologize for his very existence."

Her warning went unheeded as he caught the hand she used to ward him off. He grasped her arms, held her before him. "Is that what you think I was doing? Apologizing?"

She met his glare with one of equal intensity. "Weren't you?"

"No. I was giving you an out. I never had a real escape hatch, Maggie. I know that. I had choices, like I said, but I also know they were limited. Maybe I made the right ones, maybe not. I know now that I can't change the past, that I can't let it destroy my future.

"My mother always talked of the future, of my future, the happiness she wished for me, here, farming this place as my father had intended it to be farmed. When she died, I couldn't stay. I had never learned to be a farmer. I had learned to be a drug dealer's assistant. That wasn't what I saw myself doing for the rest of my life. And I wanted to . . . atone. If I could. But I believed that even if I had a future, it wasn't meant to be a happy one.

"Laura showed me different. She was so good inside, she made me feel like a decent human being again. I even began to believe in forever. Then she died. I stopped believing in it. It was enough to live for today."

He wiped an errant tear from Maggie's face with the pad of one thumb. "Then you came along, Maggie. You made me want not only today but tomorrow as well, and I began to believe in a future again. I want it. I want it with you."

He drew in a deep breath. "And I want it here, where my roots are." He looked at the trees. "I'm no farmer, but there's lots of room for horses. We could build the kind of house we both want, the kind where our children will be happy. I brought you here to offer you all of that, Maggie, but I also wanted you to know what I really am. Because if you marry me, there'll be no backing out of it. I wasn't apologizing, I was explaining. I have nothing to apologize to you for, Maggie."

He paused significantly before lowering her to her back on the blanket. "Yet," he added softly.

He saw a glimmer of excitement in her eyes, excitement that echoed the boiling in his blood.

"And what will that be?" she asked.

He lowered his full weight on her. "This," he said, against her mouth.

She wrapped her arms around him. "You don't have to apologize for this."

He ran his hands into her hair, sliding them around her head, feeling pins give. He rolled onto his back, carrying her with him, and spread his fingers, releasing more pins, until her hair hung free in a sunset cloud around their faces. "How about this?" he asked.

She shook her head.

"How about for not asking you to marry me last week, last month, even?"

She shook her head again. "You should have, but you obviously didn't know that, so I took care of the matter this morning."

"I noticed," he said. "So did about fifty other people, including our children. I'm sure half the town now thinks I knocked you up within hours of my arrival and you were demanding that I do the right thing by you—since I obviously didn't the last time. Do you know you gave me absolutely no room to maneuver, Maggie Adair?"

She nodded, meeting his gaze boldly. "Do I have to apologize?"

"Never," he said, sliding her jacket off her shoulders and searching for the zipper of her dress.

"John?"

He stopped, looked at her, waited. He saw her swallow. Saw a wash of vulnerability in her eyes before her glance hardened just a fraction. "If you don't soon tell me you love me, I'm probably going to roll you into the pond."

"But you *know* I do," he said, half laughing. "Maggie, Maggie, you must know that."

She swallowed. Her chin puckered just a little, and she shook her head. "No, I don't," she whispered.

"Oh, baby!" John wrapped her tightly in his arms, rolling her under him again, lest she try to escape. He was never going to let this woman get away.

"I love you," he said, his face buried in her wild, flaming hair. "Of course I love you. I fell in love with you when you were telling Elmer Abernathy off in front of his entire school."

"But you didn't want to."

He raised his head and looked down into her eyes. "That's right. I didn't want to. It scared me, darling. Not just because of the past, but because of the future. Our girls . . . God, Maggie! The responsibility! I had to think of what would happen if we got together, got the kids together, and then it . . . fell apart. We both know that things can go wrong."

She nodded. "I went through much the same kind of process, John."

"Yeah. But you knew what to do."

"Are you sure that's what you want, too, are you sure you love me enough to put up with my temper, my stubbornness, and my sometimes slightly exaggerated belief in my own rectitude?"

"Sometimes?" he echoed. "*Slightly* exaggerated?" He grinned. "Yes. I love you enough for that. I love you enough even to put up with your driving. And you want to know how I'm going to prove it?"

She smiled tremulously and slipped her hands inside his shirt. "Oh, yes. I want that . . . very much."

"Good," he said. "I'm going to tell all my patients to vote for you. How's that for proof of love?"

She slid her hands up until they were wrapped securely around his throat. "I suppose that would do, Doctor, unless you can't think of any other way to, um, demonstrate?"

He pretended to think. Her thumbs pressed a shade tighter. He grinned and bent his head, taking her mouth in a kiss that told her all the things his words could never impart.

When he looked down at her again, she wore an expression he wanted to see on her face every day for the rest of his life.

The look of a woman in love.

EPILOGUE

"Mom?" Maggie glanced up from the windowsill she was sanding, preparatory to painting it. "Hi, hon. What's up?" The school bus had just delivered the girls to the farm, where the new house was nearing completion, almost a year after she and John had married.

The third grader chewed on her bottom lip. "I got something I gotta tell you."

Maggie steeled herself as she rose from her knees to her feet. "Go ahead," she said.

"I bopped Jeremy Freemont today and knocked a tooth loose. He spit blood all over Mr. Abernathy's pants when he went to tattle on me."

Maggie sat down on a roll of carpet. "Oh, Andi! You know better! You promised you'd quit fighting. Don't you understand it's really bad for a member of the school board to have a daughter who's always in trouble with the principal?"

"Yeah. I understand. I'll try not to do it again."

Maggie looked into a pair of remorseful gray eyes and smiled. "I know you will, sweetie, and thank you for telling me. I'm pleased with your honesty, but furious that you were fighting in school." She groaned, running a hand into her hair. "And I suppose Mr. A's even madder than he normally would be, because he couldn't reach me all day?"

She had been very careful not to give out the number of the cellular phone John insisted she carry when she came out to the new place to work alone.

"I asked if I could tell you first, on account of you being pregnant and everything. I'm sorry, Mom."

Maggie hugged her awkwardly. It was hard to fit another human being against her massive, bulky belly. "I forgive you," she said. "What did Jeremy do to deserve a bop?"

"He tripped Andi."

"Tripped *whom*?"

Those gray eyes went wide as a hand clapped over a mouth making a perfect O. "I mean, he tripped *Jolie*."

Maggie's eyes narrowed. She heaved herself to her feet. "Andrea Jane!" she yelled, planting her hands on her hips. "You get in here. On the double!"

Footsteps thudded on the bare plywood subflooring, and Maggie's other daughter skidded to a halt. "Yeah, Mom?"

"Don't you 'yeah, Mom' me with those big, innocent eyes. I know which one you are." She poked a finger into Jolie's chest. "And which one *you* are too. And I want to know why you swapped clothes today, why you swapped identities."

"Well, because we figured you might be upset, knowing Jolie was fighting," Andi said, sidling protectively closer to her sister. "I mean, you're used to me doing it, and I'm used to being grounded, but Jolie really wants to go to Monica's sleepover and see *The Lion King* again."

"Is that so?" Maggie asked, her eyebrows raised nearly to her hairline. "Have I got news for you two! *Neither* of you is going anywhere this weekend, and that's that. When your father gets home, you'll see how fast he agrees with me once he learns what you've been up to."

"*I* agree with you all the time," John said, striding through the door. "It's *cucumbers* that don't agree with you, Mrs. Martin." He swept them all into a hug.

"Hi, how are my girls?"

Once the babble of noise created by two eight-year-olds trying to justify their actions had died down, John kissed his wife, feeling her lips tremble under his.

"Can we get rid of these reprobates for the evening?" he murmured.

Maggie groaned softly and whispered back, "No. I just grounded them both for the weekend."

John shook his head. "Maggie, Maggie, Maggie! When will you ever remember not to do that when Dr. Petronius is covering my calls?"

Maggie leaned back in his arms and glanced at her daughters. She couldn't help feeling a sneaking bit of pride in Jolie for having finally learned to take care of herself—and her sister.

"I could, I suppose," she said slowly, speculatively, "commute it to a suspended sentence. After all, it *was* a first offense."

As the girls reached around her considerable bulk and hugged her from the sides, John hugged her from the front, and Maggie tried to hold them all close to her heart. Her love for them grew, and grew, and grew, until she thought she would burst with the joy of it.

John stepped back and touched her face. "Tears?"

Maggie smiled through them. "Of course not. I never cry."

He nodded sagely. "I see. These, then, are mere figments of my imagination."

She grinned. "Okay, so they're tears. But they're good ones. Happy ones. Because you've given me so much."

He kissed them away. "And I haven't finished yet."

Maggie was sure of that.

THE EDITOR'S CORNER

Escape the summer doldrums with the four new, exciting LOVESWEPT romances available next month. With our authors piloting a whirlwind tour through the jungles of human emotion, everyday experiences take a direct turn into thrill, so prepare to hang on to the edge of your seat!

With her trademark humor and touching emotion, Patt Bucheister crafts an irresistible story of mismatched dreamers surprised and transformed by unexpected love in **WILD IN THE NIGHT,** LOVESWEPT #750. She expects him to be grateful that his office is no longer an impossible mess, but instead adventurer Paul Forge tells efficiency expert Coral Bentley he wants all his junk back exactly where he had left it! When she refuses, little does she realize she is tangling with a renegade who never takes no for an answer, a man of mystery who will issue a challenge that will draw her into the seductive unknown. Hold on while Patt Bucheister skillfully navigates this ride on the unpredictable rapids of romance.

The excitement continues with **CATCH ME IF YOU CAN,** LOVESWEPT #751. In this cat-and-mouse adventure, Victoria Leigh introduces a pair of adversaries who can't resist trying to get the best of each other. Drawn to the fortress by Abigail Roberts's mysterious invitation, Tanner Flynn faces the woman who is his fiercest rival—and vows to explore the heat that still sparks between them! He had awakened her desire years before, then stunned her by refusing to claim her innocence. Join Victoria Leigh on this sexy chase filled with teasing and flirting with utter abandon.

Take one part bad-boy hero, add a feisty redhead, raise the temperature to flame-hot and what you get is a **PAGAN'S PARADISE,** LOVESWEPT #752, from Susan Connell. Jack Stratford is hold-your-breath-handsome, a blue-eyed rogue who knows everyone in San Rafael, but photographer Joanna McCall refuses to believe his warning that she is in danger—except perhaps from his stolen kisses! She isn't looking for a broken heart, just a little adventure . . . until Jack ignites a fire in her blood only he can satisfy. Take a walk on the wild side with Susan Connell as your guide.

In **UP CLOSE AND PERSONAL,** LOVESWEPT #753, Diane Pershing weaves a moving tale of survivors who find sweet sanctuary in each other's arms. A master at getting others to reveal their secrets, Evan Stone never lets a woman get close enough to touch the scars that brand his soul. But when small-town mom Chris McConnell dares to confess the sorrows that haunt her, her courage awakens a yearning long-denied in his own heart. A poignant journey of rough and tender love from talented Diane Pershing.

Happy reading!

With warmest wishes,

Beth de Guzman

Shauna Summers

Beth de Guzman   Shauna Summers

Senior Editor   Associate Editor

P.S. Watch for these spectacular Bantam women's fiction titles slated for August: In **BEFORE I WAKE**, Loveswept star Terry Lawrence weaves the beloved fairy tale *Sleeping Beauty* into a story so enthralling it will keep you up long into the night; highly acclaimed author Susan Krinard ventures into outerspace with **STARCROSSED**, a story of a beautiful aristocrat who risks a forbidden love with a dangerously seductive man born of an alien race; *USA Today* bestselling author Patricia Potter follows the success of WANTED and RELENTLESS with **DEFIANT**, another spectacular love story, this time of a dangerous man who discovers the redeeming power of love. See next month's LOVESWEPTs for a preview of these compelling novels. And immediately following this page, look for a preview of the wonderful romances from Bantam that *are available now*!

Don't miss these extraordinary books
by your favorite Bantam authors

On sale in June:

MYSTIQUE
by Amanda Quick

VIOLET
by Jane Feather

MOTHER LOVE
by Judith Henry Wall

HEAVEN SENT
by Pamela Morsi

THE WARLORD
by Elizabeth Elliott

MYSTIQUE

by the *New York Times* bestselling author
AMANDA QUICK

available in hardcover

Who better to tell you about this dazzling romance than the author herself? Here, then, is a personal letter from Amanda Quick:

Dear Reader:

Any man who is dangerous enough to become a living legend is probably best avoided by a sensible, intelligent lady who has determined to live a quiet, cloistered life. But sometimes a woman has to work with what's available. And as it happens, the man they call Hugh the Relentless is available . . . for a price.

Lady Alice, the heroine of my next book, *Mystique*, does not hesitate to do what must be done. She requires the services of a strong knight to help her escape her uncle's clutches; Hugh, on the other hand, requires assistance in the hunt for a missing gemstone

—and a woman willing to masquerade as his be-trothed.

Alice decides that she and this dark legend of a man can do business together. She strikes a bold bargain with him. But you know what they say about the risks of bargaining with the devil . . .

Mystique is the fast-paced tale of a man and a woman who form an alliance, one that puts them on a collision course with passion, danger—and each other. It is the story of a ruthless man who is bent on vengeance and a lady who has her heart set on a studious, contemplative life—a life that definitely does not include a husband.

These two were made for each other.

I hope you will enjoy *Mystique*. When it comes to romance, there is something very special about the medieval setting, don't you think? It was a time that saw the first full flowering of some of the best-loved and most romantic legends, tales that we still enjoy in many forms today. Hugh and Alice are part of that larger-than-life period in history but their story is timeless. When it comes to affairs of the human heart, the era does not really matter. But then, as a reader of romance, you already know that.

Until the next book.

Love,

Amanda Quick

VIOLET

by bestselling author
JANE FEATHER

Sure to continue her spectacular rise to stardom, VIOLET is vintage Jane Feather—passionate, adventurous, and completely enjoyable from the opening paragraph.

"Take off the rest of your clothes."

"What! All of them? In front of you?" She looked outraged, and yet somehow he wasn't convinced by this display of maidenly modesty.

"Yes, all of them," he affirmed evenly. "I doubt even you will take off from the far bank stark naked."

Tamsyn turned away from him and unfastened her skirt. Damn the man for being such a perspicacious bastard.

She dropped the shirt to the ground, loosened the string at the waist of her drawers, and kicked them off.

"Satisfied, Colonel?"

For a moment he ignored the double-edged question that threw a contemptuous challenge. His eyes ran down the lean, taut body that seemed to thrum with energy. He realized that the illusion of fragility came from her diminutive stature; unclothed, she had the compact, smooth-muscled body of an athlete, limber and arrow straight. His gaze lingered on the small, pointed breasts, the slight flare of her hips, the tangle of pale hair at the base of her belly.

It was the most desirable little body. His breath quickened, and his nostrils flared as he fought down the torrent of arousal.

"Perfectly," he drawled. "I find myself perfectly satisfied."

Julian watched as she stood poised above the water. The back view was every bit as arousing as the front, he reflected dreamily. Then she rose on her toes, raised her arms, and dove cleanly into the swift-running river.

He walked to the edge of the bank, waiting for the bright fair head to surface. But there was no sign of La Violette. It was as if she'd dove and disappeared.

He was pulling off his boots, tearing at the buttons of his tunic without conscious decision. He flung his sword belt to the grass, yanked off his britches and his shirt, and dove into the river as close as possible to where he believed his prisoner had gone in.

Tamsyn surfaced on the far side of the rocks as soon as she heard the splash as he entered the water.

She leaped onto the bank, hidden by the rocks from the swimmer on the other side, and shook the water from her body with the vigor of a small dog.

Julian came up for air, numbed with cold, knowing that he shouldn't stay in the water another minute, yet forcing himself to go down for one more look. As he prepared to dive, he glanced toward the bank and saw a pale shadow against the rock, and then it was gone.

His bellow of fury roared through the peaceful early morning on the banks of the Guadiana.

Tamsyn swore to herself and picked up her heels, racing across the flat mossy ground toward the small brush-covered hill.

Julian, however, had been a sprinter in his school days, and his long legs ate up the distance between them.

She fell to her knees with a cry of annoyance that changed to a shriek of alarmed fury as Julian hurled himself forward and his fingers closed over her ankle. She hadn't realized he was that close.

"*Espadachín!*" she threw at him. "I may be a bandit, but you're a brute and a bully, Colonel. Let me up."

"No."

The simple negative stunned her. She stared up into his face that was now as calm and equable as if they were sitting in some drawing room.

Her astonished silence lasted barely a second; then she launched a verbal assault of such richness and variety that the colonel's jaw dropped. She moved seamlessly within three languages, and the insults and oaths would have done an infantryman proud.

"Cease your ranting, girl!" He recovered from his surprise and did the only thing he could think of, bringing his mouth to hers to silence the stream of invective. His grip on her wrists tightened with his fingers on her chin, and his body was heavy on hers as he leaned over her supine figure.

Then everything became confused. There was rage—wild rage—but it was mixed with a different passion, every bit as savage . . .

MOTHER LOVE
by Judith Henry Wall

"Wall keeps you turning the pages."
—San Francisco Chronicle

There is no love as strong or as enduring as the love of a mother for her child. But what if that child commits an act that goes against a woman's deepest beliefs? Is there a limit to a mother's love?

Karen Billingsly's perfect life shatters one night with her son's unexpected return from college. Though neither Chad nor his attorney father will tell Karen what's wrong, she begins to suspect her son has done something unthinkable. And Karen, the perfect wife and mother, must decide just how far a mother will go to protect her son.

Out of habit, Karen ignored the first two rings of the telephone. Phone calls in the night were for Roger—frantic parents of felonious teenagers, wives fearful of estranged husbands, the accused calling from jail, even the dying wanting to execute deathbed wills.

Karen rolled over to his side of the bed and picked up the phone.

It was Chad. She looked at the clock. Not yet five. And instantly, she was sitting up. Awake. Worried.

"Where's Dad?" he asked.

"Padre Island."

"Oh, yeah—the fishing trip. I forgot. That's why you guys aren't coming down tomorrow for the game. When's he coming back?"

"His plane ticket says Sunday morning, but Tropical Storm Clifton is heading their way—and threatening to turn itself into a hurricane. Your father's trying to leave tomorrow instead, but so are lots of other people."

"But you are expecting him tomorrow?" Chad asked.

"I hope so. Are you all right?" Karen half expected him to say he was calling from a police station. Another DUI. Or worse.

"Yeah. Sure. I just wanted you to know I'm on my way home. I didn't want you to think you had a burglar when I come in."

"You're coming home *now*?" Karen asked. "It's awfully early."

He laughed. A thin, tired laugh. "Or awfully late, depending how you look at it. The house had a big party, and I haven't been to bed yet. I need to spend the weekend studying, and with a home football game, this place will be crawling with alums and parents in just a few hours. We're already overflowing with Kansas State guys down for the game. I'll get more done at home."

"Sounds like a good idea. You might even get a home-cooked meal or two."

"That'd be great. Love you, Mom. A lot."

"You sure you're okay?"

"Fine. Go back to sleep."

Karen hung up the phone, curled her body back into its sleep position and closed her eyes. But her mind kept replaying the conversation. Maybe it was from too much beer or the late hour, but Chad's voice had sounded strained—with just a trace of a quiver, like when he used to come padding in the bedroom during a thunderstorm, back when she had been Mommie instead of Mom. "I can't sleep," he would say as he crawled in beside her. And she would curl her body protectively around his and feel him immediately go limp with sleep. She missed that part of motherhood. The physical part. A small, sturdy body pressed next to her own. Plump little arms around her neck. A tender young neck to kiss. She didn't get to touch either of her children enough. With Melissa, it was a pat every now and then, an occasional hug. Chad, after years of adolescent avoidance of his mother's every kiss and touch, now actually reached for her sometimes, but mostly on arrival and departure, not often enough.

She rolled onto her back, then tried her stomach. Her son had sounded worried.

When finally she heard him come in, she went downstairs.

He was standing inside the back door, looking around the kitchen, a backpack and small duffel both hung over one shoulder. He looked almost puzzled, like there was something different about the room. Karen took a quick look around. But it was the same cheerful room it had always been—big round table, captain's chairs, a large braided rug on the brick floor. She slipped her arms around her son who was no longer a boy. He was bigger than his father, more solid. Yet, it was hard to think of him as a man, hard to call him a man.

"Did you and Brenda have a fight?" she asked.

"No," he said, hugging her back, clinging a bit, putting his cheek against her hair. "She's in Tulsa visiting her sister. I'm just feeling shitty from too much beer. Maybe I should have done without the whole fraternity bit—the partying gets out of hand. And some of the brothers are low-life jerks."

"And some of them are nice guys. I can't believe

you're missing a home game," Karen said, relinquishing her hold on him.

"It's only Kansas State. I would have hung around if you and Dad were coming down. But I need to study. And sleep."

"Well, save some time for your sister. She could use a big brother every now and then."

Karen insisted that he take a couple of aspirin with a glass of milk to waylay a hangover. He looked as though the light was already hurting his eyes.

"You want something to eat?"

"No. We had pizza at the party. Two dozen of them."

He followed her up the stairs. She hugged him again outside the door to his room. "It's good to have you home, son. I miss having you around."

"Yeah. I miss you guys, too. Sometimes I wonder why I was in such a hurry to grow up and leave home. I don't have a mom around now to bandage skinned knees and proofread papers."

Karen went back to her bedroom and opened the drapes. The sprawling backyard looked black and white in the hazy first light. Surrealistic even. Like a dreamscape.

She went to the bathroom, then returned to her bed, and sat on the side by the window, staring out at the predawn sky. The weatherman had promised another warm day. Indian summer. Daytime temperatures once again in the upper 80s. Another balmy evening—like last night. Much too warm for a fire in the big stone fireplace in the fraternity house living room.

But her son's clothes had smelled of smoke.

THE WARLORD
by Elizabeth Elliott

"Elizabeth Elliott is an exciting find for romance readers everywhere."
—*New York Times* bestselling author
Amanda Quick

Scarred by war and the dark secret of his birth, Kenric of Montague had no wish for a wife . . . until he beheld the magnificent woman pledged to be his bride. Yet even as Kenric gave in to his aching hunger to possess her, he vowed she would never tame his savage heart. But then a treacherous plot threatens Kenric and his new wife, and now he must fight his most dangerous battle yet for their lives and for his soul.

"Would now be a poor time to ask a question?" Tess raised her eyebrows hopefully, but the baron's forbidding expression didn't change. Nor did he answer. Rudeness seemed to be his most dominant trait. Unable to meet his intimidating gaze a moment longer, she casually turned her attention to the road, ignoring his silence. "I was wondering what name I should call you by."

"I am your lord and master, Lady," he finally answered, his tone condescending. "You may address me as Milord, or Baron, or . . . Husband."

The man's arrogance left Tess speechless. She considered thanking him—most sarcastically—for allowing her to speak at all, but thought better of the idea. She would behave civilly for the duration of this farce, even if he did not.

"What I meant to ask was your given name, *Husband*. I know your titles, Baron Montague, but I do not know your Christian name."

The man had the audacity to smile at her. Tess quickly dropped her gaze back to the road, half afraid she would betray her anger and smile back. The man was much too appealing by half. That is, when he wasn't being openly rude. Thank goodness he liked to frown. She wasn't at all sure she liked the strange emotions that seemed to befuddle her senses when he didn't look ready to murder her.

"My name is Kenric."

Though her hood was between them, Tess could almost feel his lips against her ear and his breath against her cheek. She marveled at the way his deep voice vibrated right through her body and wondered why the words seemed to steal her breath away.

"You may call me by such whenever we are alone, *Wife*." Kenric expected to get some sort of reaction when he stressed the word 'wife,' but Tess didn't say a word. He pulled her hood aside, surprised to see her smiling.

"You find some humor in my name?" he asked. Her smile grew broader. "Well?"

"Hm?" she inquired absently.

"Why are you smiling?" Kenric demanded, his expression softening when she raised her head and looked up at him. The sweet, faraway look in her eyes was enchanting.

"Your voice," Tess answered dreamily. "I can feel it. Right here." She placed her palm between her breasts, a soft laugh in her voice. "It tickles."

HEAVEN SENT
by Pamela Morsi

"Morsi's stories are filled with lively narration
and generous doses of humor."
—*Publisher's Weekly*

*When virtuous Hannah Bunch set out to trap herself
a husband, she hardly dreamed she'd be compromised
by a smoldering, blue-eyed stranger. Her reputation
shattered, she promises to honor and cherish him always—never suspecting that his first touch will spark
an unquenchable flame and his secret will threaten
her life.*

"Violet! Bring me my gun!"

Inside the wellhouse, Hannah Bunch woke from
her warm, pleasant dream, startled to hear the sound
of her father's angry voice. Disoriented at first, she
quickly realized that everything was going as expected. This was a crucial part of her plan, a difficult
part, but one that was essential. Her father would be
understandably angry, she had known that from the
beginning. But it was her father who had taught her
that nothing worth having was achieved without sacrifice. A few embarrassing moments could hardly be
counted against a lifetime of contentment.

She knew that more than one couple from the
community had anticipated their wedding night, and
rather than condemning them her father had always
been understanding and forgiving. She had counted
on that spirit of forgiveness, but there was no mercy

in him right now. He was furious and he seemed to Hannah to be talking crazily, directing his anger to the man who stood silently behind her.

"People told me not to trust you, that you're a heathen with no morals, a son of a drunken squaw-man. But I said a man must be judged on his own merits! The more fool me! I invite you into my home, feed you at my table, and this is how you repay me, by ruining my daughter!"

"Papa, please don't be angry," she pleaded, leaving the door of the wellhouse and walking toward her father with her arms outstretched, entreating him. "I love him, Papa, and I think that he loves me," she lied.

Her father's look, if possible, became even more murderous. Her brother, Leroy snorted an obscenity in protest. She grabbed her father's clenched fists and brought them up to her face in supplication. "He's a good man, Papa. You know that as well as I."

The crowd of people stood watching in shock as Violet, who had heard the commotion and her husband's call for a weapon, came running with his old squirrel gun, as though she'd thought some rabid animal had got shut up in the wellhouse. Seeing her stepdaughter, clad only in her thin cotton nightgown, she stood stunned in disbelief, but retained the good sense not to give her husband the weapon.

"Papa, we want to be married," Hannah pleaded, praying silently that Will would not dispute her statement. "Please, we want your blessing."

Her brothers exchanged looks of furious disbelief and righteous indignation.

"You're a dead man!" Rafe, the youngest, threatened.

Hannah was tempted to go over and box his ears.

"Give me that gun!" Ned ordered Violet, but she gripped it tighter.

Hannah's patience with the whole group was wearing thin. It wasn't as if she were a green girl, she was a grown woman of twenty-six and was thoroughly entitled to make her own mistakes.

"I love him, don't you understand?" she lied. "I want to be with him."

"That low-down snake doesn't deserve the likes of you, Miss Hannah!" a voice just to the right of her father shouted in anger. "What's got into you messing with a decent farmer's daughter?" he yelled at the man behind her.

The voice captured Hannah's immediate attention. She turned toward it, shocked. Will Sample, the man she planned to marry, was standing in a group of men staring angrily at the wellhouse.

With a feeling of unreality, Hannah turned toward the object of their anger. In the doorway of the small building, with his hands upraised like a captured bank robber was Henry Lee Watson, a man Hannah barely knew.

And don't miss these electrifying
romances from Bantam Books,
on sale in July:

DEFIANT
by Pat Potter

"A shining talent."
—*Affaire de Coeur*

STARCROSSED
by Susan Krinard

"Susan Krinard has set the standard
for today's fantasy romance."
—*Affaire de Coeur*

BEFORE I WAKE
by Terry Lawrence

"Terry Lawrence makes the sparks
really fly."
—*Romantic Times*

To enter the sweepstakes outlined below, you must respond by the date specified and follow all entry instructions published elsewhere in this offer.

DREAM COME TRUE SWEEPSTAKES

Sweepstakes begins 9/1/94, ends 1/15/96. To qualify for the Early Bird Prize, entry must be received by the date specified elsewhere in this offer. Winners will be selected in random drawings on 2/29/96 by an independent judging organization whose decisions are final. Early Bird winner will be selected in a separate drawing from among all qualifying entries.

Odds of winning determined by total number of entries received. Distribution not to exceed 300 million.

Estimated maximum retail value of prizes: Grand (1) $25,000 (cash alternative $20,000); First (1) $2,000; Second (1) $750; Third (50) $75; Fourth (1,000) $50; Early Bird (1) $5,000. Total prize value: $86,500.

Automobile and travel trailer must be picked up at a local dealer; all other merchandise prizes will be shipped to winners. Awarding of any prize to a minor will require written permission of parent/guardian. If a trip prize is won by a minor, s/he must be accompanied by parent/legal guardian. Trip prizes subject to availability and must be completed within 12 months of date awarded. Blackout dates may apply. Early Bird trip is on a space available basis and does not include port charges, gratuities, optional shore excursions and onboard personal purchases. Prizes are not transferable or redeemable for cash except as specified. No substitution for prizes except as necessary due to unavailability. Travel trailer and/or automobile license and registration fees are winners' responsibility as are any other incidental expenses not specified herein.

Early Bird Prize may not be offered in some presentations of this sweepstakes. Grand through third prize winners will have the option of selecting any prize offered at level won. All prizes will be awarded. Drawing will be held at 204 Center Square Road, Bridgeport, NJ 08014. Winners need not be present. For winners list (available in June, 1996), send a self-addressed, stamped envelope by 1/15/96 to: Dream Come True Winners, P.O. Box 572, Gibbstown, NJ 08027.

THE FOLLOWING APPLIES TO THE SWEEPSTAKES ABOVE:

No purchase necessary. No photocopied or mechanically reproduced entries will be accepted. Not responsible for lost, late, misdirected, damaged, incomplete, illegible, or postage-die mail. Entries become the property of sponsors and will not be returned.

Winner(s) will be notified by mail. Winner(s) may be required to sign and return an affidavit of eligibility/release within 14 days of date on notification or an alternate may be selected. Except where prohibited by law, entry constitutes permission to use of winners' names, hometowns, and likenesses for publicity without additional compensation. Void where prohibited or restricted. All federal, state, provincial, and local laws and regulations apply.

All prize values are in U.S. currency. Presentation of prizes may vary; values at a given prize level will be approximately the same. All taxes are winners' responsibility.

Canadian residents, in order to win, must first correctly answer a time-limited skill testing question administered by mail. Any litigation regarding the conduct and awarding of a prize in this publicity contest by a resident of the province of Quebec may be submitted to the Regie des loteries et courses du Quebec.

Sweepstakes is open to legal residents of the U.S., Canada, and Europe (in those areas where made available) who have received this offer.

Sweepstakes in sponsored by Ventura Associates, 1211 Avenue of the Americas, New York, NY 10036 and resented by independent businesses. Employees of these, their advertising agencies and promotional companies involved in this promotion, and their immediate families, agents, successors, and assignees shall be ineligible to participate in the promotion and shall not be eligible for any prizes covered herein.   SWP 3/95